ESCAPE TO ITALY

THE COLLECTION

MELISSA HILL

SUMMER IN SORRENTO

CHAPTER 1

A balmy breeze floated through the open kitchen window and tickled the back of Maia's neck as she stood at the sink washing lemons she'd just plucked from fruit trees languishing in full sunshine at the side of her farmhouse.

Taking a deep breath, she closed her eyes and allowed her senses to take it all in.

She smelled the azaleas that had just come to life outside her window—their fragrance mixed with the scent of saltwater spray floating up distantly from the Bay of Naples below.

Opening her eyes, the view that her husband Jim had loved so much welcomed her, and she dropped the lemon she had been holding in a colander, allowing herself a momentary respite to simply 'be.'

Glancing down at the ring on her left hand, she used the fingers of her right to twirl it longingly, remembering the magical day that Jim had placed it there.

"I hope you can see what I see right now, love," she whispered to the air—her Irish accent peppering her words.

She imagined that Jim was standing next to her, remembering

how much he loved to simply take in the view of Mt. Vesuvius and the gorgeous expanse of the bay spread before them.

A sense of sadness as well as peace washed over her all at once, and she had the overwhelming sense that she was quite close to heaven at that particular moment—safe inside the nineteenth century farmhouse on a steep Sorrento hillside that she and her husband had bought upon his retirement three years before.

Smiling sadly, she gathered up the lemons. "And honestly my love," she said to the air, "I hope that you like what I've been doing with the place."

Maia glanced around the kitchen that she - along with the help of some local workmen - had just finished renovating the week before. Working on introducing the nineteenth century structure to the twenty-first century had been a labor of love at the best, and a heartbreaking endeavour at worst. She also knew without a doubt that the entire process would have been much easier with Jim around.

But fate sometimes had other plans.

The house, aptly named Villa Azalea, had been Jim's dream— and his one passion outside of love for his wife—right until the end. And as much as Maia missed her husband, she knew that she couldn't blame the house for his heart attack.

She stacked the freshly picked lemons on a ceramic bowl she had bought during a recent trip to Naples, and placed the lot in the center of the rustic oak kitchen table they'd brought from Dublin when they moved to Italy.

"Though I suppose I can definitely blame this place for some of my money problems…" she mused aloud, ruefully looking around the space, and quickly calculating how much of their savings had been spent on each part of the renovation.

Fresh paint, twenty euro. New windows, three hundred euro. Butchers block countertops, priceless, she thought to herself.

Now just to figure out a way to pay off the credit card bills...

4

As if providing an answer to her train of thought, Maia suddenly heard a car pull up outside the house. The sound of an engine idling lingered a little, before stopping altogether.

She smiled as she walked out the back door and wound her way down the dirt path that led to the main road sweeping past where the house was perched.

Trotting through the lemon trees that bordered the walkway, she raised a hand to shield her eyes as she made her way out of the shade and into the brilliant Italian sunshine.

There, she found an older couple; obviously tourists, peering at the mason jars full of olives that she had so carefully cleaned and canned the night before—displaying them for sale inside a small wooden stand that her neighbor Giorgio, had built for her at the end of last winter.

"*Buongiorno!*" she called out happily. "*Grazie per l'arresto. Posso aiutarla?*" Thanks for stopping. Can I help you?

The man, who appeared to be in his mid-sixties, looked to his wife before stating in stilted Italian, "*Salve. Si. Hai belle olive. I limoni sono piuttosto troppo. Posso acquistare un pesce?*" Hi. Yes. You have beautiful olives. Lemons are pretty too. Can I buy a fish?

"I'm afraid I don't have any fish to sell. But I can certainly help with the lemons and olives," Maia laughed. "I can also speak English if it's easier," she asked, watching relief immediately flood the man's face.

"Oh, er, yes. Fantastic. Yes, English is better as we are - British, that is. Just here on holiday," said the man.

"Your accent," his companion called out. "Is it Irish?"

Maia nodded an affirmation. "I am indeed Irish. Welcome to Sorrento. You picked a beautiful part of the world to visit. Is it your first time?" she inquired.

"To Amalfi Coast, yes. Italy, no," said the woman, walking forward to offer her hand to Maia. "Kent and Cora Beauchamp. It's nice to meet you."

"Maia Connolly, and a pleasure."

"Do you live here?" Kent asked.

"I have for three years now," she stated simply.

"Well, there are worse places," he laughed. "And you can't beat this weather, eh? We left London two days ago in drizzle and cold. Nothing beats an Italian summer."

"Indeed," Maia smiled.

Cora held up two jars of olives and a bag containing five or six lemons. "*Quanto?*" she asked in Italian. How much?

Maia did the math in her head. "Ten euro, please."

Kent reached into his pocket and extracted a note. "Thank you kindly." He shot a glance at the house behind Maia. "And you live here alone? Do you feel safe? A woman in a foreign country?"

Knowing that this line of questioning usually came eventually, she nodded and slipped the tenner in her pocket.

"Quite safe. And yes, I do live alone. You see my husband passed away two years ago. This was his dream. To buy an Italian farmhouse, restore it and make it our own. Unfortunately Jim had a bad heart."

Cora put a dramatic hand to her mouth, as if to cover up her shock. "Oh, you poor thing. And now you are left here all alone?"

Maia smiled. "Ah, well, there are worse places," she nodded ruefully at Kent, having stolen his words from the moment previous.

She exchanged pleasantries for a few more minutes with the couple, before bidding them farewell and providing directions for driving to the ruins of Pompeii, about a half hour or so away.

Waving goodbye as they got in their rented Fiat and drove down the winding hill that was essentially her front yard, Maia turned her attention back to the house. She made her way back up the pathway, only to find Camilla, the twenty-two year old local girl who helped her with household chores, standing in the doorway.

"Well?" the Italian said in heavily accented English, hands on her hips. Accusation was thick in her voice.

"Well what?" Maia said innocently. "They wanted to buy some fruit and olives. Ten euro." She took the money out of her pocket and waved it in Camilla's face before walking past her and back into the house. There, she placed the bill in a jar on the kitchen counter, where she typically kept the money she made from the roadside stand until heading to the bank in Naples once a week.

"You know what I mean," chastised Camilla. "Did you tell them you have rooms to rent? They looked like tourists."

Maia turned around to face the young woman, leaning against the counter. "Yes, they were tourists. British. But I'm fairly sure they already have somewhere to stay."

Camilla tisked. "They might have somewhere to stay *right now*, but if they don't know it exists, how will they know to return to this place, and stay *here*? Sorry my friend, but you aren't going to be able to keep this place going just by selling lemons and olives."

Maia frowned. It was true, she knew that. But she also knew that the house wasn't ready yet to house visitors.

"I just don't think it's up to scratch..."

But the young woman was already shaking her head.

"You have a working kitchen. You have several bedrooms. You have indoor plumbing. You are set on a beautiful cliffside in Sorrento." Camilla motioned to the scenery that lay beyond the kitchen window, as if Maia had forgotten where she was. "And you have friends. People like me and Giorgio, to help you. What else do you need?"

Grimacing, Maia couldn't deny the truth in her words. She had been trying to figure out how to make money off the investment that she and Jim had made in the farmhouse—and the fact was she needed money more than ever now if she was going to keep this place—and not have to return to Ireland and to her work as a graphic designer.

Admittedly, living with the spirit of Jim on a hillside in Italy was a more attractive idea. But this idyllic dream unfortunately didn't pay for itself. And Maia was almost out of savings.

"Maybe you're right, Camilla," she began thoughtfully.

"Of course I'm right," the other woman tisked afresh. "But how will you fill up rooms and find guests if you keep your mouth shut when people drive by and stop? *This* is how I know you have no Italian blood. If I were you, I would be shouting the news from the rooftops."

She stared Maia down, challenging her.

But thankfully, Maia already had an answer to Camilla's conundrum, one which thankfully didn't involve shouting.

"So what do you think?" she asked a few days later, turning her laptop screen around to face the other woman.

Camilla, who had been standing at the kitchen counter arranging freshly-picked azaleas in a glass vase, turned in Maia's direction and approached the wooden table that her friend was sitting at.

Pulling a chair out and placing herself in it, she leaned in close and examined what Maia offered on her screen.

"It's … how do you say it? *Semplice,*" she commented, looking unimpressed.

Maia smiled. "Simple? Yes, I would say it is. But I'm not designing a website for the Ritz Hotel after all. We're a private guesthouse. Or at least intending to be. Not exactly a multinational conglomerate," she remarked watching Camilla's face fall.

"You are thinking too small," her friend scolded, standing up again and returning to her place at the counter.

"I'm thinking realistically. I've put up pictures that show the house honestly. They are beautiful pictures mind you, but I also have to express that the farmhouse isn't finished yet. That yes, there are civilised comfortable areas, but if I want to make a long-term go of actually establishing a business—and not just getting bad reviews on TripAdvisor, then I need to be upfront from the start. *L'onestà è la miglio politica.*"

Camilla smiled and placed the bouquet of flowers in the middle of the kitchen table. "Honesty is the best policy?"

Maia nodded. "It truly is. Okay, the site is live. Villa Azalea is now open for business. Let's see what, if *anything*, we get."

CHAPTER 2

*J*f Maia was being honest with herself, she wasn't expecting to suddenly be an overnight success in the hospitality industry—in fact, she was still wrapping her head around the idea of hosting strangers in her home.

She'd been watching the website nervously all week, so much so that she even worried that her website design skills were more than a little rusty.

First, she decided to Google herself in order to make sure the website did show up—and then, certain that the gods were working against her somehow, called Giorgio her neighbour and friend who lived just down the road, and asked him to do the same.

She was relieved when he confirmed that yes, he had found Villa Azalea's website.

Feeling that she had accomplished something at least, though she wouldn't likely need to worry about bookings for some time, she opened a bottle of Chianti, poured herself a glass and headed to the back patio overlooking the Bay, with the intent to sit and watch the sunset over the clear, crystal blue waters of the Mediterranean.

Settling back in a wooden deck chair that Jim had built when they first moved to Italy, Maia thought back over the journey that had brought her to where she was today. Her husband had said that it was necessary to enjoy this view before all other things, including a finished or renovated house.

The breeze ruffled the branches of the surrounding lemon trees, and she felt an instant wave of calm wash over her. It was always here, in this spot, drinking wine and simply relaxing, where she felt closest to Jim.

She'd been truly devastated when he died—had never expected to be a widow in her mid-forties, and the idea of being alone in a foreign country without the benefit of family or an extensive network of friends had almost set her running back to Ireland.

But Maia had realised something.

Italy, and the experience that she and Jim had in this country together, albeit a short one, had been uniquely theirs.

Her life in Ireland had other dynamics at play—and she worried that if she went back, she risked losing the part of Jim—that essence —that had made him so happy in the days before his heart attack.

Her sister, Joyce in Dublin had told her that by staying in Italy she was pursuing an impossible dream, and living in the past. But Maia disagreed—and instead committed herself to living the reality that Jim dreamed of, but had sadly missed out on.

Now, she breathed the delicious citrus scent floating around her nose, and looked out over the horizon. She watched as an ocean liner made its way steadily out of the Bay, and toward the open sea.

"Floating hotels Jim, that's what you always called them wasn't it?" Maia smiled, talking to the air.

She chuckled at the memory; he could never understand how tourists believed that this was 'visiting' another country, taking a boat from place to place, disembarking to hit up the souvenir stalls in order to buy a fridge magnet so that they could tell people at home that they had 'seen' Naples or 'been to' Sorrento.

"Do you think I'm likely to get visitors like that here?" she asked the sky, only to be greeted by silence. She took a sip of her wine and paused for a moment to close her eyes and relish the fragrant bouquet that tickled her tongue. "No," she whispered. "It's not likely I'd get cruise-goers, not if they want to stay overnight. But I wonder who *will* visit me."

She opened her eyes and looked back over the Bay, then stood up and wandered toward the hillside, feeling a sense of wonder and history all at once.

"It really is a magical place," she sighed. "You were right about that. How many people through the ages have stood in this spot, and seen this same view?"

Maia had a tremendous sense of longing for her late husband and wished so desperately that she would feel Jim walk up behind her right at that moment, and wrap his arms around her. She tilted her head up to feel the last rays of the sun on her face and focused on remembering what it felt like when Jim kissed her throat, making his way lazily up to find her lips.

"Oh I hope I'm doing the right thing honey. I really do. I know you loved this place, and I want to make it work, so I can stay here," Maia whispered to the Italian sunset. Suddenly feeling desperate, and totally worried that she didn't have the business ability to pull off an Italian villa-style guesthouse, nor the necessary skills needed to entertain groups of people and make them feel like they were in their home away from home, she added urgently, "Jim, maybe give me a sign? If I'm doing what I should be doing—opening our place up to visitors—let me know."

She sucked in her breath, as if waiting for a bolt of lightning to crisscross the pale pink sky, but nothing came. Then Maia bit her lip and shook her head, feeling chagrined at her own silliness when suddenly Camilla's voice trilled from the house.

"Maia! Maia! *Presto!*" Come quick!

A moment later, the Italian girl tore from the house, skirt fluttering behind her. When she came into view, her face was flushed with excitement; her tanned cheeks a burst of rosy color.

"Camilla? What is it? What's happened?" Maia asked, immediately worrying there was a disaster of some sort—something was on fire, or a pipe had burst. "What's the emergency?" She thought of her bank account and the reserve she had on hand to cope with whatever tragedy had befallen them.

Or rather, lack thereof. Panic engulfed her.

But Camilla was shaking her head. *"Nessuna emergenza!"* No emergency. "It's the website. I was on your computer. It's official! We have our first booking!"

A wave of relief flooded Maia's body. There was no emergency. Then tears pricked at her eyes and she gave a wistful smile.

But she did get a sign.

Our first booking. Thank you, my darling.

CHAPTER 3

A week later, working with Camilla to fluff pillows and make beds in the guest rooms, Maia brushed a lock of errant hair out of her face and wiped a bead of sweat as it formed on her brow.

"I suppose this is what you might call trial by fire," she said as she turned to the window and threw it open to welcome in the Mediterranean breeze. "When did Giorgio say he was going to come up and take a look at the air conditioning unit? Of course it's our luck that it decides to banjax itself at just the right time…" she fretted, feeling a wave of panic grow in her stomach.

But Camilla simply waved a hand. "It's practically a new unit. Besides the air conditioning—it's no big thing. Not with scenery around us like this." She motioned to the window, as if the view of Mt. Vesuvius would make up for the fact that the greater Naples area was suddenly having one of the hottest Junes on record—and that the house felt every bit the oven that it was.

Maia smiled knowingly, certain that most tourists valued air conditioning above all things. "I suppose we will just have to deal with it. But I feel it's rather a cruel joke."

Camilla looked at her friend, puzzled. "So the visitors will find it funny?" she asked. "Well, *that's* good."

But before Maia could explain her intent, she heard a car pull up outside, its wheels grinding against the gravel of the drive before it came to a stop.

"Oh that must be Giorgio—thank goodness," said Maia, finalising laying out a set of bath towels in the room and smoothing back her hair. "Hopefully he can make this place a few degrees cooler—this is what it must feel like *inside* Mt. Vesuvius."

She left the room as Camilla called out. "How silly you are—the volcano, it's not active you know."

Shaking her head, Maia stifled a laugh. *No, her friend definitely didn't get irony.*

Going through the kitchen and to the exterior door with purpose, Maia readied herself to call a greeting to Giorgio, when she was suddenly met with a car that she had never seen before and a person who she didn't know, getting out of it.

Oh blast it, a guest—and they're early!

Since receiving her first booking the week before, Maia had been shocked to find herself with subsequent reservations - enough for a soon-to-be full house.

Indeed it felt as if by the time one reservation had come in, she just as quickly had three—a booking for each guest room—and she made the quick decision to ensure that the website was updated with the announcement that they were fully booked for the time being.

Nothing like jumping in feet first, she pondered. Though what she'd first thought was a sign from Jim that she was doing the right thing had quickly morphed into her wondering if he was playing some sort of practical joke on her from the ether.

That would be just his style.

Putting a smile on her face, she opened the door and stepped into the Italian sunshine just as the young man - apparently her first guest - closed the door of his Mercedes, an obvious rental by the sticker in its window, and opened the boot to extract his bag.

Quickly thinking back through the reservations she had received, Maia realised that this must be Jacob Bellafonte. The New Yorker. He was due to arrive today, but not until the evening.

"*Buongiorno!*" she called out. "*Benvenuto!*" Good day! Welcome!"

The man looked quickly at the house and Maia and gave a quick nod.

"Hey there," he said quickly. "Jacob Bellafonte. You must be Maia." He crossed the distance between them in five long strides and extended his hand. "Sorry I'm early. My flight got in ahead of schedule. We must have had a good tailwind from Manhattan. I hope that's not a problem."

Maia shook his hand as she noticed his strong New York accent and she wondered what brought him to Italy.

Looking to be in his mid-thirties, he was handsome and dressed in a dark suit, which she immediately recognised as a custom Armani. He had a watch with a large face on his wrist—the diamond inlay showed it was a Movado—and Maia was sure that the shoes were also Italian—Gucci perhaps? All in all, Jacob looked successful and moneyed—and she immediately wondered why he had opted to stay here.

Not that her place wasn't lovely of course, but she had priced it rather cheaply because it was unfinished, and the man in front of her looked better suited for one of Naples five-star luxury hotels.

"I am. Maia, that is," she replied with what she hoped was an inviting smile. "And no, it's not a problem. So lovely to have you with us, Jacob. Is that your only bag? Here let me get that for you." She briefly remembered the episode of *Downton Abbey* she had been watching the night before and wondered if Carson, the fictional head butler, would approve of her behavior.

But Jacob shook his head. "I can manage. It's no problem. You're English then?"

"No but close, Irish. And it's easy to tell that you're American. I mean that in a good way, of course," she grinned. "Please come inside."

Maia graciously led the way into the kitchen, where they found Camilla, who immediately straightened at the sight of the attractive young man with dark good looks. It was clear that Jacob was definitely her type, as much by the younger woman's hungry expression as the way she immediately puffed out her chest, making sure her impressive assets were introduced first.

Oh good Lord, Maia thought, she's like a strutting peacock. "Camilla, meet Jacob Bellafonte, our first guest. Jacob this is Camilla di Mariano Filipepi—my er, helper." Maia could hazard a guess as to exactly what Camilla wanted to help this particular guest with.

"*Ciao, siete I benvenuti,*" her friend purred batting her eyelashes seductively. Hello, you are *most* welcome. Maia heard the inflection of her words.

Jacob turned and looked at Maia. "Is it okay if we speak English? I mean, I hate to be that guy but…"

"Of course."

"Yes, that is fine, my English is wonderful too," smiled Camilla.

Jacob gave a weak grimace and shifted from one foot to the other. "I mean it's not like I don't speak Italian, I was born here," he added quickly. "But I just prefer not to."

Maia furrowed her brow. Seemed like a strange thing to visit Italy if you didn't like to speak Italian – and could.

"I'm assuming you are here on business then?" She again looked him up and down—the suit screamed business traveller, but again his choice of lodging contradicted that assumption.

"Not quite," Jacob shrugged. "It's family. My father lives here— in Naples. And well, to be frank, he's dying. So that's why I am here." Maia realised at once that his voice lacked both sympathy and empathy.

But Camilla didn't catch this, as she practically lunged forward —her actions were so dramatic she belonged in a Fellini flick.

"Oh no how tragic, I'm so sorry. This must be so difficult for you. Are you close to him, your father?"

A cloud passed over Jacob's face and he answered simply, "No. Which is why I'm staying here." He turned to look at Maia. "If you don't mind, could I be shown to my room? It's been a long night, getting here, and I would like to get cleaned up."

Maia rushed forward immediately, mortified that she hadn't thought to bring him to the room first thing.

Clearly she had a lot to learn…

"Of course, if you would just follow me this way—we'll get you all set up. Please forgive the heat; our AC unit is on the blink, but it will be taken of shortly."

Her curiosity piqued by Jacob's ready dismissal of his family situation, Maia gave Camilla a glare that conveyed caution, and quickly changed the topic.

Still she (and indeed Camilla) needed to remember that Villa Azalea was a guesthouse, not a therapy clinic, and that her guests' reasons for being here would of course be varied.

But more to the point, absolutely none of her business.

"Is he settled in his room?" Camilla inquired as Maia re-entered the kitchen, fresh from making sure that Jacob had all required amenities.

Wiping her hands nervously on her skirt, Maia shrugged, "I suppose in a manner of speaking—he has a bed to sleep in, fresh bath towels and a roof over his head."

"But did you hear him? His family lives close by—and his father is dying. Clearly, something isn't right between them, otherwise, why on *earth* would he stay here?" Camilla glanced in the direction of Jacob's room, a forlorn look on her tanned face. "So sad. I can't imagine not being close to my family, especially my papa. Maybe we should ask him?"

Maia's eyes widened. She shook her head.

"No, no that's very forward Camilla. We shouldn't be that direct with a stranger, regardless that he is staying in this house. Not my business." Maia then shot a warning glance at her. "Or *yours* for that matter."

The young woman shrugged and faced toward the kitchen window. She turned on the tap and began filling a pot with water, in an effort to begin making pasta noodles for whatever lunch she had planned. Instinctively Maia's stomach grumbled. Camilla was an excellent cook.

"I suppose that is the difference with Italians. We say whatever we are thinking. No holding back. Probably why we have such low blood pressure, too. If we are angry, everyone knows it. Feeling happy, well, all those around us know it too. There are no secrets in my family," she smiled, "we always say what we are thinking."

Maia laughed. "Yes, I'd kinda gathered that." Turning toward a wine rack that she kept on the counter, she grabbed a bottle of Sangiovese. "What do you think? Too early in the day? My nerves are a bit frazzled from welcoming our first guest."

"It's never too early in the day to drink in Italy," scoffed Camilla. "Please, you should know that by now."

The pair opened the bottle and savored a glass while Camilla cooked. Smells wafted from the stove as finely scented basil and garlic were added to a stewed tomato base. They swirled around Maia's head, and she had a brief flashback of sitting there at the kitchen table while Jim filled Camilla's role—cooking succulent Italian dishes, just for the two of them. She had a sudden pang of longing, spurring her to finish her glass and pour another.

"Life's too short," sighed Maia. She was speaking to herself more than anything, but Camilla answered.

"For what?" she asked, turning briefly from the stove. "Fighting with your family?"

Maia gave a meek shrug. "Yes. That. And other things, too."

Thankfully, her melancholy was broken by the fact that Camilla was finished cooking lunch and her attention was turned to the plate of delicious looking pasta that was placed in front of her.

"Oh Camilla, you have outdone yourself, once again, I hope you know that I would be twenty pounds lighter if it weren't for you."

Camilla smiled happily. "Food is the flavor of life. Now you stay put. I will go ask our guest if he wants to join us."

Happy to do as she was told, Maia dug in, working her hardest to think happy thoughts instead of the mournful bouts that sometimes entered her subconscious.

She couldn't deny that she missed Jim—horribly so—but she also knew that she had a life to live, and that he would not be pleased if she wrapped herself and her brain in a constant state of widow's weeds, dwelling only on the life that she had before everything changed.

Jim would always want her to *live*.

Feeling contentment overcome her now, she took another sip of wine as Camilla reentered the kitchen, this time with a somewhat dour look on her face. Immediately, Maia knew what had happened.

"Let me guess," she smirked, "he's not hungry."

Camilla sat down across the table from her with a definitive clatter. "Who is not hungry in Italy?" It was less of a question that an accusation, Maia thought. "*Di tutte le cose stupide...*" her friend muttered.

"Now now, it's not stupid. He's just not hungry. Let the guy get settled in before you try seducing him with your food."

Camilla narrowed her eyes at Maia. "Fine. When he is hungry, I will just make him a new dish. He cannot escape me for long."

Maia giggled. She had the immediate mental picture of Camilla standing over a cauldron, brewing a love potion that came in the form of fresh pasta and large amounts of Italian vino. However, the picture was interrupted by the sound of a small voice echoing from the doorway beyond where they sat.

"Um, excuse me. *Perdonatemi?*" Pardon me. "I'm wondering if I am in the right place?" said a properly accented British voice.

*S*tartled, Camilla and Maia both turned to find a young woman in her mid-twenties, standing in the entryway.

She had her blonde hair pulled back into a severe chignon and a pair of dark sunglasses shielded her eyes, even though she was now practically indoors. She wore a pink sundress and gold sandals and would have looked perfectly at home as a tourist in the brilliant Italian landscape, but lines of worry that etched her forehead and around her mouth gave her away.

Tension radiated from her body and Maia immediately felt the slight buzz she had been experiencing from the wine she'd been drinking, evaporate.

"It depends on where you are supposed to be," she smiled kindly, getting up from the table. "I'm Maia. And this is Camilla. And you are?"

"Amelia Crawley. I made a reservation for this guesthouse online. Just two days ago. This is a guesthouse, Villa Azalea?"

Maia nodded. "You're in the right place. And yes, we were expecting you Amelia. Did you find us okay?"

Amelia stole a glance around the kitchen, as if trying to determine if her choice of lodging had been a wise one. Her face practically screamed the words, "Stranger danger."

"Yes, it was easy. I was so glad you had rooms available. My trip was a bit … last minute. Everything in the area was booked … well except one place, and I didn't want to stay there because … just, because."

Maia and Camilla exchanged a glance, immediately wondering what Amelia meant. After Jacob's introduction, they suddenly felt on high alert about hidden messages in their guests' words.

"So are you in Sorrento on holiday?"

Amelia shook her head sadly. "Definitely *not* a holiday. My … um friend, is getting married. On Saturday. I just decided to come at the last minute."

"How nice," Camilla crooned. "Weddings are so lovely. Especially in this area and at this time of year. What a wonderful time you will have."

Shrugging, Amelia offered a meek smile. The young woman once again looked around the kitchen, her eyes finally settling on the half-eaten meal that her hosts had obviously just been sharing. "Oh I apologise, I seem to have interrupted your lunch."

But Maia jumped forward. "No, of course not. You didn't interrupt. And really, would you like to join us? We have plenty of food and Camilla is an excellent cook. Please sit down, relax, have a glass of wine."

Amelia shifted from one foot to the next and she looked poised to decline the invitation, but then her stomach gave her away. A tiny but polite grumble was heard and she blushed.

"It has been a long morning. I hate airplane food, and Gatwick is such a nightmare… All right then."

Quickly fetching another pasta bowl and wine glass, Maia made a home for Amelia at the table. Once seated, the slight-looking English girl had no trouble tucking into her dish of pasta.

"This is really wonderful. Thank you."

Camilla beamed with pleasure. There was no quicker way to win her over than by complimenting her cooking.

"So where is the wedding?" Maia asked with a smile, eager to engage their new guest.

But Amelia kept her head down, focused on her dish. Finally she spoke.

"Um, down the coast somewhere. I'd have to look at the details on the invite," she offered vaguely

"Your friends must be so happy that you made the journey here —to come to their wedding. Have you and the bride been friends for a long time?" Camilla pressed.

Suddenly, Amelia looked up and met Camilla's eyes directly. "No, I'm not friends with the bride."

Which insinuated that she was friends with the groom. Opening her mouth to inquire more, Maia all of a sudden noticed the stony look on Amelia's young face—there was pain there that was far more advanced than her years, and she felt at a loss for words.

Closing her mouth and reaching out to grab her wine glass, she caught the look of relief that washed across Amelia's face—as if she was pleased that the questions had ended.

Taking a sip of the fragrant liquid, Maia pondered all that occurred that morning.

It seemed that they had more than one mysterious houseguest on their hands …

CHAPTER 6

*L*ater that afternoon, Maia and Camilla sat outside fanning themselves, hoping to catch a breeze as it lifted off the Bay.

They were each trying desperately to avoid the hotbox that the inside of the house had become without air conditioning when Giorgio, the handyman neighbour, pulled up in his battered utility truck.

"Oh thank the Lord," Maia exclaimed, casting a quick glance at the house. "I love Giorgio but sometimes he moves as slow as molasses in January."

Camilla furrowed her brow as she attempted to understand the colloquialism. "Molasses in…"

"Never mind," she smiled, not wanting to go into the nuances with her Italian friend. "It's just great that he's here, and before the last guests arrive too. I just don't understand how Amelia has been able to put up with the heat inside all afternoon."

After lunch, Amelia had retired to her room—commenting that she was going to have a nap.

Jacob the New Yorker, on the other hand had emerged from his room as Camilla and Maia cleaned up after lunch. He took a quick look around and having successfully evaded Camilla's attempts to cook him a meal, mumbled something about the hospital in Naples before getting into his car and driving off.

Maia felt the mystery of her guests thicken with every interaction, while Camilla simply mourned the lost opportunity of wooing Jacob with her culinary skills.

Returning her attention to the matter of the air conditioning and Giorgio, who was gathering a variety of tools from his truck, Maia muttered, "I just hope this isn't too expensive."

She was weary of writing cheques and paying bills—she needed just a brief respite from the stress—and to make a bit of progress in paying back her investment.

"Ciao!" Giorgio called as he walked up the path to the house. *"Ho sentito dire che è un po 'una calda nella vostra casa."* I hear it's a bit hot in your house.

That's the understatement of the year, Maia thought ruefully, casting a glance at Mt. Vesuvius in the distance.

"Just a bit," she answered. "I'm hoping you can fix it quickly—I am close to having a house full of guests and I don't want to put anyone through any more unnecessary discomfort."

Giorgio shook his head with a smile.

"You know in Italy we have survived for centuries without the benefit of cool air—we have never worried so much about air conditioning. All through the ages, we have survived."

Maia suppressed a grin—she truly loved Giorgio, and was appreciative of everything he did for her, usually at a discount, but just then she didn't need a history lesson on the superiority of the Italian people compared to other apparently 'lesser' ethnicities.

"Yes yes, I know Giorgio—let's talk Italian history later. Now, come inside the house." She extended a hand to her friend as if to guide him to where he needed to be when she heard another car pull up.

Realising that it couldn't be Jacob returning so soon, Maia knew that her wish to have the AC fixed before her last guests arrived had been an empty thought—they were already here.

Thinking back quickly to the other reservation – this one for a couple - she recalled the names—Parish. They were also Americans, from Florida and apparently visiting Italy for their wedding anniversary.

"Camilla can you take Giorgio into the house? Some more guests just arrived."

FOLLOWING HER INSTRUCTIONS, the Italian pair disappeared into the house, leaving Maia to once again put a welcoming smile on her face as she worked to suppress the stress and nervousness.

"Hello!" she called out, deciding this time to forego the Italian welcome given that they were American and probably more comfortable with English. "You must be the Parishes?"

Maia headed down the walk to where the couple stood. Taking in their appearance, she immediately decided that they had to be in their late forties, probably closer to her in age than either Amelia or Jacob. She wondered what wedding anniversary they were celebrating.

"Hi," said Lori, "we are - the Parishes that is. And you must be Maia. We are so happy you had a vacancy—this place looks perfect."

Lori had bright red hair and Maia knew right off the bat that she was a natural redhead, as much because of her pale ivory skin dotted with freckles, as the fact that the highlights in her hair simply could not be bought in a salon.

Maia smiled at the compliment. "Well, thank you for that, but in the interests of full disclosure, I just want to warn you that our air conditioning is broken at the moment. It's a new unit though and we do have someone working on it currently. I have no doubt we will have cooler air inside shortly."

With her comment Hal, the husband of the pair, perked up. "I know something about air conditioning. For my engineering degree I worked for a heating and air company in Orlando. I can go help if you like."

Maia shook her head, touched.

"Oh, I appreciate it. But you're on holiday! You don't need to do that. Besides, my handyman, Giorgio; he's the one who installed it. I'm sure he can manage."

Lori looked to her husband, clearly in agreement with what Maia was saying. "Come on honey, she's right, it's our vacation. You don't need to go mess with the AC, they'll get it fixed."

But Hal was shaking his head. "No really, I don't mind. Point me in the right direction. What did you say his name was? Giorgio?" He pronounced it "Georgie-O" without the necessary Italian accent.

"Um," Maia said, looking nervously between the pair, and feeling immediately worried when she saw the happy expression that had been on Lori's face disappear. "I mean, yes, Giorgio is his name, but honestly he has it covered. You shouldn't feel the need to do this— you are a guest after all."

But her words had obviously fallen on deaf ears. At that moment, Giorgio emerged from the house, apparently to fetch another tool from his truck, and Hal honed in. Seemed he knew he was the AC repair guy by sight alone.

"Hey man," Hal called. "You fixing the AC? Need an extra pair of hands? I know what I'm doing in that department."

Giorgio, who had pulled a rag from his back pocket to wipe grease off his hands, cast a curious, albeit confused look at Maia. For a moment, she just hoped that her friend would pretend to not understand English in an effort to deflect Hal's help—but no such luck.

"Yes. I am trying to fix it now, but - "

However Hal didn't allow Giorgio to offer any protest.

He'd already dropped the bag that he was holding on the ground and was walking forward, ready to help.

"Great. I used to work in heating and cooling—a long time ago, but I know my way around a repair, you know? So what are you dealing with? How many BTUs? Is that how an Italian system works? I wonder if the output is the same as American units?"

Giorgio shrugged and looked at the women who were standing behind Hal. "Yes, I think so. I just need to grab some tools."

Getting what he needed, Giorgio turned back to the house with the new guest following in his wake. The bag he dropped hadn't moved, and Hal hadn't come back to fetch it. Apparently, that was to be left to his wife, who was now looking despondent and somewhat crushed by her husband's actions.

Maia wasn't quite sure what to say, so she made the simplest of offers.

"Can I help you with the luggage?" she asked quietly.

Lori looked close to tears and she bit her lip, casting her eyes downwards.

"Ten years. This is our tenth anniversary. We honeymooned here - in Sorrento. I thought that coming back here would…" Lori swallowed hard. "But no, he wants to fix the goddamned air conditioning."

Maia leaned forward and picked up the bag that Hal had dropped. "Maybe he just wants to be helpful?"

But Lori rolled her eyes. "*Right*. That's what it is. Him being *helpful*. Because at home if I have a sink clogged or need something done around the house, he simply jumps at the opportunity to help me." Lori's voice was thick with sarcasm and Maia felt immediately awkward. She had just met them after all, and was unsure what to do with the woman's candidness about her marriage.

"Well, all marriages have their rough spots," Maia said kindly.

"Really, it's okay. I'm used to this crap." She looked at the scenery around her, as if noticing it for the first time. "This place is gorgeous though…"

"Is there anything else I can do to help?" Maia asked - it didn't seem as if they had any more to carry inside, just the two bags.

The woman smiled. "Possibly, yes." She looked over Maia's shoulder at the house. "Do you by chance have any wine in there?"

Maia emitted a laugh.

Errant handyman husband aside, she knew she would get along with Lori Parish just fine.

*H*al looked very satisfied with himself, when a little later he pronounced that the job was done and that they would once again have cool air in Villa Azalea.

Giorgio on the other hand, looked frazzled and weary. Maia was betting that Hal wasn't as big of a help as he thought he was.

"Well, that's fantastic news," she said as she placed a hand in front of a vent—feeling immediate relief when cold air hit her skin. She turned to where Lori was sitting at the kitchen table, drinking her requested glass of wine.

Maia had learned an awful lot about her new guest in the time that it had taken for Hal and Giorgio to do their work. She had discovered they were indeed the same age, both were childfree, and indeed of Irish descent, although Lori had lived in the United States her entire life.

However, there was one major difference between the two of them—where Maia had a happy marriage; it seemed that Lori had spent the last couple years of her relationship with Hal sailing troubled seas.

As she drank her wine, she was more than happy to divulge the fact that her marriage wasn't blissful, and that she was using this trip as a last ditch effort to reignite the spark—or else.

Maia wasn't entirely sure what "or else" meant, but she knew that its connotation didn't bode well for the future if Hal didn't turn into a devoted and attentive husband.

"Anyway, now that's fixed, I'm sure you are both ready to have some fun." Maia had discovered that the couple didn't fly in to Italy that day—therefore, neither one should be suffering any jetlag from their journey. If anything, she was well aware that Lori was eager to get out and see the sites. "We have some bikes here that you can borrow if you like —those are great for getting around the area. Or there is a vineyard actually right down the road within walking distance." Maia smiled at the couple hoping she was effectively pulling off the role of hospitality manager and tour director. "What do you think? It's a beautiful day, perfectl for exploring."

Lori was nodding eagerly in agreement, but when Maia looked at Hal, she was met with a wide yawn.

"Yeah not right now," he said. "I'm beat. I think I'm going to go take a nap or something."

And Lori's face once again fell. Maia immediately felt sad for the woman—disappointment was clear on her face.

How could her husband not see how thoughtless he was being?

Seeing Lori swallow hard, Maia clasped and unclasped her hands, wondering what to do. But then Lori spoke. "Hal, you slept late today. Why don't we go out and do something. There's no use wasting our time—not that this house isn't lovely—but I thought we were going to find that little trattoria that we visited on our honeymoon? Why don't we do that? Maia said we could borrow the bikes—it won't be far from here."

But Hal was already shaking his head. "I really need a nap. Why don't you go?" he said, turning toward the hallway. "Which way is our room? You brought the bags in, right?"

Maia felt herself holding her breath. If Jim ever pulled something like that, she would have exploded.

But Lori didn't offer fireworks; instead she took a slug of her wine and turned to look out the window. "Yeah. It's that way. Down the hallway, second door on the left. Enjoy your nap." Lori looked back at Maia pointedly—she was refusing to meet her husband's eyes. "I hope you don't mind if I go take a walk. I need some air."

CHAPTER 8

*C*amilla joined Maia in the kitchen shortly afterwards. She had contemplated going out and keeping Lori company, but it seemed clear that the woman needed some alone time.

"How is everyone getting on?" Camilla asked.

Maia shrugged and looked out into the garden, where Lori had found a home with her glass of wine.

"I don't know really—I feel like this current group might be good for reality TV, truth be told."

Camilla joined her at the window and peered out.

"Is she out there by herself?" Maia nodded. "Well, that's not much fun. Come on. Let's get to know her." Maia was about to call out and tell her friend that she suspected Lori might need time to organise her thoughts, but before she knew it Camilla was out the door, calling over an introduction.

"Oh bloody hell," Maia cursed quietly. "Well, if you can't beat them …" She grabbed the open bottle of wine.

Moments later, the trio found themselves in the middle of comfortable conversation. Whatever melancholy Lori had been feeling obviously started to dissipate once Maia offered her another glass.

"So tell me Maia, how did you end up here?" Lori inquired.

Clearing her throat, she offered the short version, and Lori murmured her condolences when she got to the part about Jim's passing.

"He sounds like he was a great man," she said with a small smile. "Anyone who follows a dream like this …I really admire you two. I can't imagine ever living anywhere else except Florida."

Maia shrugged. "I always thought that about us too. It was hard for me to wrap my head around leaving the place I had lived for my entire life. But now, I don't know if I could ever go back to Ireland. This is home now."

Lori nodded and sat back in her chair, getting comfortable. "Not a bad place to hang your hat, if I do say so myself."

"You are from Florida?" said Camilla excitedly. "I have always wanted to go there."

"To visit Disney World I suppose?"

But Camilla tilted her head. "No, no to Miami Beach. I am not a child after all."

Maia laughed. It was true that she often forgot that Camilla wasn't a teenager, but a woman in her mid twenties. "But I mean, maybe I will go to Disney too. I love the princesses."

"There's a lot of fun things to do in the Sunshine State," offered Lori. "Not that I do many of them anymore…"

"So how did you and Hal get together?" Maia asked, hoping to change the subject to a happier topic.

With that question, Lori's eyes took on a faraway look—and Maia knew that she had asked the right thing. It was apparent that she still very much loved her husband, but was living vicariously through her memories.

"It was eleven years ago," Lori said. "We didn't date for long or have an extended engagement. I mean, we were both already in our mid-thirties. And when you get to be that age, you know when it's right. You don't have to spend years trying to figure it out. With

Hal, from day one, I knew it was right. He used to be so awfully romantic."

Apparently, Hal and Lori had met in Miami Beach—and she did a good job of painting the location for Camilla. But while Camilla wanted to know about the city's party scene, Lori was frank that she couldn't really offer knowledge about that because while she had been planning to go out with her girlfriends that night, those plans had been derailed—as she had instead gone for a beautiful sunset ride in his boat.

"By the end of the night, I just knew. He was so spontaneous back then. Nothing would have stopped him from saying, 'Hey, let's take the boat down the coast to Key West,' or 'why not a trip to the Bahamas this weekend?' Even our wedding was a bit spur of the moment. We flew to Vegas and eloped." Lori smiled with the memory. "We didn't want a big wedding—we wanted to keep it small and spend our money on the honeymoon. Here. It was perfect."

Maia nodded in agreement. "Jim and I were the same way. Small wedding, just our family and close friends. And then a wonderful extended honeymoon."

But Camilla tisked. "Small weddings. When I get married, I will have a huge wedding. If I tried to do something small, my family would disown me," she grinned. "I want a dress with a thirty foot train. It will fill the aisle of the cathedral."

"And I have no doubt that the cathedral will be St. Peter's Basilica," Maia chided and the trio laughed loudly. "Do you want some more wine?" she asked Lori.

But before the other woman could answer, Amelia stepped outside.

"Oh dear, I'm so sorry Amelia, I hope we didn't disturb you, I'm afraid we were being quite loud."

"Not at all. It was time for me to get up anyway—I just wanted to get some fresh air."

Quickly, Maia introduced her guests to each other and taking a seat, Amelia appeared much more relaxed than she had been earlier that day.

"So what brings you here, hon?" Lori asked.

Remembering the conversation from earlier, Maia quickly tried to figure out how to deflect the topic—it had been apparent that Amelia wasn't overly excited to attend her friend's wedding.

But Camilla, who had obviously forgotten the young woman's discomfort, spoke first, "She is here to attend a friend's wedding," she said simply.

Amelia looked pale

"Well, what a perfect place to get married," Lori noted.

Amelia looked around and shrugged her agreement. "I suppose. But no offense, it wouldn't have been my choice."

Camilla shot a knowing look at Maia. "Well then it's lucky, yes? That you are just friends with the groom."

A cloud passed over Amelia's face, and she turned away from Camilla's inquiring eyes, casting a longing look over the Bay of Naples. She looked as if she wanted to be anywhere except here.

"Well, actually, that's the thing.... It was ...supposed to be me. My friend, the groom, he's... he's actually, my ex. And that's why I am here, to watch him marry someone else."

CHAPTER 9

$\mathcal{T}$he three woman stared in silence at Amelia, all (except Camilla it seemed) surprised by what she had just revealed.

Amelia on the other hand, suddenly looked light as a feather—as if she had been looking for a way to get that little revelation off her chest.

Lori was the first to speak. "He's your ex? And you are *going to* his wedding?"

Amelia took a long slug from the wine glass. She seemed to take a minute to ponder the taste of the red liquid, and once again threw a look out over the Bay, as if debating whether or not to answer the question.

Finally, she nodded. "Yes. Aaron. He and I were engaged actually. And now he is marrying someone else. She's his co-worker. They were always good 'friends' when we were together."

"Are you saying he cheated on you with this woman?" inquired Camilla, disgust thick in her voice.

Amelia shrugged and brushed a loose strand of blonde hair from her face. "I really have no idea. It's just awfully convenient, I suppose. All I know is that he ended it with me—he said he wasn't

ready to get married. I'd just bought my dress the day before.
Everything was set. And he said he wasn't ready. You would have
thought this might have dawned on him before he proposed to me,
don't you?"

Camilla was nodding her head vehemently, agreeing with
everything that Amelia was saying. "So what happened next?" she
asked, seemingly on tenterhooks.

Taking a deep breath, Amelia continued. "He had asked me to be
his 'friend'. That he still loved me. That I was still the *best* person in
his life." Then she let out a small shudder. "But within six months
he was engaged to *her*."

Maia sat silently shaking her head. She sometimes couldn't
believe the drama in some relationships—and she knew that she
had been lucky. Her relationship with Jim had always been drama
free. Quietly she asked the question that all of them were thinking.

"So Amelia, then really - why are you here?"

The British girl shrugged. "To be honest, now I don't know.
When the invite showed up in the post what I really wanted to do
was put it through a shredder. I honestly saw red. But I didn't want
to be that person. I decided at the last moment to come. But I
couldn't stay at the hotel with the wedding party. His parents
would be there, and I always loved his parents. I knew I would see
the pity on their faces. So I suppose, to answer your question, I
came because I needed to see it happen. I needed the visual confir-
mation. I suppose I am a glutton for punishment really, voluntarily
attending a wedding to watch the love of my life marry another
woman."

Suddenly, tears welled up in her eyes and spilled down her
cheeks.

Maia immediately rushed forward to put her arms around the
young woman. As cleansing as her speech and her explanation
about why she was in Italy might have been, it had obviously taken
its toll on her.

"Oh sweetheart, I'm so sorry. I can say you are very strong being here, attending this wedding. I don't know if I would have been able to do the same. What you are doing is very brave," said Maia kindly.

Amelia sniffled. "My best friend said I was just sadistic."

"No," insisted Maia. "You're not. I think you have a good philosophy actually—looking for closure. But if you really want to move on, you have to realise that just seeing him get married isn't enough. I think there are plenty of people out there, men and women both, who have pined over someone unattainable—only to have their hearts broken time and again."

Lori was nodding, agreeing with Maia's words. "Watch him get married. But you have to find a reason to check out before you head to the wedding, if you get my drift."

Amelia wiped her eyes and furrowed her brow. "And how do I do that?"

Lori smiled. "I always say that the best way to get over a guy is to get under another. And hey, this is the perfect place for an Italian fling."

Maia rolled her eyes and laughed. "Amelia, I don't want to sound like an old maid—and while Lori means well—I'm not sure if immediately diving into another relationship, fling or not, is the best advice. I think what she meant to say is you have to figure out what makes you happy, outside of the way you might have felt, or feel, for this Aaron. I think you should figure out how to love yourself first, that's the way to get closure. Because a woman who has confidence in who she is and what she has to offer, will never allow herself to be taken advantage of—and her happiness will never be held in the balance because of the actions of someone else."

Camilla was once again smiling and nodding. "She's right, you know. In my life, I never let any man be in charge of my happiness. And they follow me around. I pick who makes me happy. And he is lucky for it."

Maia laughed loudly. If one thing was for sure, Camilla had no deficiency in the confidence department.

She looked at the others. "I suppose now and again, all of us could do with a reminder to never put the key to our happiness in someone else's pocket."

CHAPTER 10

*L*ater, Maia was keeping a watchful eye on the kitchen door as she and Camilla began the process of making dinner for the house.

Amelia had been gone a while now, had left for a walk to "clear her head" but Maia still felt a great deal of concern for her.

While she herself had never had children, she was pretty sure that Amelia was of the age where she could in fact, be her daughter —and feeling some maternal concern over the state that Amelia's heart was in.

No one deserved to be put through such an ordeal, Maia thought to herself as she breaded chicken breast filets, to feel like you have to watch the love of your life get married, just to find closure.

She was sure that she could never put herself through the same sort of scenario—she certainly could have never watched Jim marry another woman.

Do you think I gave her good advice, honey? she asked, turning her thoughts to the ether. It sounded like Amelia had been put through the ringer by this fellow, and while it was true that she wasn't sure if he had been cheating on her with his co-worker, the signs pointed to this.

Maia also felt confident that if there was one spot where Amelia might be able to find peace, it was here.

Maybe it was a blessing then, that the wedding happened to be taking place in Sorrento. Maybe Amelia was meant to come, and stay here in the home that Maia and Jim had created, just to find herself.

She felt comforted by the thought. Maybe she had been right to do this.

It looked like all this was about more than just providing shelter and a bed to weary travellers. Thinking of the diverse little group that was lodging in her home at that moment, Maia couldn't help but wonder if maybe they all weren't there for a bigger purpose …

"OH, he's back! He's back!" Camilla exclaimed, quickly turning her attention from the kitchen window to her cleavage. Standing up straighter and adjusting the neckline of the top she was wearing, she then brushed her dark hair back and fluffed it. Tossing it seductively, she looked at Maia. "How do I look?"

"What do you want me to say? Hot?"

"Yes. Am I hot?" pressed Camilla.

Maia nodded. "Yes, you're definitely hot."

In more ways than one, she thought with a smile.

"Good. I hope he likes *Pollo alla Cacciatora.*"

Maia hoped for Jacob's sake that he was hungry this evening—otherwise Camilla was going to be completely unforgiving if another dish was wasted on him.

The kitchen door opened shortly thereafter, and Jacob entered. His eyes quickly darted around the room, assessing the situation and finally fell on Camilla, who was all but preening under his gaze. "Welcome back Jacob ," she smiled sweetly. "You have great timing. We are just finishing dinner. I hope you are hungry now."

Jacob instinctively put a hand over his stomach and Camilla's eyes followed, no doubt imagining taut six-pack abs.

For a moment however, he looked poised to decline the invite, but then Maia intervened.

"I hope you know it's bad luck to turn down the culinary efforts of an Italian woman two times in a row," she said over her shoulder. "If your family is Italian that should be part of your genetic makeup."

Jacob opened his mouth to probably argue that point, but then he shut it again and provided them both with an unexpected, but incredibly handsome, smile. It wasn't the first time they saw him smile, but it was definitely the first time that it looked genuine.

He put up his hands, signalling defeat.

"I think you might be right Maia. I surrender. And yes I'll eat. Sorry, sitting down for dinner isn't something that I think about a lot. I haven't eaten since I was on the plane, and that wasn't much."

Camilla looked confused. "How on earth do you not think about eating? And you call yourself Italian? Now go, sit."

Jacob did as he was told, taking a seat at the kitchen table. After considering Maia's offer of a beverage and settling on a Peroni, because he said he "needed it," he sat back in his chair, and rolled up the sleeves of the white dress shirt he was wearing.

"Thanks," he said, taking a sip of the beer from the bottle. He swallowed and took a deep breath.

Maia went about setting the table for six, anticipating that all of her guests would eventually sit down and eat at some point.

"Been a bit of a hard day then?" she commented off-handedly, hoping she wasn't overstepping her boundaries.

But he appeared to be a bit more relaxed than he had been earlier.

"Understatement of the year. Kinda throws your life out of whack, when you wake up one morning and all is normal, but by the end of the day you are on a flight to Italy. Not the best time honestly, and it's hard for me to get away even when I plan a trip for months."

Maia nodded politely.

"So is it your job then? The reason you don't think about eating?" Camilla asked, unconcerned about protocol.

Though Maia agreed he seemed like your typical New Yorker, fast, urgent-minded, short of time.

"I suppose you could say that. I'm a hedge fund manager."

"Wall Street?"

He ran a lazy hand through his hair. "Yes. Go ahead, you can cast the stereotypes out there right now. I don't mind."

Maia smiled and shook her head. "Not my style."

Camilla placed a bottle of sparkling water on the table. "So you had to leave New York fast then?"

Jacob shrugged. "If I'm being honest, I wasn't going to come at all but for pressure from a persistent woman to do the right thing. And like you said Maia, it's never wise to argue with Italian women."

Camilla's eyes darted to Jacob's left hand.

"Pressure, from your wife?" she queried. She knew some men didn't wear a wedding ring. "Or your girlfriend?" she added coyly.

But Jacob shook his head and took another sip of his Peroni. "I'm single," he smiled, his eyes involuntarily and briefly appreciating the cleavage that Camilla had been intent on showing off. "It was my sister actually. She lives in Boston, but she has been here for about a month, helping out. She insisted that I get my ass over."

Maia grimaced. "So your father is badly ill then?" she commented gently.

"He's been dying for years," Jacob said, bitterness creeping into his voice. "But Adriana, my sister, said this time it's for real. He has cancer." Maia exchanged a glance with Camilla—where their conversation had been easygoing, awkwardness had now crept in. "Sorry, it's just, my dad and I don't get along."

Maia pondered what to say next. "You don't have to talk about it if you don't want to."

Jacob thanked Camilla as she placed the chicken breast and pasta dish on his plate and offered him salad and garlic bread.He picked up his fork and sat silent for a moment, as if figuring out whether or not he did want to speak.

Finally, he took a deep breath. "My mom, sister and I, we moved to New York when I was four, Adriana was seven. You see, my dad, he had left my mother—and she found that she didn't have a bunch of options here in Italy as a single mother. So she took us and left. He didn't fight her on it. And he started a new family—just like that, like we had never existed. But my mom, she was suddenly responsible for rebuilding her entire life, with two little kids, in a foreign country, all by herself. She worked as a cleaning lady, scrimped and saved, did everything she could for us, just to get by —he never helped. Hell, he could barely even be bothered to send us a birthday card." He took a bite of his meal and his eyebrows rose in appreciation. "This is great, seriously - fantastic," he said to Camilla, who looked as proud as punch at his compliment. "Anyway my mom always did well by us, and I have always been intent on paying her back for her sacrifices—I bought her a town-house in Brooklyn, she wanted something with a yard. I make sure she always has what she needs and more. But *him*, well, I don't have a lot of patience for him. Real men don't leave their wives, abandon their families. That's just how I feel."

Maia put her fork on her plate as she considered Jacob's admission. It was all so sad.

"So your sister is closer to him, yes?" Camilla ventured.

Jacob nodded. "Adriana's always been a more forgiving person. But I suppose she also remembers some of the happy times with him. She was older than me—I just don't remember him being anything other than a jerk—and my mom's struggle, after he left us, that's always been forefront in my mind. Adriana thinks that she convinced me to come over here out of some sort of duty—but I can't say that I did ... for that reason at least."

Maia finished chewing the food in her mouth and swallowed. "So why did you come?" she asked tentatively.

Jacob seemed to consider his answer. A beam of sunlight suddenly entered from the kitchen window, striking the table where they sat—its intensity fading against the pale pink backdrop of the summer sky.

"I suppose I came because I wanted to show him I am successful, and that I don't pity him—that we don't have a relationship and we never will, because soon, he'll be dead, and I'll go on with my life like he never existed."

Maia felt a bit blind-sided by just how frank this admission was. "Are you sure you want to feel that way?" she asked.

But Jacob didn't have time to answer because the backdoor opened and Amelia strode in. Her cheeks were rosy and she looked the tiniest bit windblown. She definitely looked... *happier.*

"Oh!" she stumbled. "I seem to keep interrupting when people are eating."

"Nonsense," said Maia, jumping up. "It's what you do in Italy—eat—several times per day. Please, sit down. What can I get you to drink?"

And just like that the increasingly difficult conversation with Jacob was forgotten—Maia didn't think it was right to continue, not with the new introduction of Amelia to the group, nor did she think it appropriate to ask Amelia how she was feeling.

So the table kept to neutral topics—jobs, hobbies, favourite travel spots and the like.

Through it all, Hal and Lori never showed up for dinner. Maia was pretty sure they were both still in the house—she didn't think they had left.

Deciding to check on them later, she put some food away for them, just in case.

CHAPTER 11

When dinner was over, Camilla began cleaning up with Amelia's help, and Maia walked in the direction of the Parrish's room to let them know that there was food if they wanted it.

But as she neared their door, she was immediately hit with the sound of raised, albeit muffled, voices coming from within.

"No, *you* don't understand Hal. You are one of the most insensitive people I have ever met. We are in Italy for God's sakes. And what do you do? You want to fix the goddamn air conditioning at the place we are staying. Why don't you just say it? That you don't want to be here? That you have already checked out of this marriage?" cried Lori.

Maia felt a surge of embarrassment rush through her and she slowly stepped away.

As the argument became more heated, she didn't want to be caught eavesdropping should either one of them open the door, and she also knew that this was none of her business. She hoped that her footsteps were not making any noise on the wooden floors beneath.

"What do you want from me Lori? Just tell me and I'll do it. And why would you say that? That I've checked out. I swear to God, I can't do anything right. I really can't, not with you, not anymore. I agreed to come to Italy. I agreed to this guesthouse. I agreed to this downtime because you said we needed it—I don't know what else to do for you!"

Back in the kitchen, Maia couldn't help but feel upset over what she had heard between the fighting couple.

She excused herself and went outside, where the cool evening breeze whipped tendrils of hair round her temples and the scent of lemons fragranced the air.

She walked down the path away from the house, toward the road and the cliff side, determined to find some solitude to clear her head.

And she knew just the spot.

Finding her way easily to a small overlook that gave a clear view of the Naples city lights at night, she felt herself calming as she walked.

However, she was surprised to find that when she reached her destination she was not alone—Jacob had apparently found her secret place too.

And he was so fully immersed in taking in the view that he didn't hear Maia's footsteps as she approached.

"Hello," she said softly, announcing her presence. She certainly didn't want to shock anyone when they were standing that close to the edge of a hillside. "I didn't realise this place was that easy to find," she said with a smile.

Jacob turned around, finally realising he was no longer alone.

"Oh, hey, I'm sorry, I was just walking a bit and I stumbled upon this area. A bit off the beaten path, yes? I hope you don't mind. If you needed some time alone, I can go," he offered.

But Maia waved a dismissive hand. "Please, not a problem at all. It will be nice to have some company here. I haven't in some time." She took a seat on the grass. "Care to join me? Best seat in the house." She patted the soft ground next to her, and Jacob dutifully sat.

He sighed deeply as he got comfortable and cast his eyes out over the Neapolitan vista. The seashore was dotted with lights and low lying buildings filled the Napoli harbour. The sky had not fully given up the setting sun, and off into the West, the last remnants of daylight headed south.

"It sure looks different - from the skyline of New York that is."

"It is quite different yes," agreed Maia.

"Have you been? To New York that is?" Jacob asked to which she offered an affirmative nod.

"Twice, but not recently. Once as a teenager, and once with my husband, Jim, right after we were married. It's a great city. I don't suppose I could live there though. I like the quiet this place offers. I feel like I might be a fish out of water in a city like that," she smiled, turning her eyes to Jacob, who was now looking back at the metropolis beneath.

He had a strong Italian profile—like many of the men she saw here each day. There was no denying he was handsome; she could see why Camilla was attracted, but he was more refined than most of the men she met.

Probably because he was a full on New Yorker and had been his whole life. But, Maia knew that Italian passion still drove through his veins. His feelings toward his father were evidence of that.

"Do you remember Sorrento at all?" she asked. "I know you said you were very young when you left."

Jacob shrugged. "There are snippets, I guess. Little memories. I don't know if they're real or if it's something I saw in one of my mom's photo albums. Honestly, probably one of my clearer memories is of going to Pompeii, probably right before we left for the U.S. I remember thinking it was absolutely hilarious that there were pictures of naked people on the walls of one of the buildings. I now know it was a brothel that serviced the city," he laughed. "But I was just a little boy who thought it was funny—these naked people

painted on the walls, all twisted around each other. I didn't know
what the purpose of the establishment - I guess you might say -
was." He laughed. "It's weird the things you remember you know?"

Maia nodded and smiled. "I get that. Little random things—
especially when it comes to my husband. Like the time we got into
an argument about something while sitting at the dinner table—I
can't even recall what—but during the whole thing, he had this
piece of corn stuck on his cheek. And I was so mad at him that I
just let it sit there. It honestly made me feel better. It's hard to argue
with someone who has food on their face. But I always wondered,
after he died, why did I remember *that*? Out of all things ...what
was its significance to my life?"

Taking a deep breath of sea air and closing her eyes, Maia
listened for the sounds that floated up from the valley beneath.

When she opened her eyes again she shrugged.

"I'm glad I do remember though. Even with Jim gone. It's little
things like that, that pepper my thoughts. They help keep him alive
to me."

The pair sat in silence for a moment and when Jacob finally
spoke, his statement caught her unawares.

"You asked me a question earlier, at dinner, about the way I felt
toward my father. You asked me if I was sure I wanted to feel that
way."

Maia shifted uncomfortably. "I'm sorry, I shouldn't have said
that. It's not my place ..."

"No, it's okay. It's what brought me out here. I needed to think,"
Jacob said evenly. "But can I ask you a question?" She nodded her
approval. "Have you ever had to try to forgive someone for a lifetime of unhappiness?"

Maia tilted her head. "Are *you* unhappy though? You don't seem
that way to me."

Jacob tucked his feet up closer to his body and wrapped his
arms around his legs. "No, I'm not unhappy. I have everything I
could want in life—great career, money to buy whatever I want,

companionship if I want it, friends. And quite honestly, if it were just about me, I probably wouldn't give him another thought. But it's my mom. It's about *her*. She spent the majority of the prime years of her life unhappy, overworked, caring for two children alone. I remember her crying at night when she thought Adriana and I were asleep. I remember her stressing over money. I guess that's what I find unforgivable."

It was an honest answer, Maia thought. But she also believed there was something out of kilter with his line of thinking.

"What about your mother? What does she think of him?"

Jacob sighed. "That's what I don't get. When Adriana was pressuring me to come over here, Mom told me I should come too. I mean, why? I told her if it was so important that I come here, then why didn't she come with me? To watch the old man die, to get that closure. She said that closure occurred for her when she left Italy. That she didn't need to mourn him again."

Maia smiled, understanding what Jacob was missing. "Your mother sounds like a very wise woman."

"How so?" he asked.

"It sounds to me like your mother finished mourning for her relationship with your father years ago. And what you interpreted as her dealing with a broken heart, might really just have been a woman who was doing her best to handle the stresses of making a new life for herself after the plans she thought were set in stone, crumbled before her eyes. What you perceived as unhappiness, regret and loneliness could very well have been something different."

Jacob furrowed his brow. "How do you know that?"

"Because I've been through it," Maia answered simply.

Thinking of the painful time immediately after Jim's passing, she took a deep breath and willed herself not to cry.

"I had a great love in my life. And no, Jim didn't leave me, but after he died, I knew that there was nothing I could do to bring him back. I could wish on a star all night every night, but that wouldn't change a thing about my situation. But what I could do is make a new life for myself, decide how I could make myself happy in this new reality. There have been nights where I have lain awake crying because of stress. How was I going to keep this place? What was I going to do when the savings account ran out? What happens next? I'm only in my forties - prime years of my life. And I'm all alone," Maia admitted sadly. "And there have been times where I have felt mad at Jim. It was irrational, I know. After all, he went to the doctor, he never had any health problems. That heart attack wasn't his fault. But I have carried on, because I had to. No, I don't have to support children but I didn't want to lose this place." She motioned in the direction of the farmhouse. "That was Jim's dream and Jim's baby—and it became mine. The heart is resilient, Jacob, I think your mother is proof of that. She made her choices. You shouldn't fight her battles for her—she has done that already."

"So you think she wasn't just crying over him? All of those years."

Maia shrugged. "I'm sure she did her fair share of crying over him too. Tell me, does your mother have anyone in her life now? Anyone special?"

Jacob nodded. "Yes, a nice guy. His name is Peter. He's a widower. They've been seeing each other for seven years or so. But she has no interest in getting married—Peter's asked her many times."

Grinning, Maia said, "Then I don't think you should worry about your mom's happiness any longer—she sounds like she knows what she wants and who she is, although you are a good son to be concerned. I think maybe you should focus on your own feelings about your father, and not project your worries over your mother into it. What happens if you allow this grudge to fester? Let me tell you. He dies. And whatever sins he's committed in his life, whatever bad judgment or bad choices he made, that all dies with him. If you are religious, then you have your own beliefs over what happens after that. If you're not, his life becomes dust. But Jacob, you get to *live*. And that hate, those bad feelings you carry? That festers and grows and soon overpowers you. It becomes part of *you* —and then, well, maybe you aren't any better than your father. But he's gone—and you're walking the earth with blackness inside that threatens the very happiness you could achieve in your life. Just forgive your father, Jacob. You don't have to profess your love to him. You don't have to cry by his bedside. But forgive. And let those bad feelings die when he does."

Jacob was silent, and he put his head in his hands and covered his eyes. Maia didn't think he was crying, but he was definitely working her words over in his mind.

"Just think about it," she said, putting a comforting hand on his back. She then stood up and prepared to take her leave, pretty sure Jacob needed to be alone for a bit. "Life's too short. You can't change the past, but you can decide how you want to live in the future. Your father no longer has power over you. Unless you give it to him."

CHAPTER 12

*M*aia got up early the next morning—practically rising with the sun—determined to get a jumpstart on the day.

She had a to-do list that felt a mile long as her tasks had seemingly multiplied. Not only did she have to attend to the normal everyday chores around the house, but she had to now also ensure that her guests were happy and well taken care of.

She exited the house and headed directly to the roadside stand to check stock, in order to let Camilla know what was needed, but also begin canning some olives and picking some lemons herself.

Once finished, she exited the small booth and stood in front of it, inspecting its appearance.

"I really think I need to ask Giorgio to put another coat of paint on it," she commented to herself, before turning her attention to the surrounding azalea bushes. "And those are getting way too overgrown. A woman's work is never done…" she sighed.

Deciding at once that there was no time like the present, she headed to the garden shed before returning with a pair of pruning shears and a basket.

One thing was for certain, very little went to waste around this house. Whatever she cut off the bushes would end up decorating the interior of the villa in fragrant bouquets.

"Nice flowers," said a voice from behind her. "What are they?"

Startled, Maia turned around quickly to find Hal watching her work. "Sorry, I didn't hear you approach." She noticed that she was holding up her shears defensively as if ready to defend herself.

"I didn't mean to scare you," he smiled kindly. "My apologies. I was just out wandering around and I didn't realise anyone else was up yet."

"Ah, an early riser then," Maia smiled. "And these are azaleas to answer your question." She turned back to her work. "Do you mind running back to the shed over there and getting me another basket? There's one just inside the door."

Hal agreed and did as he was bid. When he returned a moment later with the empty container, he helpfully moved the full basket of azaleas out of Maia's way.

"Are these going somewhere?"

"Yes, into the house. I'll make some bouquets. No sense wasting them. They're too pretty." A beat of silence passed between the pair before Maia spoke again. "So Lori's still sleeping?"

"Yes she's um, a bit tired," he stuttered and Maia had the immediate flashback of overhearing the couple arguing the evening before.

"So do you both have plans today?" she inquired, hoping the answer would be yes, for Lori's sake alone. The woman seemed at the end of her tether.

But Hal shrugged in a non-committal manner.

"I don't know. Maybe she has plans, there are things that she wants to do and whatnot, but I really don't know why *I'm* here," he sighed, putting his hands in his pockets. "I wouldn't say that my wife and I are getting along too well right now."

Maia tilted her head and put her pruning shears down for a moment, her attention turned fully to Hal.

"Lori and I talked a bit yesterday afternoon, while you were napping," she admitted. "I told her that all marriages go through rough patches. I really think it's just about figuring out how to work through some of those times."

Hal crossed his arms and leaned against the side of the lemon stand.

"Yeah, I know," he said sadly. "And maybe I was hoping that just being in a different place, away from home, would be an instant fix. You know, like a vacation high of sorts? But if anything, she seems unhappier now."

Maia nodded as Hal continued.

"You know the thing is, we both spend so much of our time consumed with our careers, - and I don't care what she says - Lori is just as committed to hers as I am. Having kids was never a priority for us, and we met at a time when we were both older, knew what we wanted out of life, had the means to do things. But then I guess, something changed. Most days now I feel like we live separate lives. Like we live together and go out to dinner, and do all the stuff that married couples do, but at the same time we exist in two completely separate universes. We might be talking over breakfast, but our minds are in different places, already going about our day. That's how it feels to me anyhow."

Maia considered Hal's statement, and then took in his appearance. He was well turned out, in a polo shirt and khaki shorts, but he looked tired. She wondered if Lori noticed that—the fatigue in his eyes and the lines on his forehead. It was clear that he understood his wife was unhappy; he just wasn't sure about what to do about it.

"You look like you could use some coffee. Why don't you come into the house? I had a pot brewing before I came out here."

Hal agreed, and helped Maia carry one of the overflowing flower baskets. Once they reached the kitchen, she took the load before grabbing a mug and pouring him a cup of coffee. Settling him in at the kitchen table, she began pulling vases from cabinets—she needed to get these azaleas in water.

Hal sipped his coffee and nodded his head appreciatively. "That's great. Thank you. You know, I love my wife. I really do. Please don't get me wrong there, no matter what she told you."

"Oh, I think she knows you love her," Maia said, hoping her words were true. "I suspect you guys might just be in a slump, that's all. You simply need to make an effort, change things around, do something different. Maybe the two of you need to remember how to be a couple again. If you are on different wavelengths like you say, maybe it's time to start crossing your wires again?" She smiled, hoping Hal didn't think she was implying some sort of sexual innuendo.

He tapped his fingers on the kitchen table.

"So, what do you suggest? I mean, I'm a man; you have to talk to me like I'm five—or so my wife thinks."

Maia barked a laugh as she finished arranging the flowers in one vase.

"Well Lori said yesterday she wanted to visit some trattoria you'd been to before? And she was also interested in a bike ride. What's stopping you from doing that?"

Hal shrugged and looked uncomfortable.

"I don't know, I guess there is something in me that feels like situations like that … like going on a bike ride just because you're on vacation is contrived. We would never do that back home. That's just not us."

Biting her lip, Maia mumbled, "Hmm." She remembered what Lori had said the day before about how Hal used to be spontaneous —she wondered what had happened to that sense of adventure.

Life, apparently.

She took the vase of flowers she was working on and placed it on the sideboard, taking a moment to admire it before she spoke again.

"But isn't that the point of escaping from the day to day? To do something out of the ordinary? It's called a 'vacation' because it is - a break from the norm. For example, you don't worry about things like air conditioning going on the blink, because you are too busy looking for your next adventure to care."

Hal grimaced. "Hey, I was only trying to help."

"And *I* appreciated it, thank you. But now's not the time to worry about practical stuff—it *is* time to worry about your wife, and what's happening out there." She pointed beyond the window. "Apparently, the two of you fell in love with this location and even more in love with each other, before. Why can't you do it again?"

Offering another shrug, Hal stayed silent and pondered this.

Maia took her mug of coffee and sat down at the table beside him.

"When Jim, my husband and I, lived in Ireland, before we came here, all we did was work, work, work. I was a graphic designer at a busy company in Dublin. Jim worked in finance. He had always talked about wanting to move here when he retired." She laughed at the memory. "I remember at first thinking he was just spouting off big dreams. It was only after I saw the brochures laid out all over this exact same table," she motioned to the surface beneath their coffee cups, "did I realise he was serious. Buying an old farmhouse, in Italy of all places—well, I thought he was quite crazy—the pure spontaneity of it! Can you imagine? But, supporting wife that I was, well, I finally agreed.

But then, when we got here, we worked harder than we ever worked in our corporate jobs, I think. In fact, I know we did. But something else happened in the midst of all that. Jim started doing things that I would have never pictured him doing when we lived in Dublin. Like one day, I walked into the kitchen, and the place was just a mess. We were in the process of stripping back the floors, and I knew it was going to be a very long and trying day.

But then Jim said, 'No, we are doing something different today,' and he held up this picnic basket. A picnic? I thought, seriously - in the middle of all this chaos? But that's just what we did, after he convinced me that the work could wait until another day, that there would *always* be more to do in a place like this, but that ultimately, we had come here for a reason."

"So what did you do?" Hal asked.

"We went on that picnic," Maia laughed. "We trotted off down the hillside and spent the entire day basking in the sunshine, eating bread and cheese and drinking wine. It was a perfect day." She paused, recalling the time, reliving the wonderful memory.

"And Jim was right. I can't believe it took us leaving Dublin and the hustle and bustle of our everyday lives to realise that sometimes, you need to just stop and connect with the person you love. Jim said one time - it was after we finished renovating that room, 'Well this looks great, but I've had enough for one day,' and I was so intent on just admiring our work, looking at the new paint, and walking around on the floorboards we'd just uncovered, and all this *stuff*, that Jim finally had to pull me from the room. He said, 'I love what we did, but it won't keep me warm at night—you will.' I guess my point is, this place allowed him and I, even for a short time, to find balance in our lives. I realise you and Lori aren't moving in," she smiled, "but maybe it can also work its magic on you two while you're here? If you let it."

Hal smiled. "So how do I get started on some of this Villa Azalea 'magic'?"

Laughing, Maia got up, and reached for the vase of flowers. "I thought you'd never ask…"

When Lori opened her eyes, she felt momentarily discombobulated. As her mind snapped into motion, she remembered where she was—the Italian farmhouse in Sorrento. But what confused her now was the bouquet of fresh azaleas that had suddenly appeared on her bedside table. That hadn't been there the night before, when she had gone to bed angry next to Hal—the two of them sleeping with their backs turned to each other.

It had been a million miles from romantic. Some vacation!

She sat up and edged closer to the side of the bed, dipping her face into the fresh blooms, their fragrance all at once calming her. Lori looked behind her to Hal's side of the bed only to find it empty.

Getting up from bed and putting her robe on, she opened the door and padded down the hallway with bare feet. Entering the kitchen, she found it empty, but smelling of fresh coffee and hot bread. The sound of voices outside trickled into the house and she followed her ears.

Opening the kitchen door, she was immediately met with a cool summer's morning. The heat of the day had not yet found its way up the side of the mountain to the farmhouse. She was also welcomed by her husband and Maia sitting and chatting in the wooden lounge chairs that peppered the courtyard.

Feeling immediately annoyed, primarily that her husband could just get up and carry on with the landlady, happily relaxed when he couldn't do it with her, she was about to offer her displeasure when Hal cut her off, speaking first.

"There you are, honey," he smiled. "Good morning. I hope you liked your flowers."

Momentarily stunned, Lori opened and closed her mouth—and then opened it again. "Those were from you?"

Hal nodded and Maia nudged him with her elbow.

"Yes, I was up early this morning and found Maia cutting them. I...helped. And I put some in your...our...room."

Lori tilted her head out of confusion. "You helped Maia cut flowers?" She couldn't believe her ears.

Hal shrugged, as if looking for a way to diminish his role, but Maia spoke before he could say a word.

"He did help me. And he also did something else. Hal why don't you tell her? Lori, would you like some coffee? I just brewed another pot, I'm afraid that Hal and I drank the first." Lori nodded her assent and Maia duly got up to go back into the house.

She plopped down in the chair next to Hal.

"What else did you do this morning?" she inquired, all the vitriol now gone from her voice and absent from her mind. She was curious to know what her husband had been up to while she had been sleeping.

He shifted in his seat. "Well, I, um, cleaned off the bikes that Maia mentioned yesterday. And I thought that maybe we could go on a picnic. Maia said there's a spot that she and her husband used to go to, and we are on vacation after all. I mean, unless you want to go to that trattoria first? We can save the picnic for another day...or...."

But Lori was smiling, a grin so genuine she resembled a child on Christmas morning.

"You want to go on a *picnic*? With *me*?"

Hal's face reddened and as Maia retreated inside, she smiled.

"Yes, Lori. You. I want to go on a picnic with *you*."

CHAPTER 14

*L*ater that morning, Maia was manning the olive and lemon stand, when Jacob joined her, asking if she minded the company.

The pair chatted amicably for a while, avoiding mention of their conversation the night before, and bypassing the subject of his father, until Amelia also made her way outside.

"Maia, I was wondering if you knew where Le Sirenuse hotel is? How far it is from here, I mean." The girl was holding a piece of paper in her hand, which Maia assumed was the wedding invitation.

She nodded. "Further down the coast that way, in Positano."

"So I'll need a taxi?"

"Definitely. I can call one for you—get them to arrange to pick you back up at a certain time too, if you like?" Though Amelia didn't look too happy with that, likely Maia thought, because if the day went badly, she would be at the behest of a cab driver.

She bit her lip. "I wondered if I should have rented a car when I got here. Too late now, I suppose."

Jacob, who had been quiet until this point, suddenly spoke. "It's a wedding, right? That's where you're going?" He had obviously heard some snippets of conversation about Amelia and why she was here.

She smiled. "Yes. But not just *any* wedding," she added openly. "The wedding of my ex-fiancé."

"I see," said Jacob shooting a glance at Maia. "That's an ... interesting situation." Then he smiled. "You know, I might be able to help."

Maia and Amelia both immediately looked interested.

"And just how could you help?" Maia inquired of her handsome lodger.

"Well," he said. "for starters, I have a car." He extracted a set of keys from one of his pockets and beeped the alarm on the Mercedes rental parked in front of the farmhouse. "If you're allowed, or indeed inclined to bring a plus one...."

Maia raised her eyebrows and looked at Amelia.

"It might be rude of me to bring someone though? I don't want to mess up their seating plan..." She bit her lip.

But Jacob laughed aloud—he clearly wasn't concerned.

"A messed-up seating plan isn't nearly as terrible as inviting your ex-fiancée to your wedding. Just sayin'," he added bluntly.

This made Amelia erupt with laughter. "Do you know, you're absolutely right. To hell with their seating plan."

"That's the spirit. Every wedding needs a crasher," Jacob grinned. "What time should I be ready?"

Amelia provided him instructions and looked cheerier than she had since her arrival.

"This is going to be fun. But Jacob, just so you know, this isn't a ... date, or anything OK?"

Maia smiled and said nothing while he raised his eyebrows mischievously. "If you say so."

"No, I mean it," Amelia insisted. "I've seen the way Camilla looks at you. And in the name of solidarity and sisterhood, I wouldn't dream of stepping on her toes."

Jacob appeared thoughtful, as if he hadn't noticed Camilla's attention and was just now putting the pieces together.

"Right, got it. Not a date. And Camilla, huh?" He smiled. "Well, that *is* interesting …"

$\mathcal{M}$aia found herself with a quiet house that evening.

After some gratuitous flirting with Camilla, Jacob left with Amelia for the wedding in Positano, and Maia felt accomplished knowing that two of her guest's evenings were accounted for.

She felt gratified knowing that Amelia had some very handsome backup in confident and handsome Jacob—a fact she was sure would not be lost on her ex-fiancé.

She hoped that the younger girl got through the evening unscathed, and maybe even had a little fun.

Maia had not yet seen Hal and Lori return from their outing, and assumed that the two were having a good time and enjoying each other's company. At least she *hoped* that was what was happening.

However, with a silent house, Maia also had little for Camilla to do—so she sent her home for an evening off. She could cook her own dinner—and she believed that a person of Camilla's age needed to get out and kick up her heels every now and then, especially during the Italian summertime. This was the kind of weather to drink prosecco, dance, laugh, and fall in love.

Sighing, Maia walked toward the cliff side. The dark indigo waters of the Bay sparkled in the moonlight. Way down the coast, someone set off a firework—and the explosion boomed in the distance.

She looked in the direction of the sound down the shore towards where the wedding was being held—and saw a tiny sprinkle of light like wishes from a fairy's wand, fall toward the water.

"What a perfect night to get married," she said to the air, thinking of her own wedding. It was true that she often communed with Jim in this spot, but for a moment, she wondered if she would ever have the chance to fall in love again, get married.

"It seems hard to fathom," she said quietly. "But I know you would approve." She smiled to the sky. "Thanks for encouraging me to do this. I think I might be enjoying myself."

At that moment, Maia heard some noise from behind where she stood. She turned around to see Lori and Hal pushing the bikes they had borrowed back up the hill, headed in her direction. The gravel of the road crunched under the tires and Maia knew for a fact that it was easier going down than it was coming up. However, the pair looked happily flushed, which made her feel pleased. Lori called a greeting.

"This hill, it's a bit steep," Lori laughed.

Maia went to meet the pair. "Here, let me help you. You both must be exhausted. You've been gone all day. I trust you had fun?"

Lori was glowing like a new bride. "It was…how do I put this?" She grinned heartily. "An *incredible* day. Just wonderful. Feels like we covered the entire heel on these bikes," she said, referencing Italy's shape on the map. "I just don't think you can have the same experience in a car."

Maia glanced at Hal. The look of worry that had lined his face earlier that day was gone—and in its place was a kiss from the sun and a smile.

"Thanks for letting us take these." He motioned to the bikes as he handed Maia the picnic basket they had borrowed earlier in the day. "Lori's right—having these at our disposal, we saw so much, and when we wanted to stop and have a glass of wine or explore, we did. Thank you for, um, encouraging me…*us*," he smiled as Lori nudged him with her hip. "It was a nice break from the norm."

Parking the bikes nearby, Maia immediately went into hostess mode. "Well, I'm sure you two must be hungry. Here, let me get something going for you…"

But Lori put her hand up. "No, you relax. You've done so much for us since we arrived," she said, and Maia got the distinct impression that Lori was referring to more than simply providing a place to stay and food to eat. "We actually accumulated lots of stuff throughout the day. Some wine, cheese, other little treats; we thought that maybe we'd come back here and share it with everyone."

Feeling touched by the gesture, Maia murmured her thanks. "That's great. Yes, please. Although, I'm all alone at the moment actually. Amelia went off to her wedding, and Jacob offered to be her escort. With Camilla's blessing of sorts." Lori raised her eyebrows, and her husband looked at her inquisitively.

"I'll tell you later," Lori smiled, wrapping an arm around Hal's waist. "Well then Maia, you chill out here. I'll get you some wine, and Hal will get everything set up inside. You relax."

Maia was about to protest, but then she gave in to Lori's request. The couple went into the house wrapped in each other's arms like besotted teenagers, with their bag of Italian goodies in tow.

Maia sat down after she watched a light turn on in the kitchen.

"Maybe I will just relax for a second," she sighed, feeling all at once appreciated and blissfully happy that her guests didn't seem to be just lodgers, but were gradually turning into friends.

CHAPTER 16

"*A*re you sure you're OK?" Amelia asked Jacob as she parked the car in front of the farmhouse. She stole a glance at her watch - almost three in the morning.

She hoped Maia hadn't stayed up to wait for them. She had no idea that they would be out this late. She also hadn't realised that *she* would be the one driving them home.

Amelia turned in her seat again to look at Jacob. He was a bit slumped over, but it wasn't from drinking too much—that's not why she was driving. Their night had taken an unexpected turn.

She was proud of herself—she had successfully made it through Aaron's wedding. Had wished him well, had even complimented his bride and had smugly introduced Jacob to everyone she met.

Jacob, for his part, had been the perfect date.

He had flirted with her, had pulled out her chair, escorted her gallantly on his arm and had danced with her. He had made her the envy of every woman at the party—and Amelia couldn't help but feel pleased when she saw Aaron's new wife nudge him in the ribs with a scowl, as Jacob artfully dipped her on the dance floor and returning Amelia to her seat, planted a kiss on her hand before placing a glass of champagne in it.

But then, around eleven o'clock, Jacob had received a phone call from his sister. She thought that he needed to get to the hospital, right away. It was time.

Jacob had offered to drop her back before going on to Naples, but Amelia insisted on going with him.

After all, he had been there for her—the least she could do now was be there for him.

So they had said their goodbyes and left the wedding celebration. Amelia realised as they were pulling away that it was likely she would never lay eyes on Aaron again—and it dawned on her that it was okay, that *she* was fine with that.

That the goodbye she had just uttered had been final—and the good luck that she wished to the newlyweds had been genuine.

All in all, she knew that she would be fine, better than fine actually—she was going to be *great*.

But first, she had to help Jacob—she had gathered that he wasn't fond of his father, but she also instinctually knew that he was experiencing some sort of internal crisis.

They had made it to the hospital in Naples just in time. Jacob had been stoic. He'd greeted his sister, introduced Amelia and issued an abbreviated hello to what appeared to be his extended family.

Then he had asked his sister if he could have a few minutes alone with their father. Within twenty minutes or so he returned, and she saw that his eyes were red, though she wasn't sure if it was because he had shed tears, or if he was simply tired.

Regardless, he looked emotionally spent. He sat down next to her and she patted his hand, trying to comfort him.

Within the hour Jacob's father died.

Family members who had been with him at the time were visibly emotional. Jacob's sister Adriana approached and asked him to come with her. But he declined.

"I said what I need to," he told her, not unkindly. "I think Amelia and I are going to go now."

Then they took their leave and headed back to Villa Azalea.

Now back in the car, she asked the question again.

"We're here, Jacob. Are you okay? Let's get you out of here and get you to bed. You need to sleep."

She exited the car and headed around to his side, opening the passenger door, and wondering how she was going to get him out and into the house.

"You're going to have to help me," she smiled sympathetically. "You look like you weigh a ton of bricks."

Jacob shook his head and sighed. "Sorry, I zoned out." He hoisted himself from the car and Amelia put her arm around his waist, helping to guide him toward the house.

"Lean on me. I don't mind," she said, giving him a squeeze. "You let me lean on you earlier—I can return the favour."

Jacob put an arm around his new friend, and it was then in the darkness that she heard a choked sob.

She pretended not to. She didn't know what had happened in that hospital room—but whatever it was, she knew that the man beside her had changed in some way.

Like her, he had uttered a very important goodbye tonight, and deep down Amelia also knew that just like her, Jacob would be okay.

"I really think we should dine al fresco and enjoy this beautiful weather. After all, how many chances do you get to eat alongside wonderful people, and with a view of Mt. Vesuvius and over the Bay of Naples?" Lori giggled as Camilla carefully instructed Amelia in the fine art of making fresh pasta.

"I couldn't agree more," said Hal, wrapping his arms around his wife and nuzzling her neck. "But I think we need a table."

He cast a glance toward the open courtyard—it was true that they had plenty of chairs, they just needed somewhere to put the food.

"Actually…" Maia said, remembering a table they had stowed away outside the farmhouse when she and Jim had first moved in. It was made of weather-beaten wood, and Maia had wanted to dispose of it—but Jim said that it was nothing that a coat of varnish wouldn't be able to fix.

But he had never got around to it, and Maia had barely given the table a second thought—until now.

She showed Jacob and Hal where it was, and they agreed to move it to the courtyard so they could all eat outside. Within minutes, the two men had been able to create a makeshift dining room outside.

Hal went back inside to rejoin his wife in the kitchen with the rest of the group. Maia turned to follow him, but was waylaid when Jacob called her name.

"Maia, do you have a minute?" the handsome New Yorker asked. He looked tired—she knew that he and Amelia had been out late the night before. She also knew that they had ended their night at the hospital. But up until this point, she hadn't a chance to speak with Jacob about what had happened.

"Of course," she responded, halting in her path.

The young man ran a nervous hand through his hair and then smiled. "So, I just wanted to say thank you."

Smiling, she tilted her head. "For what?"

Jacob straightened his shoulders. "I took your advice, and you were right. I had a chance to talk to my father last night—before... and well, I told him that I forgave him. For everything."

"And he was ... aware of what you were saying?" Maia asked, wondering if the man had been conscious.

Jacob nodded. "He was. He was lucid—I think he knew it was the end. He was holding out to say goodbye to everyone. Me, included. But I'm glad I did it. I'm glad I didn't hold a grudge. I'm free of those feelings, and it's because of you. I don't know if I would have done that without your encouragement. I can be a bit stubborn."

Maia smiled. "Probably the Italian in you."

"Probably."

She shifted her weight from one foot to the other.

"So what's next for you? Are you going to stay on for the funeral?"

"I am," Jacob nodded. "And that's actually what I wanted to talk to you about. I was thinking of staying a little longer after that too. I thought maybe I would help my sister with some stuff, you know, settling things. And I thought I might stay and get to know some of my step-siblings. I have another brother, two sisters, maybe we have something in common, outside of sharing the same father. I figured I have vacation time that I never use, so…"

"Well, that's great. So do you plan to go to Naples and stay with them?"

He smiled bashfully. "Actually, I was hoping I could extend my reservation around here—for a bit. If that's okay of course, I don't want to intrude. But I am also happy to help out. I mean, I know you've been doing things on your own, trying to get this place in order. And you've done a hell of a job, but I don't mind helping if you could use another set of hands. I was thinking too that if I did that, then I could ask Camilla out, maybe get to know her properly."

Maia laughed. "I think that's an excellent idea. You are most welcome, Jacob. I would love it if you stayed on here for a bit."

He looked relieved, as if he had been unsure what Maia's response would be.

"And just for the record—I'd be happy to give you any other advice you need—about this place," he added. "I don't want to toot my own horn, but let's just say that I know a thing or two about how to make money off an investment. You want to turn Villa Azalea into a proper business? I can help."

*A*s they all settled down to dinner beneath the stars, Hal and Lori then shared their plans about where they were going to go next.

They had decided to extend their stay in Italy too, because they were having so much fun. But better yet, and much to Lori's delight, it was Hal who suggested they head to Venice for a few days later in the week, just to "check it out."

"I'm impressed," Maia laughed. "How very *spontaneous* of you."

Hal grinned and wrapped an arm around his wife, pulling her closer. "I suppose living in the moment is a bit like riding a bike; you might not do it for a while, but the moment that you decide to, you realise that you haven't forgotten how."

"And of course Maia, please know that we are going to write an absolutely *wonderful* review on TripAdvisor. You have a gem of a place here, and I think everyone needs to know about it," Lori said, raising her glass. "Cheers to Maia. Come on everyone," she encouraged. "I cannot thank you enough for opening up your home to us. You are a wonderful hostess. And I hope that you will also allow me to call you my friend."

Maia felt her eyes become misty as the rest of the group raised their wine glasses and toasted in her honour.

Embarrassed, though grateful for Lori's kind words—she looked to try to take the spotlight off herself and turned to Amelia.

"And you, sweetheart? What's next for you?"

The young blonde smiled and shrugged her shoulders.

"I don't know. I suppose we'll see. Head back to England. I think I've been just … existing for too long, and not truly living. I need to reconnect with some friends, go dancing, drink champagne, laugh, travel, be young. I realised that last night, with Jacob's help …" she looked at her new friend and winked, "… that I'm going to be great —single or otherwise. No one is going to be in charge of my happiness except me—I'm doing what you told me, Maia. The key is back in my own pocket."

THE NEXT DAY, after Lori and Hal had departed for Venice and Jacob left with Amelia to drive her to the airport, Camilla and Maia sat in the kitchen—falling back into their old routine.

"So are you excited that Jacob is going to stay on a while?" Maia smiled, as she opened her laptop, realising that she hadn't checked her email in days.

Camilla looked over her shoulder from where she stood at the counter, slicing lemons.

"What do you think?" she replied a sparkle in her eyes.

"I think Jacob has no idea what he's getting into," Maia laughed at the same moment her email pinged with a new message. "Oh a notification from TripAdvisor. We got our first review!" she said gleefully, knowing it must be from Lori and Hal.

Clicking on the link, she accessed the website and within seconds, was reading Lori's carefully worded, and incredibly complimentary review.

"*My husband and I stayed at beautiful Villa Azalea, and I cannot rave enough about this wonderful spot. Set in an idyllic location, right above the Bay of Naples, you will not find a more beautiful private residence in Italy. You wake every morning to the fragrance of lemons and azaleas, you go to bed at night under the bright stars of the Neapolitan sky and the location provides you the ultimate opportunity to explore and delight in the countryside—something you would never get staying at a big hotel. However, what makes this spot even more wonderful is Maia, the 'hostess with the mostest' who does all in her power to not only make her guests feel welcome, but like they are a member of the family. In the few days that we spent there, Maia became our friend, and I wouldn't hesitate to go back, just to see her. If you are a considering a stay in Sorrento, this is the place to be."*

Maia felt a tear escape her left eye as she finished reading Lori's words. She wiped it away quickly, but Camilla had seen. "What?" she frowned. "What does it say?"

Maia duly turned the laptop around and pushed it toward her friend, who bent down to read the words on the screen. When she was finished, she gave a huge smile.

"So, that's a great review! And it's just our first. I think this will be good for business. What do you think?"

But right then, Maia's thoughts were back with her beloved, Jim.

Seems this truly is what I'm supposed to do, honey. And I think I'm going to be doing it for a very long time …

A TASTE OF SICILY

CHAPTER 1

"Sicily?" Olivia Bennett narrowed her eyes at her features editor and annoyedly blew a strand of hair out of her face. "Come on, Erica, you can't be serious…"

"Why not?" her colleague replied. "Sicily is beautiful—especially in the spring. *You* get to sit in the sun, eat loads of Italian food, and come back fifteen pounds heavier. Who *wouldn't* want to do that?"

"Me, actually," Olivia responded, irritated. "The place is packed full of tourists, ugly beaches and pushy men. And *everything* smells like fish."

"Jeez," Erica rolled her eyes, "did somebody from the island kick your dog or something?"

Olivia held her tongue and stared past Erica out the window.

Four years before coming to *The Wanderer*, one of the USA's premier travel magazines, she'd started out her brand new travel-writing career by following her then-publisher Richard on what was supposed to be a grand tour of Sicily—and double up as a romantic holiday for them too. Excited for a shot at romance and set on finding the hidden gems of Italy, she eagerly accepted the offer.

But three days later, she found herself alone on a Sicilian beach vomiting undercooked garlic prawns and unable to find a decent area on the island that wasn't a tourist trap.

When she finally got home, broken-hearted and miserable, she'd almost considered giving up travel writing altogether. Or at least anything vaguely related to Italy, which was forever soured in her mind.

Snapping back to reality, she turned her gaze to Erica and sighed.

"I just—I thought I might've earned a little bit of leeway, I guess."

Erica had recruited Olivia to *The Wanderer* based on her large established online following, and evocative articles on East Asia, South America, and the Middle East.

Her first assignment for *The Wanderer*, an exploration of glaciers in Patagonia, had been hailed as revolutionary, and was already generating buzz for a slew of awards.

But Sicily was quickly becoming the *it* place in Europe for American vacationers, and the combination of a hyped location, and popular writer was just too enticing to pass up.

"Look," Erica conceded, "I know this isn't ideal. But we need our best talent covering the trendy regions. And Sicily truly is *it* this year. We've gotten hundreds of enquiries about this self-taught chef running a cooking class there that's supposed to be incredible. And I need *you* to check it out to see what the hype is all about."

She slid a glossy paper brochure towards Olivia. On the cover was a photo of a woman in her seventies. Dressed in a striped floor length dress and her silver hair pulled back in a tight bun, she had the look of an Italian grandmother who spent hours fussing over her sauces.

"Oh come *on*," Olivia cried, exasperated. "I write about authentic culture, not this touristy nonsense." She shook her head. "I can't take this assignment. There's no way this ends as a positive for Sicily, not with this whole cookery thing going on too."

"Even better," Erica said eagerly. "Readers *love* negative reviews.

Half the travel shows on TV now are about crusty expats irritated with their surroundings. If this thing is a crock of crap than expose it."

Olivia rolled her eyes, but Erica could see she was reconsidering. "Besides," she continued, "it's only five days. Kick butt on this, and we can send you wherever you want on your next assignment."

Olivia took a deep breath. She reminded herself that she was lucky—at twenty-nine, she had an incredibly enviable position and wasn't tethered to a desk. She knew she had to consider it.

"Can I think about it?" she asked.

"Take the night," Erica responded over the ring of the phone on her desk, "but I'm gonna need to know in the morning."

CHAPTER 2

*A*fterwards, Olivia pushed open the door to a coffee house up the street from the office.

She found the crowds of busy professionals oddly soothing—it helped her clear her head and think.

And she sure needed to think after that meeting. She ordered a black coffee and found a place at a bay window. She sat there for a few moments, sipping occasionally from her coffee.

Suddenly, she remembered the pamphlet Erica had given her. She pulled it from her back pocket and began reading.

THE FOOD OF LOVE
CHEF ISABELLA'S SICILIAN COOKING CLASSES

Experience all that Taormina has to offer in this four-night, five-day culinary vacation.
Visitors have the chance to work with self-taught Sicilian chef Isabella Bottaro, whose work has been featured in countless cookery magazines and books all throughout Italy.
Spend your days exploring the enchanting Sicilian town of Taormina—its

sprawling mountains, sloping hillsides, luxurious beaches, and classical Italian and Greek streets that bring out the best of Sicily.
Evenings at Isabella's Villa are spent feasting on authentic handmade Sicilian recipes specially picked to match the skill level and needs of students - beginners and experienced chefs alike.

"RIGHT," Olivia muttered under her breath, "even cheesier than I thought."

It read like the thousands of other tourist brochures she'd collected over her travels. They all advertised "authentic cultural experiences" that usually turned out to be based on stereotypes than local flavor.

It was exactly this kind of cultural disintegration that she strove to combat in her writing.

Still, she'd promised Erica she'd give it a chance. She scanned the rest of the brochure.

ISABELLA'S PHILOSOPHY

Experiencing the world begins at the dinner table. While it is easy to find "authentic" in any corner of the world, what makes Isabella's class different is the attention she gives to each and every student. Isabella believes that cooking is a personal experience meant to be lived and enjoyed in the moment. Whether the student comes with no experience or has professional training at top cookery schools of the world, Isabella will provide one on one guidance and insight. After all, as Isabella always says,
"Non c'è megghiu sarsa di la fami."

ALWAYS ONE TO DO HER homework, Olivia pulled out her phone and entered the Italian phrase into her translation app.

"*Hunger is the best sauce,*" it said.

That made her laugh; the phrase was pure kitsch—but it *had* elicited a response. It was sufficient at least, to make her start looking up travel site reviews of the cookery course.

All gave the Isabella's Villa high marks, most saying the same laudatory things. But then, she came across one in particular that caught her attention:

"*MaryEllen87*:

I'm not one to fall for touristy things like classes or tours, but my girlfriend insisted we take Isabella's cooking classes together on our trip to Sicily. I only agreed after looking at pictures of the grounds and the proximity to Mount Etna. However, when we arrived, I was instantly taken aback by the sheer beauty and warmth of the villa. Its stone walls shone brightly in the sunlight and glimmered in the moonlight. The patios became a place of refuge, a perfect setting to release all of our travel woes.

"But what really won me over was Isabella herself. I'm not a cook by any means. I prefer a hamburger over a fancy seafood dish. I was skeptical at what I could possibly learn in five days, but here I am, back in Chicago a month later, and I am still in love with cooking. Isabella made her "classes" accessible, personable, and I left her villa feeling like I could conquer the world. I cannot thank her enough for it. This place and experience is not one to miss. See Taormina and meet Isabella. It will change your life."

"IT WILL CHANGE YOUR LIFE?" Olivia muttered. "Please."

But it was a challenge if ever she heard one.

As she finished her coffee, she began composing an email to Erica; she'd made her decision.

CHAPTER 3

*I*mpatiently tapping her heel on the linoleum floors, Kate O'Toole fidgeted listlessly in the plush chair of her doctor's office in Cork.

It had been at least fifteen minutes, but Dr. White still hadn't arrived to go over her test results. The wait was almost unbearable, and it didn't help that the chair next to her remained unoccupied.

Normally, Ed would have gone with her to these appointments. As they waited for the doctor to arrived, her husband would hold her hand gently, reminding her that everything would be okay, no matter what the doctor had to say.

But month after month, payment after payment, Ed's enthusiasm for the process had dwindled. And when it came time to make today's appointment, he'd opted out altogether, blaming a work issue he couldn't get out of and Kate had to get through it by herself.

At this stage, she should have been used to it. Infertility treatments had become just another part of her daily routine.

At the start of her cycle each month, they would visit the office for a consultation and a plan of action. She and Ed would quickly accept whatever the doctor had to suggest in terms of treatment.

Then, over the course of about a month, she would subject herself to painful shots, horrid medications, and endless blood draws and ultrasounds.

All of that just to conceive a single baby.

It had been over a year since they had started the process. Before that, they had tried for five years to conceive naturally with no luck.

Now, at thirty-five, hope seemed to fade away faster with each passing day. And these end-of-cycle appointments were just another opportunity to remind Kate of her age, her health, and her diminishing chances of ever holding her own child.

Doctor White gingerly knocked on his own office door. Kate stood to greet him, shaking his hands heartily, hoping that he would glance her a smile, a wink, a nod—anything that would give her a hint that good news was about to come. But just like all the other appointments, the doctor had his nose in their paperwork, eyes remaining stuck on the large stack of documents.

"No Ed today?" His concern struck her as another sign that this appointment was not going to go as she had prayed.

"No. Work wouldn't let him off today. You know how that goes…" She couldn't bring herself to lie much more about the situation. How could she tell her doctor that her own husband had given up on their chances?

"That's a shame. We'll just have to talk the two of us, then." He looked back down at the paperwork, clearing his throat a bit as he seemingly searched for what to say next. With a burst of air, he let the news out, "I'm sorry, Kate, it's negative again. I'm afraid your body is just not responding to the medication and treatment plans."

Kate stared at him with a blank face. While in past appointments, she had allowed herself to show a hint of sadness, even cry, she was far past that now. She had heard Doctor White say the same thing for the last fourteen months, and this point, she wasn't sure what an appropriate reaction would be. Instead of reacting with all the hurt and anger she had bottled up inside, she simply said, "Okay."

"I think we need to reevaluate the whole thing at this point. Obviously, what we are doing at the moment is not working. And by the look of you and the fact that Ed isn't here, I think it is best that we all take a break."

"A break?" That word frightened her. A break meant no trying, no medication, nothing. It meant time away from fighting this thing. And at this point, time meant the world in terms of conceiving a healthy child.

"Sometimes being in the right headspace is what you need to conceive. Stress and fatigue can take a huge toll on the body, let alone on a couple, and after six years of trying for a baby, you and Ed need a break. So I am giving it to you. Take the next month or two to get away, go on a holiday or something, enjoy each other's company. You deserve it."

She wiped a few teardrops away from her eyes and focused on sounding as clinical as possible "Maybe," she said, "but there's got to be something else we can do. I'm just—"

"Kate," Doctor White said, smiling sadly and sympathetically, "I want to keep going. I really do. Seeing you deliver a beautiful baby would be amazing. But given where we are, I… I'm just afraid I can't continue working with you, at least not like this. All I'm asking is that you give it a month. Just one. And after that we can start again."

With this, Doctor White stood up and turned towards his filing cabinet. He placed her manila folder into the metal organizer with the rest of the stack. Kate's heart thudded along with the sound of the drawer door slamming shut. She too stood, hastily saying her goodbyes, and walked out the door of his office.

CHAPTER 4

*B*ack home, she headed straight for the bedroom at the top of the second floor, passing by the open doors of the empty rooms.

When Ed and Kate had purchased the place in the suburbs of Cork city nearly ten years ago, they had intended to fill the space with many children.

Now, the rooms were ghosts, occupied by office desks and guest beds. The rest of the house stood eerily silent as it always had.

Kate fell onto her bed, her head smothered into the pillows, waiting for tears to come. Instead, she found herself strangely restless and devoid of emotion, so she moved to the computer.

She started by looking up other fertility specialists in Ireland, but she quickly realized that switching doctors would likely mean starting this entire process over again. She couldn't put her marriage through that again—she couldn't put her*self* through that again.

And so, her mind wandered back to the doctor's office and that word: *holiday*. Because of the price of treatments and the pressure to be near her doctor, the couple hadn't ventured out of the country in years.

Maybe it was time for a break away from this empty house and the stuffy doctor's office? Maybe it would save her marriage from eroding even further.

She began a quick search online. Ed had always mentioned Italy as one of his dream destinations. If she was going to persuade him to go anywhere, picking a location that he wanted the most was probably her best bet. But prices for trips to Rome or Venice were astronomical. He would never agree to that.

Then, she came across Sicily. Looking at the average temperatures for the time of year, and the pictures of the beautiful sandy beaches, it seemed to have everything a couple could want. There was culture, art, beautiful scenery, nice hotels, etc. Compared to the rest of the Italian hot-spots, a quick break there would be a steal.

Kate spent the rest of the afternoon researching the island of Sicily. She made spreadsheets of ideas and itineraries with prices and breakdowns. She included activities and sites she knew Ed wouldn't be able to resist. Her mind was flooded with thoughts of holding hands strolling down stone piazzas while eating fresh gelato.

SHE WAS SO PREOCCUPIED with her activity, she didn't even hear the bedroom door open. Ed quietly snuck in, throwing his suit coat on the bed as he striped off his tie and belt. Hearing the thud of his body hitting the edge of the bed, Kate turned to face her husband.

In his mid-thirties, he still looked just the same as the day she married him. His blonde hair was shorter, but he still had those baby blue eyes pinched by laugh lines. The only difference was he looked more tired now, almost defeated. Darker lines under his eyes became more puffy. The way he held his body was a bit more hunched and subdued.

"So what did the doctor say?" His face showed no sign of hope.

"He said we need a holiday." It came out a bit blunter than she'd intended, but she didn't regret it. Blunt might well be the best way to broach the subject.

"A holiday?" He stared at her quizzically, almost mocking her. She just gazed back at him with a tired expression. "No, seriously," he continued, "What did Doctor White say?"

"He said," she repeated with a sigh, "that we needed a holiday, Ed. He is not going to treat us next month. He recommended that we get away from everything."

"Are you joking?" His face contorted in annoyance. "We're paying that guy God knows how many thousands to tell us we need a damn holiday? We don't need a holiday; what we *need* is a baby!" He placed his head in his hands, covering his eyes out of frustration. Kate stood up from the desk and sat next to him, rubbing her hand down the small of his back, undoing the top button of his shirt.

"Love, I think he's right. We need to get away from all this for a while. Being in this house all day, alone, with nothing to think about except the fact that I can't conceive is just adding on stress and pressure. It's not good for my mind or my body. And it's not good for us."

He remained motionless, refusing to glance up from his hollowed palms, so she pressed on. "You have some holiday time saved up, and we could put together the money for something cheap and cheerful. I was thinking we could take that trip to Italy we've always talked about doing? The mainland's a little pricey, but if we stay in Sicily, hotels and food are working out fairly cheap. Think about it: we could go climb mountains, see Greek ruins, relax in the sun by a pool. Anything you want to do."

The two sat in silence, her attempting to comfort him while he bore deeper into despair.

Finally, he broke. "No, Kate, I can't."

"You can't... what, get the time off?" She had expected him to resist the idea, but he was so definitive.

"*This*, Kate," he said, looking directly into her large almond eyes,

"I can't do *this*." His hand swept back a length of chestnut colored hair that had fallen from behind her ear.

She pulled away from him, tears stinging her eyes.

"Ed," she said, her voice wavering, "*I* have to go. I *have* to. I can't stay here another month just… *waiting*." Her voice pleaded with him to understand her. "And if you're not going to go with me, well then, I'll go on my own."

He stood up and shuffled to the dresser on the opposite side of the bed. Then he pulled out his wallet and tossed her a silver credit card.

"So go." With that, her husband opened the bedroom door, walked down the stairs, and turned on the television in the living room.

KATE GRASPED THE CARD, unsure of what to do next. She inhaled a shallow breath and went back to the desk. OK, if that's what he wanted, she would do it. She would go alone to Sicily. She was going to take a trip all for her. She wanted to sit on the beach, the ocean spray licking her feet. She wanted to walk up the side of a volcano and stare at the valleys below. She wanted to do everything that Sicily had to offer.

With that train of thought, Kate sat down at her computer and brought up the list of options she'd been searching through earlier.

CHAPTER 5

*A*fter an eight hour flight from Toronto, Martha Walters was relieved to finally have her feet on the ground.

She was never one for travel.

And despite flying at least twice a year to visit her children across the United States, she still couldn't breathe right until she had safely made it out of the terminal.

Today's flight marked the longest trip she had ever taken, and that return of breath was more heavenly than ever.

The relief was short lived when she regained her bearings. This wasn't just another airport in States.

Leonardo Da Vinci Airport was packed with tourists speaking every foreign language imaginable while gesturing towards signs written in Italian.

To Martha, it might as well have been hieroglyphics. She sat down on a metal bench and started scanning her translation book in an attempt to figure out how to find her connecting flight from Rome to Palermo.

A man in a dusty brown suit sat next to her tying his leather loafers. She knew that she would have to be brave.

"Sir? Pardon me. Sir?" She tapped his shoulder gently, unsure of what the cultural protocol was here. He glanced up at her, his graying mustache twitching in annoyance. "English? Do you speak English?"

He lifted his hands and gestured a clear no. She glanced back to her translation book where the phrases were. She started slowly,

"Dov'è terminal due?" Her looked at her and smiled. Pointing his tanned finger upwards and to the left, he motioned towards a large lit up sign with arrows pointing the direction.

Relieved, she smiled and stood quickly. As she walked away, she shouted towards the gentleman "Grazie, grazie." He watched her petite frame go off on a small sprint towards the direction of the arrows.

TERMINAL 2 LOOKED JUST like the rest of the airport she had come through. Lofty with large white beams over her head, the space reminded Martha of the airport hangers her husband worked in years ago. She had wished William was here with her today. He would have loved this adventure.

In fact, when her children had presented her with the airline tickets to Sicily and the brochure for a cookery holiday in Taormina, it took all that she had not to break down at the thought of going alone.

She had been a widow for five years now. William had passed away suddenly, without little warning. The loss was crushing, but Martha had powered through knowing that her children needed her to be strong. They needed a mother and a father, and she would be tasked with playing both roles.

However, reality hit her fast. Only a couple of years after William's death, her children began leaving the nest. And worse, leaving Canada. The twins, Julia and Jennifer went down to college in Boston first. A year later, Christopher followed his father's foot-steps and enlisted in the airforce. April was married nearly three years ago and now lived in California.

For the last two years, the large brick bungalow in the suburbs was shared by only Martha and her youngest son, Kurt.

However, just last week, she said goodbye to her baby as he unpacked boxes and rearranged his college dorm room, his new home for the foreseeable future.

She was no longer a mother - or at least, it wasn't her primary job anymore. She had taken up classes and spent hours volunteering, but her children grew concerned when Martha lost her luster for life.

Things that had interested her previously, such as church or playing her violin, had suddenly gone stale. Most nights were spent watching television or writing emails to her children in hopes they would reply quickly.

And now, she was here alone, overwhelmed and culture-shocked at the thought of being in Europe.

Her children had intended for this to be a life changing experience. "You get to go somewhere new, see the world, learn how to cook a real Italian meal!" they'd insisted enthusiastically, while presenting her with a new set of luggage filled it to the brim with glossy pictures of Sicily's coastline. The twins had even gone to the trouble of calling the community center Martha volunteered at to arrange her days off.

And that night, Kurt led the group as they sang "Happy Birthday" to her in Italian, as she blew out the fifty candles affixed to a cannoli cake April had made.

But the truth was, Martha hadn't wanted any of this. At her age, travel was out of the question. Just lugging around suitcases in the airport was enough of a chore, let alone attempting to get to grips with Italian or figure out menu options. If she wanted a beach, she could have gone to Florida. And if she wanted to learn how to cook, there were plenty of cooking shows on TV or books in the store. Italy just seemed like a waste—a way to get her to leave home and stop hounding the kids, probably.

Martha took out her cellphone and turned the WIFI signal back on. Searching her email inbox, she had hoped to see something from her children. Instead, it was as empty as usual.

She drafted a short, cheerful group email letting them know she had arrived in Rome safely, and that she had another twenty minutes until her plane to Palermo boarded. She promised to call one of them when she reached Taormina in the afternoon.

Glancing around the gate, she saw she wasn't the only one with her head in a cell phone or computer. Directly seated across from her, a woman in her late twenties was also busy typing away at a laptop.

Her dark brown, pin straight hair fell into her face as she looked furiously at the screen. When she was done, she dramatically closed the laptop and tossed it into her leather bag. Seemingly exasperated, she sat back with her arms crossed tightly across her chest, muttering to herself in English, and what Martha was sure was an American accent.

Noticing Martha staring, the woman put on a quick, almost guilty smile, obviously embarrassed by her display of irritation. Martha's motherly instincts kicked in immediately. "I know the feeling," she said with a little laugh. "But we must remember that it is still only midnight or so back home"

"Yeah, I guess you're right." Olivia glanced back at her open bag and then again at the woman seated next to her. Not unused to striking up conversations in airports, she turned back to the woman who she guessed was not US-born but Canadian, "Are you headed to Palermo too?"

"Yes, but then I have to take a bus to a place called Taormina. I'm there for a cooking retreat—a gift from my children. How about you?"

Olivia beamed curiously at the coincidence. "I'm also heading to Taormina. My editor set me up to review a cooking class believe it or not. Is yours the one taught by Chef Isabella?" The woman smiled and nodded. "Olivia Bennett. I write for *The Wanderer* magazine." She stretched out an arm towards her companion.

"Martha Walters, just a mom. That's why I'm here actually. My children, for some reason, conspired to get me out of the house and off to an entirely different continent." She blushed slightly at her honesty.

"You don't sound too excited to be in Italy. Is it your first time?"

"Yes. My late husband had always wanted to go to Europe, but we never got the chance with raising five children. I never really had much interest. I'd rather be back home in Canada. I'm not one for travel."

"To be honest, I'm not too keen on this trip either. Sicily was on my do-not-travel list, but my publisher went nuts over Taormina and this cookery vacation, so it was either go check it out, or find a new job. Luckily for us, it's only a few days, right?"

"Right." Martha smiled, thankful to be in the company of someone much more secure about the situation than she was. The two continued chatting, Martha transfixed by Olivia's stories on the road, and the places she had traveled over the years.

For Olivia's part, she was glad to find someone to chat to, and especially happy to have met a fellow culinary student.

She was used to being alone and independent that it was kinda refreshing to just chat with a fellow traveller and share the experience. Perhaps this whole Sicily thing would be a change of pace?

Already she got the feeling that this trip would certainly be different.

CHAPTER 6

*S*pringtime in Sicily was as gorgeous as Kate had imagined it.

The sun-drenched, cramped streets opened up to an expansive blue-green bay, and the low-lying stone buildings reminded her of what she had envisioned for the settings of fantasy stories of her youth.

The island was a mixture of Greek, Arabic, and Italian classical architecture, and wandering the pavements of Palermo, she wanted nothing more but to open one of the many red and brown doors and step into a Sicilian resident's life.

She only had a couple of hours to explore the place before the next bus left for Taormina, the beautiful hilltop town set high above the sea, where the cookery holiday she'd booked was located.

Unsure of where to start, she had her cab driver leave her at the Piazza Pretoria and instantly, she spotted the iconic Fontana della Vergogna. It was striking with its nude figures bursting out of the low lying pools of water. Certainly, it was not something you'd see everyday back home in Cork.

Taking a seat on the steps leading up to the fountain, Kate pulled her small suitcase and backpack towards her. She watched as

Italian women in their large, floppy hats and flowing earth-toned skirts passed her by. Even the men seemed effortlessly chic in their pale colored suits and small lensed sunglasses. All breezily unaware of the raw, unique beauty they were a part of.

She breathed it all in: the sea air, the warmth of the Mediterranean sun, the delicious scents coming from the local restaurants. She allowed herself to lean back and take a moment to release her thoughts and fears. For just a moment, Kate didn't have to focus on the baby she didn't have or the husband that was equally absent. This moment was just for her alone.

But in the back of her mind, there was one thing she couldn't let go: Ed.

She wanted him here, next to her, so that she could lean her head on his shoulder and talk about her desire to look so effortless as the Palermo women. She wanted someone to stroll the Italian streets with, point out the beautiful scenery and discuss what they might eat at lunch.

Hearing his voice would surely bring him here to her in spirit, even if it was just for a couple of minutes. She grabbed for her phone, searching for her husband's name in her list of contacts. She held her breath while she listened to the phone ring on the other end. She was almost giddy with excitement of all the things she wanted to share with him. A smile grew wide on her face as the familiar, soothing voice of her husband answered.

"Ed," she gushed. "Guess where I am right now, at this very second?" She listened closely to the sounds on the other end. She could hear voices, voices other than her husband's.

"Can I call you back?" Ed said then. "I'm, ah, a bit busy right now."

Disbelief overcame her.

"Excuse me? Ed? Where are you? Why do I hear in the background? Aren't you supposed to be at work?" A million questions washed over her. She couldn't understand why Ed would just forget about her so suddenly without another thought. He didn't even care enough to check if she was safe, or actually in Sicily.

For all he knew, she could be in China wandering along the Great Wall.

"Its just the, television you hear. Everything's grand. But I'll have to call you back." With that, she heard a click, and the sound on the other end go from flooded with sound and movement, to nothingness.

Kate wasn't sure what to feel. She angrily tossed the phone into her bag. Sitting in this spot, with the happy tourists passing her by, she began to feel light headed and sick. She needed to get away. She needed some sustenance.

*U*nsure of exactly where she was heading, she turned right past an ancient cathedral near the fountain.

The winding streets became a maze of curves and criss-crosses as she passed through corridor after corridor.

Stores and shops buzzed with commerce. Outdoor vendors set up shop with all kinds of wares: flowers, newspapers, seafood stands, gelato. The smell of briny winds grew nearer, indicating that she was nearing the bay. *Thank goodness*, she thought to herself.

As she rounded the next bend, her stomach rumbled audibly; she needed something to eat. With only an hour or so to spare before the bus left, it would have to be a quick bite, but she was not allowing herself to skimp out on quality or experience. Her plan was to stop at the first restaurant with an outdoor patio to get the true Palermo experience.

Rounding a stone corner, she stumbled into the outdoor seating area of a pretty little cafe. She glanced around nervously looking for an English menu, but with no luck, she took her seat at the very back of the patio and put a menu to her face. She took out her phone once again and this time pulled up her translation app, quickly looking up menu items.

Two tables away, a young man of about late-twenties, in a white button down shirt, watched Kate intently, smiling at her panicked expression. He stroked his stubbly beard, debating if he should take pity on the poor foreigner. Subtly, he took his cappuccino and napkin and moved to the table next to her.

"Pardon me." His accent was thick, but gentle. It had hints of humor in it. "Do you need help ordering?"

Kate barely registered the younger guy now sitting less than ten feet from her. "Oh. No, thank you. I'm grand."

Just as she was about to turn away, a female waitress approached. She spoke quickly in Italian as Kate nervously looked away. She was sure she had asked her what she wanted to drink, so Kate responded by pointing to a random wine on the wine list. The waitress chuckled a little and repeated what she said again slowly and deliberately. Kate again held up her menu and pointed a finger at the same wine.

The woman held up her hands and firmly said, "No. No today." Kate pointed to another wine on the list, and looked up at the dark-skinned Italian with hopeful eyes. The woman shook her head furiously. Reaching over, she flipped the large food menu to the back page and pointed annoyed, at the bottom selections. Kate still could not comprehend what was going on.

The man next to her again leaned over. She is saying that those wines are not for this afternoon. Those are dinner wines. You must order a lunch wine."

"Oh. Really?" Kate felt flushed as she realized what a fool she must look: just another ignorant tourist.

The man continued, "Would you allow me?" She nodded and he began to speak to the waitress, who scribbled furiously on her pad as he ordered. When he finished, she smiled brightly at him, ignoring Kate altogether, and headed back inside.

"So, what did you order?"

"A white table wine to start," he winked, "and a glass of flat water. For food, I started you off with an octopus salad and then ordered my favorite meal, the caponata. It's an aubergine stew. If you're sharing, I may even order you dessert."

Despite his forwardness, Kate smiled. The guy was certainly blunt and outgoing, but she liked how friendly and charming he was too. She agreed to share a dessert with him if he ordered her something with chocolate, her ultimate indulgence.

The wine and octopus salad came out quickly, and immediately, the mouthwatering combination of olive oil, lemon, and oregano melted away Kate's residual anger towards Ed. Without a care in the world, she tore into the plate, devouring each oily and lemon zested morsel. The juices trickled down her chin carelessly, freely. She didn't even dare to use a napkin in fear of losing another taste.

As she cleared her plate, she turned back towards the man. "Thank you so much. That was... I don't even know. I don't think *delicious* would describe it accurately."

He laughed and outstretched his long arm to her.

"Marco, and I am glad that you enjoyed it."

"Kate. It is great to meet you."

"Ah," he said, clapping his hands together, "Like the English princess!" She blushed slightly as he continued. "So, what brings you here to Palermo, *Principessa* Kate?"

She beamed back at him. "Just passing through," she said. "I'm actually supposed to be moving on in about," she checked her watch, "about thirty minutes, actually. Heading to Taormina."

"Taormina? Really? I am actually headed there as well. My business is there. I am just in Palermo to check on some family. Are you taking the 2:30 bus?"

"Yes, that was my plan. I need to be at my accommodation by five." She was leery about giving this stranger more detail. Yet, everything in her said he could be trusted, that he was relatively harmless. Still she knew that as a solo female traveler, she had to be a bit more aware and less 'chatty Irish'.

"Well, if you would like a guide, I would be happy to accompany you to the bus stop. It isn't far from here, but it can be tricky to find if you only have a tiny tourist map on hand." He gestured to the wrinkled mess of a map sticking out from her carry-on bag. Again, she blushed, embarrassed by just how obvious it was that she was a tourist. She couldn't even pass for an experienced traveler.

Still, before she could agree to him joining her, she felt she needed to make it clear to this guy that she was married. After all, she didn't exactly know what his intentions were…

"That would be great, thank you. But before we go, I need to call my husband back home. I like to tell him when I plan on boarding foreign buses with strange men." She laughed at herself, trying to lighten the mood.

To her surprise, Marco responded with an equally jovial laugh. "Ah, I know you Americans think us Italian men are only about one thing, but I can assure you that I am just in it for the conversation and potential dessert." He winked at her, and his accompanying smile gave him a sly fox appearance, just as she had imagined flirty Italian men to be.

CHAPTER 8

The two enjoyed the rest of their meal, each keeping to their own table.

Kate found the stew to be almost as delicious as the octopus salad. Fresh and juicy, it was the right mixture of hearty and comforting without being overwhelming. And as she promised, the two enjoyed dessert, a shared chocolate tart.

When the time came to catch their bus, she realized how thankful she was for Marco's help. The cobblestone Palermo streets were a massive spider web, yet Marco navigated them effortlessly.

He bypassed the heavily traveled areas while managing to skim minutes off of their would-be journey time with shortcuts and alleyways.

The whole way, he still managed to play tour guide, pointing out the most interesting points along the way: a bookshop that only sold antique texts in Latin, a record store frequented by the hippest Palermo citizens, the entrance to a palace, the top of the Greek theater popping up from behind a building.

The bus stop itself was the least impressive sight. Attached to the train station, it was as dreary as any back home in Ireland. As the bus wasn't any more luxurious or exciting, Kate secretly lamented the end of her Palermo adventure.

First stop was a Catania, another costal town equal in charm as it was to views. Marco pointed out the looming Mt. Etna, describing it as the center of all Sicilians' world. A volcano that contained all of the famous Italian tempers.

When boarding the bus, she and Marco had taken a seat across from two women travelling together. One with slightly graying hair and a disheveled look, and the other a slick twenty-something who looked as stylish and effortlessly chic as the other Italian women on the bus. The two chatted animatedly in English about their journey and Kate quickly deduced from their accents that they were American.

After a little while, Marco, sitting on the outside seat, interjected himself into the women's conversation.

"*Buongiorno*, ladies! I am sorry to interrupt, but are you headed to Taormina also?" He oozed charm, and he knew it, Kate thought chuckling to herself.

The older woman ignored him, evidently more off-put than Kate had been by this Italian stranger's insistence to strike up conversation. The younger woman however, happily replied. "Yes, yes we are. We are on our way to Villa Isabella."

"Villa Isabella?" Kate perked up. "That's where I'm headed too."

"Yes, we're there for the cookery class. Are you as well?" The older woman now seemed just as enthused to meet a fellow student as Kate was.

She nodded, "I am. I hear it is amazing. I'm not much of a cook, but I suppose there's really no better place to learn Italian cooking than Italy itself." She grinned, hoping their response would be equally enthusiastic. "I'm Kate."

"Great to meet you. I'm Martha, and this is Olivia. Olivia is a travel writer. We met on the connecting plane from Ro—"

The information was enough for Marco to pounce, "Olivia. What a beautiful name! Almost as beautiful as mine, Marco. Tell me, how long will you stay in Italy, Olivia? And is your trip for business or pleasure?"

Olivia took it all in her stride. It was easy to see that out of the three women, she was the most experienced in dealing with flirtatious foreigners. "Just here for the cookery break. That's my assignment."

"What a shame to call Italy an 'assignment.' Italy is life… it is art… it is love! There is no country like it." Marco gestured wildly, his arms dramatic yet inviting.

"I'm sure I could argue that," muttered Olivia in reply. She smiled at the other women. "But we'll all have to decide for ourselves."

Marco laughed, and continued to argue, trying to keep his conversation just between him and Olivia. Kate watched patiently, noticing Martha behave almost like a protective mother hen, ensuring that her younger companion was not getting in too deep with this stranger.

As the bus edge slowly up the hill on the zig-zag roadways leading to Taormina, finally coming to a stop near the centre of the town, Marco helped the women gather their bags from the overhead storage.

Ever the gentleman, he kissed each of their hands as the three loaded into a taxi bound for Villa Isabella.

Before the driver could take off, he peeked in "Before I let you leave, I have to ask… what did you bring to give to Chef Isabella? It is rude to go to a Sicilian's home without a gift of some sort."

"Oh, I didn't bring anything!" Martha and Olivia nodded in agreement to Kate's reply. "Should we pick something up on the way, maybe a bottle of wine?"

"No!" he exclaimed, almost offended. "It is even worse to bring a bottle of wine to a Sicilian's home."

"Why so? In the US, it's almost customary." Olivia was intrigued, taking out a notepad to jot down his reply.

"It is akin to saying that your host does not have good taste in wine. In Sicily, we grow up knowing what wines are the best and what are not so good. Plus, as a chef, your host will already have wines paired with the meals."

The three women sat in silent contemplation. This sudden injection of cultural mores was both valuable and telling.

"What I suggest you do is bring her flowers," Marco went on. "It's not the best, but good for when you meet a stranger for the first time. I'll have the driver bring you to a shop a street down from the villa." Without giving the women time to interject, he began speaking in Italian to the driver, both nodding in agreement.

"Ciao, till later. I'm sure I shall see you around." With his hands in his pocket, Marco let go of the open window, and watched as the car sped off towards Villa Isabella.

*T*he taxi curved up the winding driveway to the entrance of Villa Isabella. Peppered with lush, leafy olive trees and bushes, and bordered by tall Italian pines, the terracotta yellow mansion shone as brightly as the sun.

While Olivia had checked out the estate online before departing, the sight of the home in person was enough to take her breath away. Her jaded facade slowly melted away as she spotted the clear blue pool jettisoning out of the landscape, and the expansive patio overlooking the scene.

This alone was worth the visit ...

Standing by the brown wooden door was who Olivia quickly identified as Chef Isabella. The woman's black and white pinstriped dress engulfed her petite, yet stout body. Her silver and black hair was knotted in a loose braid that dripped over her collarbone. She fit right in with the Italian renaissance scene.

The women disembarked, each slowly approaching their host with gentle caution. Olivia gingerly carried the bundle of sunflowers they had picked out from the flower shop Marco had directed them to.

"*Che meraviglia*! You all arrive together! The fates must have been on our sides today." Isabella smiled brightly at the group, as she outstretched her arms first to Martha, embracing her in a large hug and exchanging gentle cheek kisses. Kate was next, but instead of a hug, Isabella grasped her hands tenderly.

Olivia, flowers in arms, was never one for affection. Even though she was worldly and had grown accustomed to the traditional European greeting, she still shied away. For some reason, Isabella seemed to sense this, and instead took the flowers from her and gently touched her cheek with the soft, wrinkled palm of her hand.

"*Grazie*, my dear. *Grazie*. These are beautiful." Isabella deeply inhaled the scent of the sunflowers, genuinely impressed by the gesture.

"The flowers are from all of us." Olivia went down the line, introducing each of the other women. "We wanted to thank you for welcoming us to your beautiful home. It is breathtaking."

"Well, you must see inside first before you say that." With a quick turn on her low heeled leather shoes, Isabella opened the large wooden doors and walked inside with a motion for the women to follow.

All three silently took the cue, grabbed their bags, and rushed to catch up with the sprite Sicilian.

"These are the bedrooms. Each of you have single rooms, but you will all need to share the two bathrooms on this floor. My room is downstairs, near the *cucina*, the kitchen. I like to sleep where the action is." She grinned as Kate giggled.

Isabella glanced at a dangling gold pocket watch that hung from her dress. "*Accidenti!* We only have a couple of hours till the market closes. Unpack quickly and meet me downstairs in the living quarters. We have lots to do if we are to get dinner on the table by eight."

Olivia walked into the room closest to her. Alabaster walls and white linens dominated the speckled bedroom. Even the furniture was painted in an antique pale yellow that fit right into the scene.

Stark white, translucent thread curtains floated softly in the air, as a soft breeze pushed from the open window.

Setting her suitcase on the chair, she pushed back the drapery further and fully opened the shuttered window.

She let out a gasp as all of Taormina came into view. The villa itself sat on the lofty hillside, with the town itself sparkling right below her.

To the right was Mount Etna, the volcano. Straight ahead was the sea, dominating the landscape, its turquoise color glimmering in the fading sun.

The rest of Sicily circled around, forming a classic U-shape that gave Olivia the impression of being so close, yet so far away from civilization.

EAGER TO SEE the rest of the property, Olivia joined the other women and Isabella on the bottom level of the villa. The living room was expansive and also decked out in all white. However, colorful accents like the red throw cushions or the yellow woven rug popped out from the scene.

Connected was the massive kitchen which Olivia instantly identified as a chef's paradise.

The white and tan work stations were decked out into five designated areas. Each had its own stove, oven, and sink along with an apron hanging from the counter drawer. Simple cooking utensils were tucked away in a decorative metal pot. In the corner of the room was a hanging display of pots, pans, lids, and cutlery hung on hooks and magnetic strips.

Isabella sat on a wooden stool at the center station, furiously writing on brown parchment cards. She only took a moment to acknowledge the three women as they entered the space, speaking as she continued to write. "Welcome to the kitchen! Each of you have a workspace along with your apron. Two hours before breakfast and dinner, we will gather here. I will hand you a recipe card outlining what you will make, and then walk you individually through what to do. Normally, I would get to know you all a bit better first, so I will simply guess at your skill levels tonight.

"Each of my classes are different. I never pick the same recipe. What fun would that be for me? Tonight, I am thinking we'll start with some of my favorite recipes. Martha, you shall make the *antipasti*, the appetizer, *melanzane alla parmigiana*. Kate will make the *primo*, the first course. It is typically a pasta, so I say we try *linguine al limone?* Olivia will make the *secondi*, the *Fettine alla Pizzaiola*. And I will make the dessert."

As their tutor assigned each student their mission for the evening, she handed out three cards with a recipe written in English.

Olivia studied her small stack, each card crunched with specific instructions and notes. Her own recipe didn't appear quite intimidating as the others. It was a simple meat and tomato sauce dish. However, she was relieved that her cooking skills wouldn't necessarily be put to the test just yet.

"In Sicily, eating isn't just a thing we *do*." Isabella went on. "We say *sperimentiamo*: we *experience* it. In order to make a good Sicilian meal, you must know the basics before you become a master. I do not expect you to walk out of here in four days as authentic Italian chefs. Instead, I expect you all to learn about what it means to be an *artista*. To do so, you must know that there are rules when it comes to eating here." She emphasized the world 'rule' as if it was something they should take heed of, like a law or a commandment. Olivia rummaged in her bag for her notepad, hoping to take all the wisdom she could get for her article.

"Your first rule is that not everything is in season. I have been to America, and I have seen your giant markets with your fruits and vegetables lined up on display. That is no good, to have so many options at all times. The best in life is what available now, what is *fresco*. There should be no worry about the future or the past. In Italy we say, *Ciò che conta è oggi*—what matters is today. We work with what God has given us, not with what we wish we had. So when we plan our meals, we plan with the season in mind."

Olivia scribbled away furiously as Martha continued to stare at her card. Kate, on the other hand, looked directly at Isabella with a quizzical look on her face. Her eyes widened with each bit of wisdom.

"Before we get started, we obviously need ingredients. So we will go to Taormina's best shops and markets before they close. I will show you how to shop for what you truly need."

114

CHAPTER 10

The three women duly followed Isabella out of the kitchen and down the stone steps that jutted out from the hillside.

The actual town was about a ten minute walk straight down the steps to reach the centre. The stone steps changed quickly into light and gray checker board pavement, and the streets soon became overrun with tourists from cruise ships and nearby hotels. Yet Isabella took everything in her stride, seamlessly pushing through the crowds, with her students following closely behind.

Most of the market's vendors and shops were located along Porta Catania. Lined up with their colorful fruits and produce on tables, and on the beds of trucks, the owners of the mobile stalls shouted loudly at their customers and other proprietors.

As they stood at the foot of the market, all three women looked at each other and shuddered. Shopping here would not be as easy as it was in supermarkets, Isabella was right about that.

The chef turned towards her group before starting, "I have made list of the ingredients we need for *la cena* tonight, as well as breakfast tomorrow morning. We'll start first with vegetables and then work our way to the outside for the meats and seafoods.

Always get last the things that will smell. Plus, meat vendors are more desperate to sell than the produce men."

She handed each a copy of the list. With only about ten items, it did not seem like it would take too long—just a quick shopping trip.

However, Martha quickly realized she had misjudged the task. Isabella insisted on stopping at each vegetable and fruit stall to squeeze, smell, and inspect each item. She would hold up an onion or a tomato and loudly point out the imperfections, much to the ire of the cart's owner. The women, stunned by her boldness and her ease of spotting rot or ripeness, nodded in silence.

About twenty stalls were ventured through when Isabella go to the end of the staircase street. "So, *miei cari*, who can tell me where we should get the best tomato from?"

Kate and Martha averted their eyes, obviously stumped by the question. Olivia chimed in confidently, "Nowhere. None of those vendors had a perfect vegetable or fruit."

Isabella placed her hand on her chin, studying the words as Olivia said them. "Let me ask you this: is life ever perfect? Have you ever found the juiciest peach or the ripest tomato? Have your beans ever been the most green that you've ever seen them?"

Olivia shook her head in reply, duly chastened.

"So, why should we look for perfection? None of these vendors will have it here. But even the dullest pea can taste as good as the next. A tomato with a bruise can still be as flavorful as before. Instead of searching for something that doesn't exist, we seek out what we think - in our hearts - is the best of what is presented to us."

With their heads held a bit higher, the women went back into the heart of the marketplace, again stopping at each stall. Kate decided on the onions while Martha hunted down the beans. Olivia cautiously selected the peppers, unsure of what Isabella could mean by 'best of what is presented to us.'

When they were sure of their choices, Isabella would approve of the selection and then haggle with the vendor loudly in Italian. Each of the burly, sweaty men would at first appear off-put by Isabella's boldness and her instance at getting in the final word. When they would not relent, she would walk away to the vendor next to them, cooly passing them off until the owner would run towards her with a counter offer.

The meat was an easier adventure. With only beef on the menu, they glided effortlessly pass the men with meat on a spit, or hoisted on the top of a tent, to a small building in the corner of the market.

Inside, a balding man with a handlebar mustache greeted Isabella enthusiastically.

"The best way to buy your bigger items," Isabella said as she turned from the butcher back to her group, "is to find the person you trust the most. Federico has been selling me my beef for thirty-five years. I know that when I need the best of the best, Rico will provide."

The man returned with a package wrapped in red string and brown paper.

He kissed Isabella on the cheek and waved goodbye to the women as they marched back to the villa with their marketplace wares in paper sacks.

ONCE THEY SETTLED BACK IN, Isabella showed each student to their station. Olivia took her place at the one nearest the window. She donned her red apron and white chef's hat as she shook the tension and nervousness from her hands. As a traveler without a constant base, she rarely prepared for anyone, let alone had a home-cooked meal. The thought of cooking for three other women, one a professional chef, scared her senseless. Yet, she powered through, following Isabella's delicately written instructions word for word.

As she began to mix the sauce with the meat, Isabella appeared behind her shoulder, startling her. Previously, she had been keenly focused on Kate, who was struggling to find the right balance of lemon zest for her linguine. Now it was clearly Olivia's turn to be in the pressure spot.

"You seem nervous, *mio bambino*. You shouldn't be. Even if you ruin the recipe, the trick about hosting with a group of friends and loved ones is that we care enough to lie to you." She smiled at her own joke as she placed her hands upon Olivia's shoulders, squeezing the tension away. "But let's try a taste anyway. Sampling is the best part of being a chef." She grabbed a large fork from the metal utensil pot and tasted a bit of the meat.

"Slightly overcooked, but still delicious. Try a bit."

Olivia took a bite herself as the tomato sauce she created burst into her mouth, the hearty beef texture following second, and the onion leaving a gentle kick.

"It's good, but I still overcooked it. It should be more tender, right?"

"Yes, it should. But it is as I said in the market: sometimes, even the food with imperfections can taste as good. No point in searching constantly for 'perfect' or 'best.'"

Olivia looked back down at her pan both messy, yet a work of art. Using her phone, she snapped a picture and debated who to send it to.

She could upload it on her social media pages where her followers could find it. But this felt like something so personal, something she wanted to share with those she cared for deeply. However, there was no one in Olivia's life worth this intimate accomplishment, she realised sadly.

Instead, she tucked the phone back into her pocket, and began plating her food. Tonight, she wouldn't think about what was truly on her mind.

Instead, she would join the rest of the class as they feasted on their dinner at the table overlooking the crystal, navy blue sea.

$\mathcal{T}$he cell phone vibrated incessantly, shaking the antique bedside table until it rattled itself off the shelf and onto the wooden floor. It kept buzzing, the constant "zzz" "zzz" "zzz" echoing off the floorboards until Martha could take it no longer.

Rolling over, she grabbed in the dark for her pair of black reading glasses, knocking over a book in the process. She finally found the lamp switch and, the room now illuminated, found her phone still vibrating. Looking at the caller ID, she cursed mildly and answered the call.

"Kurt!" she hissed into the receiver, praying that the ruckus she was making in her room hadn't woken anyone else in the villa. "Do you know what time it is here? It's—" she held the phone away from her ear and checked the time "—four in the morning!"

"Mom." The voice on the other end was flat and even, and Martha's anger melted. Kurt, her youngest, always had a way of twisting her emotions around with just that pleading sound of his voice. "Something's happened. I need help."

She quickly sat up, brushing her hair wildly from her eyes. "What's wrong? Talk to me. I'm awake now." Her coddling voice was almost too eager.

"It's school. I, uh, got caught…" he waited for her to catch on. Martha's silence begged for more, "I was at this freshman party and there was beer …I didn't know any better."

Martha swallowed and attempted a tone that could be lecturing without coming off as angry. She only partly pulled it off.

"Kurt," she said in a measured tone, "you knew that was against school policy. You're still underage. I warned you about this." She listened as he murmured incoherently into the phone. Obviously, the matter was much more urgent than she had previously thought. "So, what does the school want to do about it?"

"They're suspending me!" he wailed, his usual emotional control failing. "What am I going to do? They want me to move out in three days. I can't move out in three days! And what about my classes? What about my major? I'm not going to be able to graduate on time. I'm not going to be able to pledge this year, Mom. What if they don't let me back?"

"Honey, slow down. Everything will work out. I will call later today when the school opens. I'll get this sorted out for you. For right now, just hang tight and stick to your room. Okay?" Her motherly instincts had kicked into high gear.

"Yeah, okay. You promise you'll call, Mom?" Her youngest sounded just like he did as a child: vulnerable and afraid.

"Yes. Now, I need to go back to sleep. The sun hasn't even come up yet in Italy. I love you." With that, Martha hung up the phone. A smile popped on her face.

For the first time in ages, she felt needed again.

CHAPTER 12

*K*ate woke to birds singing outside her window. Early morning sunlight drenched her white room, giving it an almost ethereal appearance.

The entire scene looked as charming as she had envisioned it when she first decided to go on this trip. Stretching out her arms, she instinctively looked for her phone first.

No missed calls.

Getting up, she grabbed her robe, a towel, and her travel bag of toiletries. As she opened the door to head to the communal bathroom, she stopped short.

Outside her room sat a large floral bouquet full of large yellow sunflowers, not too dissimilar to the ones they'd brought Isabella yesterday. But as their host had arranged these in a vase in the hallway she knew these were different.

Probably Isabella's way of returning the gesture.

She grabbed the bouquet, unsure what to do with it, and glanced at Olivia's and Martha's doors. Not seeing any matching bouquets, she assumed they were up and about and had already collected theirs.

She placed the flowers on her bedside locker and inhaled their earthy, succulent scent. It had been years since she had got flowers.

She had always insisted to Ed that it was a cliched, overpriced gesture, but the truth was, she was slightly envious of other women whose husbands went out of their way to pick up flowers for birthdays or special occasions.

The dissatisfied thought caught her attention instantly, and she shook her head wildly as a way to remove her from the moment. Today was not about her disappointments.

Today was about her, her relaxation, and her quest to learn Italian cooking. With determination, Kate grabbed her towel, and went to get ready for the breakfast lesson.

Once showered and dressed, she joined Olivia and Martha in the kitchen. Isabella was already busy preparing the ingredients and mixing bowls. However, it seemed the foursome wasn't alone this morning.

Kate was surprised to see Marco, their helpful stranger from yesterday, standing right in the kitchen alongside Isabella, chatting rapidly in Italian.

"Ah! Our *traversina* has arrived, and just in time." Isabella's attention whipped from Marco and onto a bashful Kate. "Come join us. And meet *mio nipote*, my grandson, Marco. We're learning how to make briosce to go with our morning gelato."

Grandson?

"Gelato?" Olivia chimed, seemingly more intrigued by the idea of dessert for breakfast than Marco turning out to be a relative of their host.

Marco looked at her pointedly. "*Si,* gelato. We sometimes have our pastries with shaved ice, but today, I brought gelato as a celebration of my triumphant return to Taormina." He winked at her and smiled.

Martha laughed heartily, "Wait until I tell my Kurt about dessert for breakfast!"

The three women gathered around Isabella's station as she

began mixing flour, egg, milk, sugar, and butter into a giant jewel-colored mixing bowl. "Most chefs are lazy," she sighed. "They buy their breakfast from shops or cafés. But the best breakfasts are the ones you make yourself."

The women mimicked her actions as they formed balls of dough in their white powdered hands.

Marco joined in, more confidently than the women, placing himself shoulder to shoulder with Olivia.

"Keep your flour to yourself, please," she said to him as he lightly tossed a handful of flour onto the top of her kneaded dough. Cupping her hands around some flour of her own, she blew the remains into his hair.

"I look like my grandmother now." He turned and brushed it away, grinning over at Olivia as she continued to mold her briosce.

TWO HOURS LATER, the briosce was taken out of the oven as the students gathered their own trays, each admiring their handiwork.

"In all my life, I've never made my own bread without a mixer." Martha looked down at her golden brown pastries with newfound pride as they moved to the wooden communal dining table.

Marco followed the group with a large, clear plastic tub of glossy, creamy gelato. He served Isabella first as she cut lightly into the center of the pastry. Marco placed a dollop of the coffee-flavored cold treat in the center of the bun.

Kate and Martha seemed unsure of how to approach such a strange, rich breakfast. But Olivia, being the adventurer she was, jumped in headfirst, taking a large bite.

The sweet and eggy taste overwhelmed her senses, bringing back memories of childhood treats and simple, country meals. It was heavenly. The other two joined in, each having a similar reaction. All almost too overwhelmed to speak.

"The reward of a good meal is sometimes a quiet guest," Isabella smiled as she stared at the girls. "When you are finished, leave your plates here. I will clean up and store the rest of your buns and gelato for tomorrow. This afternoon, you may explore Taormina. I'm sure Marco can guide you around if you wish. The beach, if that interests you, is only a short distance down the hill. I need you back here by four o'clock to start dinner."

Marco turned towards the women, as Isabella excused herself.

"Would you like to join me in my shop? It is only a short distance from here. I can show you how to make glass just like my ancestors."

"I'd be interested." Olivia tried her best to sound unenthused, but genuinely cultural experiences had always excited her.

"I had actually planned on checking out one of the hotel spas. Do you have a recommendation?" Kate had looked forward to a spa day since she had stepped off the plane in Palermo. Pampering was exactly what she needed.

"I may stick around here actually, Isabella if that's OK. I need to be near my phone in case my son calls. He needs my help with some school thing." Martha was a bit timid with her news, but she couldn't help but smile at the same time.

A little later, Kate, Olivia, and Marco said their goodbyes to the others as they rushed out the door to begin their Taormina adventure.

Alone together, Isabella turned to her guest, "It's a rare treat for me to have a friend around for the day. Most students want to escape on their vacation, not stay here. Is it an emergency?"

Martha considered her words. *An emergency?* It wasn't something she needed to fly home over, but hearing Kurt yearn for his mother was so different and unique for her. The last time she could remember him needing her help was when he first started high school almost five years ago.

"No, not an emergency as such, but he needs my help. You know what it's like to be a mom. You're always on call!" Her chipper voice floated with her words.

"How old is your son?" Isabella asked, as she and Martha began clearing the table of the remaining breakfast dishes.

"Kurt's nineteen. Just started college, but it sounds like he got in trouble with some of the rules, and needs my help getting out of a jam."

"I see." The older woman kept her head down, focusing on

tidying up the table. "Before you go off to make your phone calls, would you like to help me set up some lunch?"

"I would love that." Martha lied. She wanted to be on the phone with the school as soon as possible. Preparing lunch when they'd just finished breakfast couldn't be farthest from her mind.

Isabella went to her fridge, taking out a platter of uncut meats.

"When my sons were younger, all they wanted was meat, meat, meat. Lamb, pig, cow, goat… whatever they could get their hands on. I would say to them 'one day, you will need to make your own meat.' So I would have them go down to the butcher and watch him work. Now, my oldest owns a butcher shop in Agrigento that my youngest works at. Best in the town!" She began slicing the meat into thin circles using a large silver carving knife.

"My second son, though, he never wanted to go. He'd stay at home or sneak away from his brothers. He would watch the others and think that he would always be provided for. When he left home to work at the docks, he would write to me about how horrible the food was. Complain, complain, complain. I blame myself for that." Her body shuddered for a second.

Martha looked at her curiously. "Why would you blame yourself?"

Isabella sighed as she finished up. "I always thought, maybe like a fool, that he could rely on his brothers or me if he needed. But I'm getting older; there's no doubt about that! And his brothers are grown men with families of their own. They have their own children to teach their trade."

Martha watched as Isabella spread the slices of meat she had cut onto a platter of thin brown crackers and golden-colored cheeses.

But instead of a celebrated Italian chef, she watched another mother twenty or so years older than herself, suffer just as she did.

The woes of motherhood crossed every generation and every border.

For both Martha and Isabella, the thought of releasing a child not fully prepared for the realities of life was immeasurably frightening.

Martha thought back to the satisfaction she felt this morning hearing Kurt plead the words "mom" and "help" because he knew - he knew that she would jump to his side, hold his hand once again.

But, as Isabella said, maybe he would have to learn to make his own mistakes? He could not always rely on her to help him.

And likewise, she realised, chastened, she should not wish for her children to remain as they once were: needy and helpless.

With sadness in her eyes, but fire in her belly, Martha understood what she had to do.

"Isabella, I think I *am* going to go down to the beach today. Can you tell me how to get there?"

Isabella smiled as she offered to pack Martha a small lunch for her day in the sun.

CHAPTER 14

The light in Taormina was almost overwhelming.

Between the white and dusty browns of the stone walls, and steps down to the gleaming blues of the ocean, the town itself had an opulent glow.

Olivia was almost too overwhelmed by the sheer beauty of it to care about the tourists and the hawking vendors that spread themselves throughout the streets. Normally, this wouldn't be her scene at all. But today, she was oblivious. Today, she was in love.

Marco had doted on her since leaving Kate at a nearby hotel spa. His tour of the city was fascinating as he pointed out the charming cathedrals and ancient ruins of the Greeks and Egyptians that still remained behind.

Taking a detour, he insisted emphatically that the two make a stop at his favorite place in the city, the Giardini della Villa Comunale.

"What is that? More ruins?" she quizzed him.

"No, not at all. It's a park. The best park in the world."

"Why do you say that? How many parks have you been to that you can declare it as the best?" She smugly reminded him of her international knowledge.

"You know, you do not need to go everywhere to know that some place is the best," Marco replied easily. "Sometimes, you just know, in your heart, that you do not need to search any further than what is right in front of you."

He stopped walking and turned towards her, offering his hand. It was such an unexpectedly gentlemanly gesture that Olivia was a bit taken aback. Almost without thinking, she gingerly placed her small white palm into his, allowing him to squeeze a bit.

The two walked the rest of the way in a blissful silence, hand in hand, as they entered the park's grounds. Marco guided her expertly through the greenery, pointing out the remains of the old city zoo, and the base of the stone of Lazarus pagodas that jutted out as almost as naturally as the trees and other flora.

"Can you see why I think that this is the best park?"

Olivia nodded eagerly as Marco spun her around towards the outside walls. She could instantly spot the reason as the trees disappeared and the Ionian Sea opened up before her.

The panoramic view allowed her to look down at red and brown brick roofs of the buildings of Taormina with widened eyes and a fuller heart.

She had seen some resplendent views on her travels, but this was truly one of the most impressive ones. As she spun again, she spotted the tip of Mt. Etna peaking at her from a distance.

After a moment of taking in the salty sea air and listening to the breeze drift in the Italian pine trees, she turned back to her companion.

"While I see why you love this place, I have to ask.. Why would you not want to go out and see if this truly is the best park in the world? Are you not curious?"

"Of course I am!" He laughed without mocking. "But Taormina will always be home. It may not be Central Park or have the Eiffel Tower in the background, but it will have my heart, and I want to be where my heart is."

His words shot through her. Of course she had many times

heard the saying *Home is where the heart is*, but she had always put little faith in it. Her heart had always been wherever her suitcase was. Sure, it was a little battered and beaten from the road, but she had managed to keep it from heartbreak and sorrow. It was full of experiences, not love, and she was fine with that. Or at least, she hoped she was.

"What about you Olivia. Where is your heart? What place is your *villa comunale?*"

She sunk into deep thought as she retraced her travel memories, all of which were now a blur of deadlines and rewrites.

As a travel writer, her stories from the road were dissected and dismantled by people other than herself. Her photos and notes were just keepsakes, until she had moved on. She had little time to actually take in a moment, let alone find the unique treasure of it. "I don't know if I've found it yet," she admitted. "Is that a bad?"

"You'll find it," Marco said, giving her a reassuring smile, "but in the mean time, you can borrow this park." His playful brown eyes softened as they caught hers. It wasn't pity that she saw inside of them though; it was a powerful warmth and fortitude she had not experienced before.

She longed to let go of his hand and place hers on to his chest, just to feel if his heart was beating like hers, fast and in a rhythm all new.

But she didn't dare do so. Instead, Olivia turned back to the sea, content on taking this moment in.

CHAPTER 15

"*Y*ou've reached Ed O'Toole. I am unable to answer my phone at the moment. Please leave me your name and phone number, and I will get back to you as soon as possible. Cheers."

Beep.

"Hello, love. It's noon here in Taormina, and I'm pretty sure you're in the thick of things at work. I am assuming that is why you are not answering. I just wanted to let you know that I am fine. Well, I'm better than fine. This place is amazing, and Chef Isabella is, well … amazing too. She left sunflowers for us all this morning. How lovely is that? Anyway, we have the afternoon off, so I am going to a spa at this place her grandson recommended. I hope you're not too jealous. It would, of course, be better if you were here with me, but I understand why you are not. At least, I think I understand. I'm not sure. I …I really want to talk to you and tell you more. Will you ring me when you get back from lunch or when you're not so busy? Okay. I think that's all. I love you."

Kate felt instant regret settle over her. She had promised herself that morning that she wasn't going to call Ed or even worry about why his phone seemed to just ring and ring whenever she tried to get through.

Yet, here she was leaving him a long and rambling message whereby she practically confessed her frustrations and need to see him.

The thought of the spa had never sounded more appealing to her than this moment. Marco had been able to convince the best spa in Taormina to take her for the day. Though the Hotel Lusso already looked packed with guests wrapped in white downy robes and slippers, the manager guided her to a private room where he handed her an English menu of their offerings.

She carefully selected the stone massage with Sicilian oils, a dip in the salt water pools, a manicure, and a pedicure. Many of these treatments were things Kate had always wanted to try, but the high price of the fertility treatments had kept her from indulging at home. Even a trip to the beauty salon would have triggered instant guilt that she was spending too much on herself and not on the future of her family.

But as the manager came back with towels, robes, and slippers, the need for self-deprivation melted off as Kate stripped down her layers of clothing. She removed her wedding ring last, placing it carefully in the safe assigned to her along with her still silent mobile phone.

The orange umbrella Martha rested under glided back and forth gently in the wind, and the pink concoction the bartender at the beach had made her, was just what she need to cool her nerves. Stretching a seemingly endless distance, the pale sand and pebbles of Letojanni beach beckoned her and the hundreds of other sunbathers surrounding her, to give in to its charms.

She had never been one for the beach. When the children were young, she and William took regular family trips to the shore in the summer months. But as a mom, she considered those vacations more like business trips: there was always sunscreen to apply to someone's nose, and sandwiches to protect from sand and bugs. Her time to relax was more or less limited to the moments in which her husband would distract the children long enough for her to take a nap or read a chapter of a book.

But today, Martha was without worry or care. On the ride in on the beach bus, she had left a message for Kurt basically telling him that there was little she could do from Italy, and that he would need to deal with it as a man.

She hated doing it, but she understood that she needed to let him stand on his own two feet. It wasn't as though freshman drinking exploits were anything new to a college principal - or indeed serious - and certainly nothing she needed to get involved with.

Anyway, a little scare like that would only stand her son in good stead for the remainder of his time in college.

So Martha decided, for the rest of this trip, a trip given to her as a means of escape from her children, she was off the grid.

And on her first day as a free woman for the first time in almost thirty years, she went to take a swim in the Ionian sea.

While all the other women her age sat dry and baking, she boldly removed her cover up and marched herself into the sea.

The waves gathered and nipped gently at her legs, and the salt water frothed and foamed around her body as she waded deeper in.

She dipped her head back, soaking her hair in aquamarine sea, and eventually, she placed her whole body in, letting it rise to the surface to float lazily on her back.

As Martha stared up at the cloud-speckled sky, with a weight off her shoulders, suddenly the world seemed to open up to her like never before, and she imagined all of the other seas and oceans she could experience now.

She imagined herself trekking in Brazil, diving in Egypt, and snorkelling in Australia.

It was all so new and fresh.

A dream that was once her husband's, to travel and explore, had now taken over and become her own.

*K*ate blew quickly on her nails, attempting to speed-dry them as she hurried up the stone steps back to Isabella's home. She was late—almost twenty minutes now—and hadn't had time to wait for the blue light machines to work their magic.

So instead, she ran, hoping to keep her freshly painted pink fingernails safe from harm.

She wasn't late on purpose. In fact, she had been watching the time meticulously, acutely aware of her obligation to be back at the villa for dinner preparations. But instead, it was the hotel manager that had kept her back. As she had requested the bill for her day at the spa, he had insisted that she had already paid.

"*Signor*," Kate explained, "there must be some mistake. I haven't paid for anything, and I am in a hurry. Can you just process a bill for me so I can pay and be on my way?" Her impatience was growing thin and the benefits of her relaxing day quickly wearing off.

The manager's thin mustache twitched as he looked her over.

"*Signorina* O'Toole," he explained, "I am telling you that your bill is already paid. You are free to go whenever you need."

"I don't understand," she countered impatiently, "How can that be possible? I haven't even given you my credit card!" She curtly handed him her Bank of Ireland debit card, insisting that he take it. The man's hands rose quickly as if to guard him from it, and she finally sighed and gave up, returning the card to her purse. "Fine. I will take my *free* day at the spa then..."

She waited for him to reply, but he instead walked from behind the long birchwood desk and graciously walked her to the door. "I hope you enjoyed your stay," he called, "Please do visit us again."

As she strolled along the cobblestone path outside the hotel, she found herself at a loss, wondering what to make of the situation.

Would another less charitable employee track her down later to try to get more money out of her than she owed?

Just in case, she sped up a bit, attempting to retrace her steps from earlier in the day when Marco had shown her the way to the hotel.

Rounding the corner, she spotted Martha, who brushed a patch of yellow sand from her skirt with a pink-tinged hand.

"Kate! Were you at this hotel?" the older woman gushed, running up to her. "Did you check out the beach at all? It was to die for."

"I thought you were staying back at the villa?" she replied distractedly. "Did you get everything sorted with your son?"

"No," Martha admitted, "but that's the thing, I figured that if I am on vacation, I should actually *be* on vacation. So, instead, I spent the entire day at the beach drinking these pink little cocktails and reading this brilliant book I picked up from the library back home. I totally lost track of time!"

"That sounds great," Kate smiled, pleased to see her looking so happy. "I spent my day at the spa here. For some reason, there was an issue with my bill, but I guess it worked itself out."

She didn't dare tell Martha that her opulent day of me-time was apparently on someone else's account.

The two women instead spent the rest of their quick walk back to Isabella's villa recounting their day, from the pedicurist who spoke nine languages to the bartender at the beach who purred at Martha while calling her "carina."

Olivia was already back at the villa.

Still glowing from her own day in the sunlight, she moved around the kitchen effortlessly as she worked on her assigned recipe.

Marco walked her through a new, more efficient technique for chopping up tomatoes. Both stood arm and arm, sharing laughs and long glances.

Joining them at their workstations, Martha and Kate couldn't help but raise eyebrows at the pair of the them, a budding couple if ever there was one, Kate thought.

As they made their sincerest apologies for being late, Isabella quickly handed them their handwritten recipe cards and dinner tasks of the evening.

Kate had the *secondo*, a swordfish chop, while Martha was assigned the *primo,* a most famous Sicilian recipe, the *pasta alla norma.*

Marco would make the dessert, a Sicilian version of cannoli.

Fluttering between stations, Isabella guided each woman with their dishes. She tasted everything, savoring even the simplest of spice combinations. When assisting Kate with chopping the swordfish into smaller pieces, she didn't flinch as she deftly added even more olive oil to the pot.

All the while as the dishes cooked, she hummed a sweet tune while pointing out opportunities for what she called "vista breaks" to take in the sight of the sun floating lower into the sea.

Occasionally, she stopped for lessons. For Martha, she applauded her instinct to double the garlic cloves to the pasta's already flavorful palate. Looking over Kate's seafood dish, she reminded the women that patience is a virtue. Cooking a meat on low was sometimes the only way to get the best results.

And for Olivia, she reassured her that perfection wasn't necessary in a dish's appearance; and that sometimes, the look of a meal was deceptive with the worst tasting often being the most eye-catching.

As the group finished their final touches, Isabella gave her last lesson of the night on the virtue of wines.

None of the women admitted to being big fans or frequent drinkers, giving Isabella time to speak.

"Most of you probably only serve one wine per meal," she explained, "but in Sicily, we know that not every meal will have its perfect pair for each dish. Instead, we drink a glass with each course. For tonight, we have Olivia's *arancinette.* Deep fried rice balls probably doesn't seem like any match for a wine, but every meal has its mate. The heaviness of it calls for something red, light, and full of flavor. Martha's pasta needs something to balance, rather than to detract, so a simple table red that is low on acidity is best. And finally, with Kate's swordfish, we will drink a glass of Inzolia, a white grape wine."

"That's a ton of wine!" Kate exclaimed, as she held her first glass high while Isabella poured a generous helping of the first red. "How does anyone stay sober in this country?"

"We drink slow and savor," Isabella smiled. "It would be a waste to drink too fast and spoil our food. With nowhere else to go and good company, who would want to spend their time too ill to take in the fun?

Marco gestured to the open doors leading out to the patio over-looking the seafront. The group followed, bringing their plates out to the main patio for an *al fresco* experience. Isabella too had brought out a handful of small table candlesticks to illuminate the white linen tablecloth and the shimmering blue ceramic dinnerware.

CHAPTER 18

The evening air was light and fragrant.

While the lights of Taormina glittered, and the sounds of people on the street filled the night, the tranquility of it all gave the scene an almost out of body atmosphere.

In her mind, Olivia recognized it as one of the most authentic travel moments she had experienced in years. It was free from obligation and pre tense and as natural as sitting with her own family.

Her heart ached as she remembered that there would only be one more dinner like this.

With her wine glass raised, she instinctively stood, turning towards the front of the table where Marco and Isabella sat, "To our host. To this beautiful, mythical town. To new friends. To new hopes and dreams. To life and food."

"*Cent'ann!*" Marco chimed in, tapping her glass with his. "100 hundreds of life and love!"

"*Cin Cin!*" followed Isabella joyfully as she looked over her table. The group dived into their meal ravenously; the mixture of the swordfish, pasta, and rice warming over their senses and awakening their tired minds.

Isabella talked endlessly about the tucked-away Taormina vineyards she traveled to for their drinks and her favorite vendor at the docks who always gave her the best deal on her seafood when the market was low.

"Isabella, what do you do when you are not hosting your cookery course? Do you spend the time alone in this big home?" Martha asked with genuine curiosity.

"Oh no! I go out on friends' boats. I travel to see friends. I tend to my garden. And sometimes, I have my sons or grandsons take me dancing."

"Dancing?" Kate's eyes lit up. Before she married Ed, she had loved to go to local night clubs and discos.

"Of course! There are several dance halls here. And sometimes, I'll even go to the modern clubs along the beach for young people. But that is when I am feeling my bravest."

Marco laughed, "You should see her! I've taken her to several beach bars and she will ask anyone to dance. She especially likes the men with longer hair... right, Grandma?"

Isabella gently brushed him off with a wave of her hands as she stood to go retrieve the desserts from the fridge.

Kate continued, "I would love to go dancing tonight if we could. Where would you recommend, Marco?"

"I would say Passaggi. It's a good mix of not too young, not too old. And it's very romantic being out on the main square. Plus, the drinks are always strong. I could take you if you would like."

"Seriously, would you? That would make my night!" Kate clapped her hands excitedly and bounced like a child in her chair. "How about you, Olivia and Martha? Will ye come?"

Martha readily answered yes, excited to continue on her adventure from earlier in the day.

Olivia, on the other hand was reticent. She had spent all day with Marco, and she found him becoming less of a character for her travel article and more of a fixture in her own mind. Venturing out with him in such a charged environment might well push her in a way she wasn't exactly ready for.

However, she also knew that seeing some of Taormina's nightlife was almost essential to getting the city's entire profile. She had learned early on in her days on the road that what a town may appear to be in the day could totally change in an instant when the sun went down.

This was her shot to capture the entire experience.

*T*he four quickly demolished their cannoli along with the final wine of the night, a syrupy sweet *passitos*. The women then went back into their rooms, changing into more formal attire.

Kate chose a black halter dress with a plunging neckline. Martha stuck with her long, golden maxi dress and a black sweater over her shoulders.

Olivia spent the most time preparing, as she rummaged through her backpack for the pearly white shift dress she had picked up in Barcelona several years back.

She paired the look with the teardrop earrings a friend from Tokyo had gifted her, and a quick dab of ruby red lipstick - a rare luxury she typically didn't indulge in while on the road.

Marco and the others waited for her down the terrace stairs near the front entrance.

His eyes lit up at the sight of her descending the steps. She had swept up her blonde hair in a slightly messy ballerina bun atop her head, revealing her dainty neck and the slight curve of her bare, lean back.

The light from the villa bounced off her white dress, almost giving her a halo as she glided down to meet Marco's outstretched arm.

As the group approached the town, the sounds of music, laughter, and shouting grew closer. Taking a prominent place right in the center of Taormina, right then it looked oddly part of the scenery, with its open air tables, and white and tan linen awnings.

Locals and tourists mingled, chatting amongst each other on the tan sofas and huddled in secluded, corner tables.

The music was a mixture of standard club songs with thumping bass and vibrating lyrics to softer, more traditional Italian standards sung by crooners with booming voices.

Young couples danced dangerously close, locking their bodies to one another as they swayed with the beat. Older men and women sat circled around the dance floor, watching and pointing at the movements. When the music would suddenly, almost disjointedly, switch to a familiar tune, they would jump up effortlessly, weaving through the younger dancers to find their place in the center with their partners.

Kate watched one older couple contentedly.

The man, hunched over from age, removed his gray cap to reveal a wisp of waspy, thinning hair. He reached for his partner, a woman of equal age and stature, and guided her slowly out to the floor where they danced as they must have twenty, thirty, maybe even forty years before. Cheek to cheek, they swayed, not even whispering a word - both sets of eyes closed firmly as if they were picturing another scene from when they danced years before.

A twinge of guilt overcame her as she remembered her first dance with Ed at their wedding. She could almost feel him cupping her back with his large hand, guiding her to the center of the empty floor. When their song ended, he dipped her dramatically back with such ease and poise.

And at this moment, now at the Taormina club, she couldn't help but wish he was there with her, dancing like this couple, too full of memories and moments to care about the present.

Martha noticed the pained look on her dewy face. As Olivia and Marco slipped off to the bar to gather the drink orders, she asked her new friend, "Are you all right?"

"Just thinking about my husband. I haven't heard from him since yesterday when he was too busy to talk. He never called me back, and he hasn't answered the phone yet." She felt a bit foolish to be talking about her marriage problems.

Martha placed her hands tenderly on Kate's.

"That's too bad. He's the one missing out though, not you. There were so many things my husband missed out on, when he became too wrapped up in life—first moments with the kids, day trips to visit our friends, opportunities like this… But, in the end I guess it's the quality of time spent, not quantity. While it is amazing to have a partner to share things with, sometimes, it's best to be our own companion."

Kate nodded, understanding her words. She was her own companion here in Sicily, and it was time to start enjoying and loving herself.

Suddenly, the music switched over as an oldie, a popular American dance song came on.

She grinned as she tugged on Martha's hand.

"Well, since you and me are own companions tonight, we might as well partner up on the dance floor."

"Marco, look." Olivia tapped on her companion's shoulders attempting to gain his attention. She pointed at Kate and Martha as they jumped and spun around on the dance floor. Their careless, uninhibited dance moves had gained attention as both young and old infectiously joined in around them.

Olivia laughed as an older man dressed completely in white reached for Martha's raised hand and spun her body into his. Martha dipped her head back and laughed as she greeted her new partner fearlessly.

Kate had also gained the attention from several young Italian men, but she continued to dance by herself, her black dress blowing in the breeze as she twirled and dipped to the rhythm of the music.

"They look happy," Marco shouted over the music, handing Olivia the drinks. He led her back to their table near the exit. Compared to the stuffy interior and the shuffle of sweaty, youthful bodies, the terrace's nearly empty chairs and tables were a relief.

"So, what did you order me?" She stared at her orange-ish red drink with orange rinds floating near the top.

"Negroni. It's like a burnt orange gin martini with a twist. It's my favorite."

"If this is your favorite, then what are you drinking?" She glanced at his pale pink drink.

"Bellini, of course. But actually, I though if you did not like yours, we could always trade. The bellini is a little more gentle." He eyed her laughingly.

"Gentle?" She pretended to be taken aback, "I've had sauki with samurais and whiskey with the Irish. I can certainly handle this." With that, she lifted her glass to her mouth and carelessly sucked back the liquor. The gin was sour and almost tart and her face puckered in reaction and she coughed a bit into her hand.

Marco laughed at her as he spun his glass in his hand.

The music slowed to a melodic waltz.

Martha and Kate bounded from the crowd, shaking with laughter and excitement. They found their chairs next to Olivia and Marco as they continued their conversation. "—he didn't speak a word of English, but I'm pretty sure whatever he was saying to me wasn't exactly romantic!" Martha's face was a bright pink as she raised her champagne to the sky "To Taormina men!"

"I will certainly toast to that," chimed in Marco meeting her glass with his own.

"Olivia, are you going to dance? I'll join you once I catch my breath if you like?" Kate panted a bit, not even turning to face her. She was focused on getting back onto the dance floor.

"I'm really not that much of a dancer actually. I once broke my foot in a disco in Thailand. I prefer to sit back and watch."

"Well, that's unacceptable," Marco insisted, "you have to dance." He gently yanked at her arm till she could no longer protest.

She glanced back at the others, unsure of what to do; Martha shooed her away and Kate just smiled, knowingly.

Olivia turned her gaze up to Marco. "I'm really not much of a slow dancer either," she said, feeling like she was repeating herself. "I'm not even sure how to do this."

Marco stood arms-length from her, towering over her petite frame.

"Just take my hand," he said. She tentatively offered hers, and he lifted it shoulder level, pulling her slightly towards his deceptively muscular frame as they headed back out to the dance area.

SWAYING TOGETHER TO THE MUSIC, his hand went around the crook of Olivia's back as she could feel his body moving tenderly and slowly. Her right hand found its way to his chest, and she mindlessly toyed with the black buttons on his shirt.

His head arched down to lean on the side of hers. She took in his scent, warm and sweet, almost like a mixture of ginger and exotic fruit. His hand felt rough from years working in his trade, yet it wasn't any less soothing as they fell into a trance.

"I was thinking about our conversation earlier at the park," he said softly into her ear.

"Mhmm" she whispered, not fully paying attention to his words.

"I've decided that it isn't my favorite place anymore." Olivia glanced up at him, unsure of why he was suddenly bringing this up. "You are. I mean, I want you to be. I want you to be my place."

The two came to a stop, now standing at the far corner of the stone-tiled floor. She looked back at him, releasing her hand from his chest. "I don't understand."

"Can you stop looking, stop searching for your perfect place?" He lifted her chin to meet his eyes as he bent down a little to be face to face to her. "Olivia..." Marco's mouth met hers, gentle and firm. He grasped both arms around her waist making for an impossible escape, yet she didn't struggle. Her own arms twisted around his neck and into the soft brown threads of his hair.

After a long few seconds, the lights and the sounds of the thundering feet on the tile knocked her back into reality.

Marco instantly sensed the change as well, as she moved away from him, taking two steps backwards.

"I know that it is very soon. I know that you have a life, a job on the other side of the world, but I cannot let you leave tonight without asking you to think about it. Please?"

"I … uh, I have to go. Tell the others I'm feeling ill, okay?"

She spun around on her heel, leaving Marco standing alone on the packed dance floor. The crowd formed around him, sucking him into the scene of Taormina as Olivia made her escape out of the club and back onto the stone steps leading to the villa.

The starry evening and the lanterns from the streets, broke through her whirling thoughts and confusion, guiding her home.

CHAPTER 21

The following morning, Kate once again woke to the sound of silence.

No phone call, no email pings, nothing. But for whatever reason, she wasn't perplexed or upset over it.

Instead, she took it as a sign that life was as it should be. Plus, after a night like hers, she was grateful to be without interruption to process the raging headache and dizzy spells that overwhelmed her.

Moving a bit slower than usual, she went about her morning routine, and joined the rest of the class downstairs.

Martha was assisting Isabella with the pastry recipe they had made the day before, while Olivia was wrapped up on the couch, typing away furiously on her laptop. She briefly registered Kate's presence and went back to her determined work.

"*Buongiorno!*" Isabella greeted Kate excitedly at the entrance to the kitchen. "It's certainly good to see you out and about. Martha has told me all about your night on the town."

Kate looked down and laughed lightly at the flour-caked hand-print Isabella had left on her shirt. "Can I help with breakfast?" she asked.

"Of course! Olivia learned how to make the Sicilian version of Bloody Marys, and Martha is making the briosce. You can make the eggs in a tomato sauce. Simple recipe, but it's tricky."

She went to the bowl in the corner of the room where a stack of brown eggs sat. She then had Kate follow her into the pantry where she stored all of her homemade tomato sauces and pastes.

"How do you know which one is which?" Kate asked. "They all look the same to me." There had to be over a hundred clear jars full of red, chunky sauces lining the walls of her back room.

"Easy. I try them." Isabella pulled out a spoon from her apron and slowly began tasting each sauce, one by one. "I make these in the winter with my grandchildren. They each make two or three of their favorite recipes. Sometimes I write their name on the lid, but it wears off and I have trouble remembering who made what." About a quarter of the way through, she stopped, grabbing the one she had last tasted.

They returned to the kitchen where Martha had just placed her pastries in the oven. Both women gathered round as Isabella showed them the proper way to crack an egg, and the right temperature to cook sunny-side up. Once the shape of the egg started to take form and the white was showing, Isabella gently added spoonfuls of blood red sauce. Adding diced peppers, onions, and a bit of feta cheese, she expertly flipped the egg over with such ease the others let out a small gasp.

Kate took over the next one. Following each of the steps, she mimicked Isabella's movements and instructions precisely. But when it came time to flip, she hesitated nervously and the egg slipped off of her spatula and back onto the pain making a chaotic mess of vegetables, yolk, and sauce.

Defeated, she turned towards the chef unsure of how to proceed.

"No problem. We'll scramble this one." Isabella walked her through the steps to puree the egg mixture without burning.

"Even in our messiest mistakes, we can find beauty." The chef handed Kate a fork and encouraged her to try a taste of the scrambled egg. The sensation of the runny egg was marvellous as it mixed with the spicy, peppery flavor of the sauce. All Kate could do was give her food a giant thumbs up and she attempted to swallow.

The rest of the women joined in around Kate's station, not bothering to sit at the communal table. The briosce finished soon after and Isabella retrieved the remained of yesterday's gelato. Olivia's Sicilian Bloody Mary was the perfect follow-up. For Kate, breakfast was enough to awake her from her stupor and put her back in the real world.

Olivia however, was in her own little world, oblivious to all that was around her.

The night's romantic twist with Marco had her reeling. Sure, she'd had flirtations and even boyfriends while traveling. But none had been serious. No one had certainly ever asked her to stay or to even consider it. There would be promises to write, some video chats, and even gift exchanges, but eventually the long distance relationships would unravel, leaving her in a mess of emotions.

But what Marco had said last night was completely different. He wasn't asking her to travel with him in mind. He wasn't asking for a long-distance relationship, a couple of phone calls here and there. He was asking her to stay here in Taormina. It was a proposition that terrified and, suspiciously, excited her. Especially as he had been so forthright and so honest, given what little time they'd spent together. *I want you to be my place.*

She had spent all night going over his words, and most of the morning going through her work, analyzing her last steps as she traveled.

She made a pros and cons list, and wrote late night emails to a couple of trusted friends. She even opened up her secret travel journal, a notebook in which she kept of all of her true feelings regarding her life on the road.

Instead of glossing over the bad or making it more editorial or readable, she put it out on the line. And the words seemed to be saying that while life on the road was a joy, there was obviously something missing.

Maybe that piece of the puzzle was someone special, someone with whom to share that joy?

CHAPTER 22

*A*s the breakfast lesson finished up, and Isabella gave the women instructions to be back by 3pm for dinner, the women dispersed to their afternoon activities.

Kate and Martha planned on shopping some of the boutiques in the town. But for Olivia, hunting for new dresses or a pair of shoes was nowhere near what she had planned on doing.

She instead rushed out of the villa and towards Taormina in search of Marco's glass shop. She had found the address online, but navigating the streets was much more difficult than she had considered. She jogged past the medieval fortresses and cathedrals full of picture takers and tour guides and past the children playing football in the narrow, shadowed alleyways.

Eventually, she found her street and instinctively took a left. She sped up as she spotted the sign for Marco's glassware shop, almost running to the entrance.

But the doorway of the red and white store was locked.

Olivia knocked loudly, hoping that someone would hear her.

Her heart deflated with each unanswered knock. "Marco?" she called out, frantically looking into the shop. "Marco," she called out again. Still no reply. A crowd of nosy Italian men and women gathered around her, all curious as to the strange tourist shouting at the empty shop.

And then, she heard the door heave and the chains unlock. A tired, haggard looking Marco answered. She ducked under his arm and inside.

"What's wrong? What is it?" He guided Olivia to a row of red chairs in the corner of the gallery. She hadn't even taken a second to look at the beautiful glass wares and sparkling vases. She was instead fixed on Marco. He was wearing a dusty rubber apron and gloves. His work pants were frayed at the bottom and his gray shirt was tattered and full of paint and acid marks.

"You were working—" she said, in the midst of catching her breath, "I shouldn't have—" Olivia shook her head in irritation with herself, feeling silly and childish. What on earth had possessed her?

"It's nothing," he insisted. "But what is wrong? Why are you here? I thought that after last night, you would—" Marco couldn't finish his words. Instead, he took to his knees in front of her. He removed his gloves and placed them next to her. His hands cupped Olivia's as she fidgeted with her thumbs.

"I didn't run from you because of what you did or said. I ran from you because … I was afraid. I ran from you because when you kissed me, I felt something I have never felt before. It's the reason why I never want to run again. I don't want to run from you Marco. I want to stay here and give this a shot."

He stared at her, stunned and apprehensive. He looked about the room, unsure if she was a figment of his imagination.

But Olivia couldn't wait any longer.

She took his scruffy face into her own small hands, cupping his jaw and cheekbones. His hair ruffled in her fingertips. Bending forward, she kissed him with such urgency she could feel her own heartbeat rush to her head. Not letting go of their embrace, Marco scooped her up by the waist and picked her small frame off the chairs and into his arms. Her feet could only float above the tiled floor.

There they remained the rest of the morning, tightly coiled, neither daring to move.

CHAPTER 23

The outside world wasn't oblivious to the new couple. Kate and Martha, amidst their shopping trip, had stumbled upon the quaint shop.

Recognizing the name above the door and recalling what Marco had said before about his line of business, they quickly deduced who the owner was. And by the looks of what was going on inside, he didn't look too prepared to open shop today.

"Oh to be young and in love again," Martha sighed as she and Kate moved onwards.

"It certainly reminds me of Ed and I when we were that young and naive." A tinge of sadness spiked Kate's words. "But I guess it all wears off eventually."

Martha stopped and faced her. "No, honey, it doesn't. The feeling may change, and yes, it may diminish. But that essential feeling, that feeling of tenderness and wanting doesn't just disappear overnight. To break down true love… well, that would take much more than a couple of fights."

"Did you and your husband have disagreements though? Did you ever feel him slipping away from you?"

"Of course, every married couple does. I felt like our relationship was slipping away many times, especially when money was tight or our children took too much of our time and energy. But we would always find one another in the storm, eventually. Even if it took months, sometimes years. The other one would be there—the answer to all the questions."

"Did I tell you why I am here - in Sicily?" Martha shook her head as Kate continued. "We can't conceive. We can't have a baby and it is my fault. My body doesn't want me to have a child, and Ed, well, he can't handle that. We've been trying everything, treatments, even considering surgery, and nothing. Now all he wants to do is break away from me, and all I want to do is run to him."

"Oh Kate, honey…" Martha's voice softened as large welts of tears trickled down Kate's face. She slumped onto the hot paved pathway against a smooth, yellow painted building.

She sniffed as she continued. "My doctor told us to take a holiday to get away from it all. So I picked this place. Ed always wanted to see Italy. I thought he would jump on it. I had hoped we could reconnect. Now I can't even get him to answer my phone calls or texts. I'm not even sure what I am going home to after this. I'm so afraid that he won't be there." Her hands hid her eyes as her body shook, her confession pouring out of her.

"We have to have faith in the ones that we love." Martha reassured her. "We have to believe that they will do the right thing. We can't try to keep them or shelter them. Eventually, we need to set them free if that's what's necessary. And if Ed isn't there, if he's stupid enough to leave someone so amazing as you, then you're strong enough to see this through alone."

She encircled her arms around Kate's slim, pale shoulders, brushing the strands of flaxen hair from her hands and face. "Now honey, dry those tears and let's go and find some lunch. I'm sure Isabella would say that a good meal works wonders."

CHAPTER 24

"*I*sabella …how do you pronounce this?" Martha studied her recipe card.

"*Timballo Polizzano*" Isabella enunciated the words slowly, accenting the hard "p."

It was later that evening, and all three students had returned to Isabella's villa in time for the dinner preparations. As always her recipe cards waited for them at their station.

But their ingredients were nowhere to be found.

"When do we begin making dinner?" Olivia's card displayed a recipe for a complex and intimidating prawn salad.

"Well, that's the surprise!" Isabella threw up her hands as if she had practiced this moment countless times before. "On my last dinner, I try to treat my new chefs to the most authentic Sicilian dinner I can think of. And that is why, instead of what is on those cards, we are spending the rest of the evening making …. pizza!" She beamed at them, her toothy, gapped smile widening as she awaited their reactions.

"Pizza? You're going to teach us how to make Italian pizza?" Kate, now feeling much better after confiding in Martha earlier, was thrilled. She had always wanted to learn how to toss and spin dough like pizza chefs in the movies.

"But, wait, why the recipe cards then?" Olivia was dubious, waiting for the other shoe to drop. She was extremely relieved to hear that they were making pizza though. Cooking fresh prawns had seemed way too much even for her.

Especially with the crazy mess her mind was in.

"They go in your books," said Isabella. "Check in the top shelf of your station. You'll find one for each of you."

Martha pulled hers out first. It was a tan leather bound photo album. In each of almost all the one hundred slots were recipes that Isabella had written out by hand. They were sorted and arranged by meal.

"Oh, this is beautiful." Kate carefully felt her own book, covered in blue vinyl with golden sunflowers blooming from the edges.

Olivia's was a fire engine red hardcover with a large strap to keep the pages intact.

Each woman placed their final recipe card in their new cookbook and shut the pages.

Returning their attention back to Isabella, she spoke again, "In Italy, we believe that the real pizza, the original pizza is from Naples. But because I do not have the proper oven, we will go into the town and learn from the experts."

THE OTHERS FOLLOWED her back into old Taormina where they stopped at a hidden corner *panifico.*

An older gentleman about Isabella's age, slowly moved from around the corner and greeted her festively. He spoke Italian as Isabella translated, "This is Tomas. He is the owner of the bakery, and he welcomes you here today. He wants to let you know that he has been friends with my husband and I since pizza was first invented."

The women chuckled at the joke, as the two chefs stood arm in arm together. "He is going to walk you through making the dough for the Neapolitan, and then how to add the sauce and toppings."

The petite man silently led Kate, Olivia and Martha to the back of the tiny bakery, where mixing bowls and ingredients were already waiting. Pointing out each item, he walked the students through each step as Isabella translated tips and tricks he would occasionally shout out.

When it was time to spin the dough, the women watched in awe as he transformed a large ball of dough into a spinning, hypnotic wheel.

Olivia attempted to throw hers first, but it landed with a thud onto the wooden table. Martha followed, and while she could catch it, the actual spinning alluded her. The only one that seemed to possess the ability to throw, spin, and mold the dough was Kate.

And even she was shocked at what seemingly came natural.

The lesson was then followed by a taste testing of various white and red sauces. Some chunky, others runny. Finally, Isabella talked to them about cheeses and why goat's cheese in Sicily was so important, pointing out that the region's cows were in short supply, and that in the summer, transporting non-hard cheeses like mozzarella was almost impossible for small vendors like Tomas. Instead, he improvised with goat's and harder cheeses.

As the three waited for the oven to finish warming their pizza, Marco slipped in the back entrance, greeting his grandmother first by handing her a small, note written on one of her recipe cards.

Isabella read it and then glanced back at her students who were chatting merrily over some red wine.

"Kate." Isabella called out and the Irishwoman duly joined the two in the corner of the store. "It seems like there is a change of plan for you this evening. Marco is going to take you to the docks. Apparently, you have somewhere to be."

"What? What do you mean? I don't leave until tomorrow night."

"No, no, nothing like that. You're going on a boat trip around the bay. It departs in one hour, which gives you enough time to grab a change of clothing. Marco will see to it that you get to where you need to go."

"I don't understand…" Marco offered Kate his arm and escorted the dazed woman out of the bakery, as Isabella returned to the rest of the lesson.

CHAPTER 25

Without any more details other than that she needed to be on the docks by 8pm, Marco was of no help to Kate.

He showed her back into Isabella's villa so that she could change into warmer clothing, and grab a sweater from her backpack, and then he rode with her in a taxi to the nearby town of Messina, where the main docks were.

He pointed out a large white yacht with the name *Mariano* painted in golden letters on its side. The captain, dressed in traditional sailor white and black chatted with Marco as he confirmed the details with him.

"Kate, this is Captain Alfonzo. He says your companion is waiting and you will take off as soon as you are ready."

"I'm sorry, but I really do not know what is going on. I don't have a com—" Her words cut off as she saw a figure ascend the stairs up from the yacht's cabin. "Ed!" Without thinking, she jumped down into the boat and ran towards her husband, catching him in a hug.

As she finally let go, he tentatively cried, "Surprise!"

"Surprise? I don't understand. How are you here? *Why* are you here?" The sight of her husband in Taormina was too overwhelming.

"I arrived on the flight after yours, and I've been here ever since. Didn't you get my flowers or wonder who paid for your insanely expensive spa day?"

Her mind whirling, Kate laughed as she put the pieces together.

"I wanted you to have the time of your life away from me and the pressure to conceive," Ed told her gently. "I had hoped this little break would be a way to bring you, the *real* you, back to me. But when I saw you crying on the path in town this afternoon, I knew it was time to let you in on the surprise." He stretched his arms out wide, as if revealing his big moment.

"I never wanted to hurt you, love. I am so sorry for how I have acted and how I have pulled away from you. It was never my intention. Our adventure has just begun, whether we have kids or not. And this trip, watching you from a distance, I don't want to miss a moment of this journey with you ever again. Please forgive me."

"Ed—" the words caught in Kate's throat as she struggled to see him past the tears in her eyes. "I, I …" She struggled to find a response to his eloquent words. Instead, she chose to shout out, "I love you!"

He moved towards her, unable to contain his emotions anymore. As he kissed her, Kate could feel the passion and the romance that was once lost rekindle slowly like a new fire. It burned brighter this time and lasted far longer. Whatever had divided them had now brought them here, in Taormina, on the Ionian Sea together at last.

She knew that no matter the obstacles they faced, however long life had to give, she and Ed would never again be parted.

Behind the married couple, the yacht had left its place on the dock as the choppy green seas parted swiftly for its travels.

It floated quickly on, past the Sicilian island and its beautiful, glimmering bays. Ahead of them was only the sea with its endless possibilities, but neither were scared.

Instead, the two relaxed as their vessel chased the setting sun, putting all over their troubles behind them.

CHAPTER 26

SIX WEEKS LATER

The red envelope addressed to her caught Isabella's eye.

It had been weeks since she'd received a personal letter, and intriguingly, this one was from an address in her own town.

She quickly tore into it. But instead of finding a letter, she found a clipping from a glossy magazine.

It read:

A Taste of Sicily

By Olivia Bennett, Chief Travel Correspondent

When you have traveled for as long as I have and collected as many stories as postcards, cities and places - even those straight from legends and lore - pass as a blur.

And while the life of a perpetual nomad may seem appealing, it certainly has its downsides.

As a travel writer, for the most part I have little say on where I go or what I will be doing. When Erica, our fearless editor assigned me a story set in Taormina, Sicily, I was hesitant. Sure, I've been to Italy before. I have seen the ancient Roman ruins and tasted authentic pizza. But unlike so many others, for me, that country has never felt much more than bricks and history, with great fashion thrown in as a bonus.

And for that reason, I begged not to write this article.

But now, here I am, in Taormina. Over three days in the spring, I stayed at a villa overlooking the Ionian Sea and the awe-inspiring beauty that is the central hub of Southern Sicily, Mount Etna.

(A friend once told me that Etna, a once powerful volcano, held all of the Italian native's infamous tempers...).

I came here to learn how to cook under the guidance of Chef Isabella and to investigate why her skills and hospitality have gained almost a cult following amongst tourists and foodies.

I did learn how to cook, as well as shop for fresh produce, enjoy gelato for breakfast, and fearlessly chop swordfish. But more importantly, I walked away with more than just a cookbook full of handwritten recipes and friendships to last a lifetime.

I walked away with love.

That's right; fearless wanderer Olivia Bennett, has developed not only a taste of - and for - Sicily, found love and settled down.

Taormina, the picturesque historical town residing in eastern Sicily, has claimed me.

I should have realised it the moment I got off the bus from Palermo. The clear blue skies, the air that smelled like tomatoes and kumquat...this place was magical. Its residents with their wide grins, effervescent attitudes, and open hearts its magicians.

With each morsel of briosce and pasta from Isabella's Kitchen, I was becoming more and more Sicilian. And I was welcoming the change even as I pretended to resist it.

Then, on one afternoon, a handsome Italian called Marco took me on a tour of the city. We stopped at the public gardens and took in a panoramic view of the area. My companion had not traveled as much as I, and had rarely been outside of his home country. Yet, he told me that he did not need to go anywhere to know that this park, the very one we stood in, was the best in the world all because it was home.

It was a corny sentiment I thought, one reserved for movies and cheap romances. But on another night, I found myself dancing cheek to cheek with the same man and wondering, "When have I ever felt so at home? Where have I ever felt so whole?" And suddenly, I knew that this man was right.

So many of us travel because we long to find better, more exciting places. And if you do it enough, you may just find it. I have.

Taormina is it, at least for me.

For some, it may indeed just be another tourist trap in the middle of the ocean, but you do not need to travel the world to know when your world is perfect as is. You do not need to perfect perfection (a lesson I learned very quickly from Chef Isabella).

That is why I have requested to stay here, in Sicily, for the time being at least.

I am giving my newfound home and love a chance. We will find our new chapter, our new dish, our new park together. And I suspect will not need to go much further than Isabella's Villa to find them.

I hope you will continue to follow my journey as I, and my new fiance Marco, travel through Italy and the rest of the Mediterranean together.

Until my next correspondence, I wish you all happy travels.

Isabella placed the article down on her wooden table and took a deep breath. The kind words from her soon-to-be granddaughter-in-law had touched her more than she had anticipated.

To know that she had helped and inspired someone so deeply, had made the labors of her life worth it, in many ways.

But for now, she couldn't dwell on her part in the fate of Olivia —or of Kate, who had too recently written about a baby on the way.

Or even that of Martha who had taken it upon herself to go on a year-long cruise around the world - alone.

Instead, Isabella had only enough time to focus on writing out tonight's recipe cards.

In a few hours, this large wooden table would again be

surrounded by new visitors, eager to take advantage of her culinary knowledge and soak up her wisdom.

And perhaps inadvertently find what they were looking for, right in her Taormina kitchen.

A WEDDING IN ROME

CHAPTER 1

"*M*olly?" a voice called up to where the blonde twenty-eight-year-old sat gazing out the window as a dusting of snow fell softly outside.

Molly O'Brien barely noticed the noise. She was captivated by the magic of this first snow – even if it was just flurries - and which she knew would have melted away by the time she and her parents boarded the plane to Italy later that morning.

There was just something about Christmastime – the brisk cold weather, greenery around the hearth, candles and fairy lights, holly and mistletoe – that filled her with such joy she could hardly contain herself. And with everything building to an even more joyous occasion now just a couple of sleeps away, Molly was entranced.

"Love?" her mother's voice came again, this time from just down the hall.

Molly sighed and returned to the suitcase laid open on her childhood bed, folding up the last of her clothes and stuffing them in the remaining spaces.

A long packing list rested nearby. She glanced through it as her mind raced. Forgetting anything for this trip would be disastrous. She couldn't afford to be distracted or unfocused.

A gentle knock came at the door, followed by a creak as it opened. Her mother Helen stood in the doorway.

Just then, Molly was struck by the greyish streaks in her mother's blonde hair; surely they hadn't been there before. But her ever-glamorous mum was getting older. They all were.

However, despite the strands of grey and the faint lines around her lips, Molly couldn't remember a time when Helen looked better. The years agreed with her.

She smiled. "Hey, Mum."

'We're all set to go, love. Have you packed the last of it?"

Molly nodded and took her mother's arm, bringing her over to the window. "Look," she smiled. "Isn't it beautiful?"

Helen sighed. "It is, honey, yes," she said wistfully. "I remember you and Caroline sitting here as young kids for hours just watching the snow fall in winter. We could barely peel you two away for anything. Well, except maybe for a few Jammie Dodgers…"

"Feeling nostalgic?" Molly asked casually. She looked at her mother who had the same dreamy look on her face she herself had. It ran in the family apparently.

Helen shook her head. "Just a bit, maybe," she admitted. "It's hard to see your baby grow up before your eyes. And now, well I suppose I'm just wishing we could have the wedding for you that your father and I always envisioned. I always knew you would get married at this time of year with that love of Christmas of yours, but I never expected that you would do it somewhere else."

"Ah, mum," Molly replied, "we've been through all this a million times already." She was exhausted. Her parents had barely let up with their complaints since, she and her fiancé Ben had announced their intentions to get married in Rome.

Helen put her hands up defensively. "I know, I know," she responded, "and it is of *course* your wedding – yours, and Ben's."

Helen thought back to the little girl playing weddings with her best friend, Caroline. There was always a beautiful red and green bouquet, teddy bears and dolls representing friends and family - and snow boots under an old white costume.

"Mum," Molly said gently. "Look around this room. What do you see?"

Helen looked at the walls of the room that had been Molly's bedroom for most of the last three decades.

Framed posters of the Colosseum, St. Peter's Basilica, and the Trevi Fountain graced the walls.

On the bookshelves were everything from Italian phrasebooks and texts on Roman history, to tomes by Dante Alighieri and Italo Calvino.

Even the wallpaper, though a bit frayed and yellowed now, featured a watermark of the Arch of Constantine.

It was in effect, the most Italian room in all of Ireland.

"I've been dreaming of this forever," Molly continued. "A Christmas wedding in Rome has *always* been the dream. And finally it's coming true."

Molly was as in love with Italy almost as much as she was with her fiancé.

She had studied Italian literature in University College Dublin, and had even taken several Italian cooking classes for fun. While she may no longer be that little girl dressing up teddy bears and 'marrying' her best friend, she was still the woman with Italian posters, books, and maps in her bedroom.

Helen nodded. "I know, love," she said kindly. "And your dad and I want to give you the wedding of your dreams. Even if it happens to be in another country."

She had struggled to come to terms with her daughter's decision, but at this point, there was no turning back. Molly and Ben were getting married in Rome on Christmas Eve - two days from now.

"Girls!" Molly's father Paddy yelled at the two women from the foot of the stairs. "It's time we headed off."

Paddy O'Brien had also been staring out the window at the snow rolling in and wondering how long they would be stuck at Dublin airport because of it.

"We're coming now," Helen called down to him. She turned to Molly. "Ready, sweetheart?" she asked with a smile.

Molly looked through the packing list once more, nodded and pulled her stuffed suitcase off the bed.

She grinned. "Ready as I'll ever be."

CHAPTER 2

"Tell me again why we couldn't fly First Class?"

Patricia Pembrey did *not* like flying steerage – and she certainly did not approve of the sort milling about in Luton Airport just then.

She made a horrified face as an elderly couple slowly walked past her, chewing gum loudly and clicking their canes against the tile floor.

"Because, mother," her son Ben said flatly, "we're going to travel like normal people for once."

He had predicted his mother was going to be a pain, but he had no idea she would be this intolerable. The complaints had started months ago and it looked like they were not ending anytime soon.

"Oh, nonsense, Ben," Patricia said coolly, adjusting the foxtail scarf over her shoulder. "We do travel like normal people, normal for our class." She stuttered, lifting her arms in frustration, "Tell him, James."

Lord James Pembrey, 15th Earl of Daventry, was nonplussed.

"I know, dear," he said pompously. His travel usually included a private boarding area at Heathrow away from the public, waitresses with endless champagne flutes, and takeoffs scheduled around his agenda.

This was too much like roughing it for his liking.

Ben shook his head, completely frustrated with his parents' inability to see past their own wants and needs.

"Look," he said, his brown eyes darting towards the fast food lines. "I'll pop over to Costa and pick us up some coffees. Will that do?"

He loved his parents, and they had given him a wonderful life filled with opportunities many only dreamed of – but they could be such woeful snobs that he sometimes wondered whether he'd been adopted.

He had been so completely different to them that when he'd gone off to university, he'd deliberately chosen not to go to Oxford or Cambridge but instead to University College Dublin – much to his parents' chagrin.

And he was glad that he had; it's where he'd met Molly.

He remembered clearly that first night he'd laid eyes on her at a social in a pub following a big rugby match.

Molly and her friend Caroline had come in, and Molly's large doe eyes met Ben's from across the crowded room.

He was normally confident, but something about her had told him that she wasn't the type that would instantly fawn over him, as so many other girls did once they found out he was bona fide English gentry.

But, unlike in the UK, that kind of thing meant little in Ireland. Part of the reason Ben had shipped out of England in the first place.

He took a deep breath and marched over to talk to her – and promptly knocked a drink off a server's tray and down the front of her top. Horrified, she'd stomped out of the pub with Caroline following at her heels. It was as awful a first encounter as any had ever been.

He counted himself lucky, then, that only two weeks later, they happened to meet again at a college party for Italian & Classical Degree students.

Ben had been invited by a mutual friend after he offered to make a pasta dish his old nanny cooked up for him and his brother every time his parents were off travelling.

Molly had made her way into the kitchen, the smell of the homemade sauce tempting her. When she saw the idiot from the bar, she'd immediately turned on her heel but Ben was faster. He grabbed her arm as she was leaving, apologising the entire way.

She'd looked at the man in the dirty apron, red sauce splattered on his cheeks, with his dark hair, deep brown eyes boring apologetically into hers, and couldn't find a reason to be angry any longer.

They'd ended up talking the whole night through, eventually watching the sun rise over campus.

As he watched her in the glow of the early morning light, the warm sunshine reflecting in her wide blue eyes, Ben knew, even at that early moment, that this was the woman he was going to marry.

On Christmas Eve five years later, he had it all planned out as he took them on a journey of their old college haunts. They'd gotten fish and chips from the chipper they'd always gone to after a night on the town, went for a drink before closing at the pub where they'd had that first run in, and eventually wandered into St Stephen's Green.

With light snowflakes swirling around them, and fairy lights shining amidst the trees above, Molly pushed her bundled-up body closer into his as they sat down on one of the benches.

As she talked about their Christmas plans for the next day, she turned to him expectantly, her eyes shining with excitement.

But Ben was not there, at least not where he had just been sitting. He was down on one knee, and pulled out a little black velvet box, his hands trembling as he searched for the words he had rehearsed for months – before promptly dropping the ring in the snow.

Ben was horrified as he squinted his eyes and searched the

damp snow for the sparkling diamond once belonging to his grandmother.

But Molly only laughed and bent down, easily picking up the antique ring with its beautiful three off-centre diamonds, tears in her eyes.

She brought her red-gloved hand to his face. "Oh, you don't even have to ask," she told him, beaming. "Of course I'll marry you."

There hadn't even been a question of where - or indeed when - to get married. Winter in Rome, at Christmastime.

While Ben had suggested that Molly's family might be more comfortable with a traditional Irish ceremony at home, she wouldn't hear of it.

She also knew Ben too well – particularly, that his family's wealth and prominence embarrassed and irritated him.

Anything traditional would have been dwarfed by the excess and pomposity the Pembreys would no doubt insist on bringing to the table.

So in the end they'd both known that a small, intimate gathering at an historic church in Rome – just family and friends - was exactly what they wanted. The arrangements had taken nearly a year, though they'd had lost of help from a wedding planner in Italy to navigate the details.

And now days before Christmas, Ben found it hard to believe that here he was, ordering coffees at the airport, about to board a plane to Rome to meet his soon-to-be wife.

He grinned and thanked the barista as he picked up the coffees, leaving some change in a small jar next to the register. "Thanks - Merry Christmas."

He returned to their boarding gate to find his mother, daintily dusting off the plastic airport seat with his father's handkerchief.

"Oh, you have *got* to be joking, Mother," he said, rolling his eyes and thrusting a cup her way.

"What?" she inquired innocently. "We'll have to find a reputable dry cleaner once we have landed in Italy. I am not packing this handkerchief in our luggage."

Ben handed his father his coffee and strode away. "Ben?" his father called from behind him, "where are you going now?"

"To find a bar," he grumbled. "I need a stiff drink."

CHAPTER 3

"*C*aroline!" Molly darted excitedly towards her best friend, her trainers nearly bouncing off the tiled floors of Rome's Da Vinci Airport.

Yes it had been a couple of months since they had last seen each other, as Caroline now lived in Cork, but by Molly's reaction, one would think it had been years.

Caroline Davison giggled and bounded in the opposite direction and the two embraced forcefully, their collective weight tilting to and fro from their exuberance, eventually causing them to almost fall over in a fit of laughing and hugs.

"Oh my God, Molly, you're getting *married!*" Caroline exclaimed, her green eyes sparkling and dark curls bouncing, as she helped her friend to her feet.

"Wait - I'm doing what?" Molly teased, a wicked smile filling her face.

"Grand. Well, we're here now, so to hell with Ben, let's find you a nice Italian Romeo!"

The two laughed hysterically as Molly's parents joined them near the baggage claim.

Helen's arms stretched out towards Caroline, embracing her in a familiar, gentle hug. Caroline gave both O'Briens a kiss on the cheek, wishing them a Happy Christmas.

"How was the flight from Dublin?" she asked.

"The flight was fine," Helen replied. "It's everything since that…"

"*Mum,*" Molly scolded.

"All your mother is saying," Paddy picked up, "is that maybe the natives could be a *bit* more helpful."

"Dad," she groaned, "Italians aren't required to speak English, you know."

"No," Paddy agreed, "but when you go to an airport cafe and order a cup of tea, they should at least have *some* idea what you mean."

"Relax, Mr O'Brien. It's nearly Christmas…though you wouldn't know it here," Caroline said, casting a dubious glance around the airport.

Unlike Cork airport from which she'd flown earlier this morning, she was surprised to find that the festive decor in Italy seemed lacking. While airports back home were usually all holly and ivy and Christmas trees, here, everything seemed a bit more subdued.

Only a few strands of fairy lights and some signs reading *Chiuso per Natale* ("Closed for Christmas") let travellers know that any sort of holiday was imminent.

But perhaps the Italians didn't make such a big deal of it? As it was Caroline's first time in the country and she knew very little about the place, she couldn't be sure.

But no doubt she would soon find out. In any case, her best friend adored the city and was looking forward to not only her wedding, but also showing everyone around.

Molly was about to speak again when a pair of hands covered her eyes and a familiar voice whispered in her ear.

"Guess who?" She grabbed the hands, turned around, and found herself face-to-face with her fiancé. She held Ben's face in her hands, stood on her tiptoes, and kissed him.

"Here comes the groom," Caroline laughed, as Ben then bent over to kiss her cheek.

"Great to see you, Car," he said. "How's life in Cork?"

"Fine as ever, Ben, how are you?"

He opened his mouth to reply, but as he did, came the sound of someone complaining on approach "...and I swear to you, James, if there is no butler service, I won't stay. I simply won't!"

"And I wouldn't hear of it, darling," Ben's father replied. He searched the crowd, finally finding his son in the mix of faces. "There you are. We've been looking for you. We have a driver waiting."

Molly shook hands awkwardly with both Patricia and James Pembrey. She'd met his parents a couple of times over the years, and was well used to their snooty behaviour.

At first, she wasn't sure what to make of them, especially considering Ben was as humble and down-to-earth as they came. Fortunately because they lived in the UK, she and Ben didn't have much to do with them.

"And you remember my parents, Paddy and Helen?" Molly said quickly, while the rest of the wedding party exchanged muted greetings.

Both sets of parents had met briefly after the engagement, but as her working class parents had little in common with English nobility, it had been somewhat ... strained.

Caroline watched the whole scene unfold as she waited at carousel belt. After a few more beats of awkward quiet amongst the families, she cleared her throat.

Molly looked to her confusedly, then added, "Oh of course! And Caroline, my best friend and bridesmaid."

Caroline smiled and approached the Pembreys. "Hello there," she greeted, beaming.

She got little in response. Instead the Pembreys, the O'Briens, and Caroline all stood there in complete silence as the conveyer belt clanked and clattered around.

"So," she said, attempting to break the ice, "who's ready for some wine tasting?"

"As long as it's not one of those so-called 'Super Tuscans,'" Patricia groused. "Never had a more overrated wine in my life."

The awkward silence resumed. Caroline smiled tightly and stared down at her feet until she was tapped on the shoulder by a small man with a wiry moustache.

"Scusi?" he said in a heavily accented voice, "You are Miss Davison, yes?"

She nodded. "I am. Can I help you?"

"Can you come with me, please?"

She followed him, perplexed.

"Signorina," the man said once they were away from the crowd, "I am afraid I have some bad news."

"What do you mean, 'bad news?'" she repeated, frowning.

"Your package," he said.

She was puzzled. "My... package?"

"No, scusi, that is not the right word," he apologised. "Sorry, my English, it is not so good. I mean, *luggage*. Your luggage – it did not arrive."

CHAPTER 4

The lobby of the Hotel Marliconi was gloriously opulent, a mix of old-world wood, Italian marble and art deco stained glass.

White stone statues of women with water pitchers stood in a small fountain in the centre of the massive reception room, giving it the extravagant feel of something from a movie, while overhead a magnificent fresco depicted a classic Renaissance scene.

Additional Christmas-themed decor – a tree, nativity scene, and a few red-and-green bows dotted here and there – gave the hotel a somewhat more festive look, though Caroline couldn't help but notice again how much more subdued it was compared to the glitzier stuff back home.

Still, any Christmassy decor paled in comparison to the inherent beauty of the city itself.

Caroline was still reeling from her first sight of the Colosseum on the approach to the city of Rome from the airport. And everywhere she looked were jaw-dropping sights of Renaissance architecture and Italian grandeur.

A gigantic structure of Corinthian columns, fountains, and equestrian sculpture in the centre of the city that Molly pointed out as the Victor Emmanuel monument was awe-inspiring, as was a passing glimpse of the Roman Forum, and the myriad Baroque fountains and pretty piazzas that gave the picturesque city an almost other-worldly feel.

Now she and Molly approached the reception desk arm-in-arm. Molly still seemed jittery, bothered by the absence of Caroline's bridesmaid dress and she thought, a little put out by the fact that her best friend seemed to be the only one in the wedding party impressed by the city sights.

On the way in the taxi, the O'Briens seemed distracted and uncomfortable, and only nodded in passing when Molly pointed out areas of interest and beauty.

For someone who loved Italy as much as her friend, and was so eager to share her great passion for the city she'd chosen as her wedding destination, it was no doubt disappointing.

She rubbed her friend's shoulders reassuringly.

"The dress will come in time, Mol," she soothed, guiding her to the front desk. "Don't worry. It's just a hiccup – nothing to worry about. It wouldn't be a wedding without a little bad luck."

Behind them, Molly's parents gazed around the hotel reception, a little taken aback.

"It's a bit … grand, isn't it?" Helen commented.

"It is," Paddy responded. "I don't mind paying for a nice hotel, but I certainly didn't expect a palace."

At the back of the group, James and Patricia Pembrey shuffled into the lobby, followed by Ben, whose voice echoed off the marble walls as he barked into his phone.

"Mark, this is simply ridiculous," he said testily. "No – no – I don't – listen to me, I don't *care*. This is my *wedding*. You're my brother, my best man. I think it's fair of me to expect you to be here at least … okay." He hung up the phone and shoved it back in his pocket.

"So where's Mark?" Molly asked when Ben caught up with her at reception.

He sighed. "Still back in London working on some kind of 'server issues,'" he said in an irritated voice. "He says he's 'trying' to get away, but it could be well be tomorrow night by the time he arrives." Then he took a deep breath and put his arm around his fiancee. "Look. Let's just get everyone checked in and then we'll all go have a drink and chill out a bit, OK?"

Molly nodded, and turned back to the check in desk. The young Italian woman behind the counter had a bored, almost lackadaisical look on her face as she leaned against the back wall, gazing at her phone.

Ben threw a quick glance towards Molly and called out, "Um, excuse me?"

The woman sighed, put her phone in her pocket, and walked up to her computer.

"Buonasera," she greeted with fake cheeriness, "how can I help you today?"

"Buonasera," Molly replied with a smile. "We'd like to check into our rooms please. There should be four in total, all under the name O'Brien."

The woman typed some info into her computer, and the machine beeped. "I'm sorry," she said, "I have no rooms under that name. Would they be under another?"

"Erm, Pembrey, perhaps?" Ben offered.

She typed the letters in. This time there was no beep, but rather a chime, followed by a look of sheer confusion on the part of the clerk. "I am sorry," she said, not looking particularly apologetic, "I must speak to my manager. One moment, please."

Caroline joined them at the desk. "What's going on?" she inquired.

Molly shrugged. "Dunno," she said. "She just looked really confused and then bounded off."

A few moments later, the clerk returned with a short, bald, mustachioed manager, a grave look on his face. "Buonasera," he greeted them, "are you Signorina O'Brien?"

"I am," she nodded. Ben's parents now huddled close to them, attempting to hear what was going on. "What's the problem?" Molly asked the manager.

"It seems we have a small … issue," he stated. "Our hotel – it is fully booked, and though we have your reservation, it seems we have sold the rooms."

Molly's jaw nearly hit the ground. "You've done *what?*" she demanded.

"It was a mistake, I assure you, Signorina, and not one that happens at this hotel often." He looked towards the staff member suspiciously, as if she personally were the one to blame.

Molly threw her hands up in the air and walked off. Ben looked to his parents – at which point James stepped in – and he darted after his fiancée.

As he went, he heard his father assume his most pompous, House of Lords voice: "Now see here, sir, this is our son's wedding, and we were assured of having four suites at this hotel. It was *guaranteed*, so do you know what you're going to do? I'll tell you what you are going to do. You will…"

BEN WAS out of earshot when he found Molly at the other end of the lobby, staring out the window towards a picturesque piazza. He went over and put a hand on her shoulder. "Molly, hon," he said consolingly, "it's going to be okay – "

"'Okay?'" she whispered, as she turned to face him. "Ben, *nothing* is okay. First, Caroline's dress doesn't get here, my parents do nothing but complain about the place, your best man isn't even sure he'll make it… and now, they can't find our room reservations. What exactly is okay?"

"That we're here in Rome to be married, like we always wanted."

"Oh, Ben," she cried, tears threatening. "I know that, but …I'm wondering if doing this at Christmas was a mistake. This has been nothing but a disaster so far – and we've only been in the city less

187

than an hour. To say nothing of the fact that it doesn't feel very Christmassy at all."

Ben hugged her close. "Do you trust me?" he asked, a glint in his eye. She looked up at him, wiped her eyes, and nodded. "Then trust me when I say it's going to work itself out. I promise." She sniffled a bit but nodded again.

A few moments later, Patricia and James rejoined the group, along with a handsome Italian man in his late thirties with deep brown eyes, and a smile that immediately sent both Caroline's and Molly's hearts aflutter.

He went straight up to Molly and kissed her on both cheeks. "Signorina," he said, still smiling, in perfect English but with a delicious Italian inflection. "My name is Fabrizio, and I am your coordinator for your stay with us here at the Hotel Marliconi."

He turned to Ben, who held out his hand for a handshake, but Fabrizio leaned in and kissed him on both cheeks as well. "Here in Italy," he explained, "we do not shake hands usually – we are a passionate people. We enjoy intimacy."

Molly's father rolled his eyes. He leaned forward and whispered to his wife, "A handshake will be intimate enough for me, thanks very much." Helen stifled a laugh as the wedding planner introduced himself to the rest of the group.

"Firstly," Fabrizio said after his introductions, "please accept my apologies for the mix-up with your reservations. Signor Pembrey – "

James cleared his throat. "*Lord* Pembrey, actually," he corrected pompously.

" – sorry," Fabrizio apologised, with a twinkle in his eye, "*Lord* Pembrey. We are not yet very certain what happened, but rest assured, we will do everything we can to accommodate you."

Molly brightened immediately. "So we're getting our rooms then?" she asked.

The smile left Fabrizio's face. "Well," he said, immediately causing her face to fall, "that is what we hope. We unfortunately have all of our suites currently occupied. However, we can for now put you in our also beautiful Deluxe Room, and if a suite becomes available, we will of course move you there."

Molly opened her mouth to protest, but Ben took her hand and wrapped it in his.

"It's better than nothing," he said.

"*Fantastico*," Fabrizio said enthusiastically, his smile still in place. "Now, I will call someone to help you with your bags. Perhaps you would like to bathe, relax for a bit. Can we meet at our terrazza restaurant in, say, one hour to discuss plans for your wedding?"

"Sounds good," Ben replied.

"*Eccellente*!" the Italian man grinned. "I will send up the luggage with, maybe, a bottle of wine for each of you? Will that be acceptable?"

Caroline perked up at the words she'd been waiting for. "*God* yes, please," she said. "We could *definitely* use some of that."

CHAPTER 5

*P*atricia rubbed her damp hair with a towel, a scowl on her face.

"Dear God," she complained, "what is this made of, sandpaper?"

James lay on the bed, scanning through Italian broadcasts on the TV. "How was the water pressure, dear?"

"Awful," she frowned. "And the bathroom has some kind of... odd fragrance."

"I think they call that 'soap,' darling."

"This really is intolerable, James," Patricia replied, exasperation in her eyes. "I understood that this hotel would be acceptable to our standards."

James shook his head. "The concierge chap assured me that they're going to get this taken care of, my dear," he told her. "For now, we'll just have to... make do. Though I agree this bedlinen does seem quite garish."

NEXT DOOR, Molly and Caroline opened the bottle of wine that had been delivered to their room a few minutes before.

Molly took a long, deep sip while Caroline kicked off her shoes and put her feet up. "This really isn't so bad, is it?" she asked her.

"It's not," Molly agreed, gazing out the window at the Roman rooftops below. "But I really wanted a suite."

"Oh come on, Mol," Caroline chuckled. "When in Rome - isn't what they say?"

Her friend sighed and sipped her wine. "Is it so wrong to just want this to be perfect?" she asked after a long pause.

"Every bride wants her wedding to be perfect," Caroline said soothingly. "But it very rarely happens that *nothing* goes wrong."

"It just worries me, a little that's all. Like, is *this* how my life with Ben is going to start?"

"You mean, in one of the romantic cities in the world at Christmastime?" Molly took a large swig of her wine. "Nasty."

"Ah, you know what I mean."

"Yes," Caroline nodded – but she smiled teasingly.

"Of course I know what you mean. In your head you're been planning this perfect Italian wedding for most of your life. But you are putting too much pressure on yourself. At the end of a wedding day, is just a *day* – no matter where it is. It's going to be brilliant of course, but don't put *too* much emphasis on it."

"That's easy for you to say," Molly countered, finishing her wine, "seeing as the closest you've come to getting married was when we were four and you and Raggedy Andy were an item—"

She stopped short, realising what she'd just said. She looked over to Caroline, who stared at her, the slight tremor on her friend's lips making it that clear Molly had hurt her.

"Oh, God, Caroline," she began, "I – I don't know – I'm so sorry. That was *literally* the nastiest thing I could've said to you. What is going on with me?"

"It's fine," Caroline said softly.

"No, it's really not," Molly continued. "I'm really – "

"I know, Mol," Caroline said, a half-smile on her face. "Besides, maybe I'll meet a gorgeous, bronzed Italian while I'm here."

"Like Fabrizio?" she teased.

"Ew," Caroline replied, horrified. "He's so…"

"Charming? Handsome? *Dreamy?*"

"…cheesy, I was going to say," Caroline concluded. "The guy is every bad stereotype of every movie set in Italy ever." She finished off her own wine and poured another glass. "Why can't life just be like *Pretty Woman?*" she asked.

Molly looked at her quizzically. "You want to be a prostitute with a weirdly expressive mouth?" she asked, giggling.

"Okay, right, not *Pretty Woman* – the other one – *Runaway Bride?*"

"*Not* the best comparison," Molly said, dissolving in a fit of laughter. Then she sighed and reached for her friend, enveloping her in a tight embrace. "You know I love you, don't you?" she said. "And that I'm proud beyond belief that you're going to be bridesmaid."

"Enough of the Hollywood smaltz," Caroline berated but she was smiling. "Now, drink up. We have a lot of work to do before we meet up again with Fabio this evening."

"Fabrizio," Molly corrected. "*Fabio* is the dude on the cover of romance novels."

"Same difference," her friend grinned.

CHAPTER 6

*A*t seven pm, the wedding party reconvened on the hotel's rooftop terrazza, taking in the extraordinarily beautiful cityscape.

Ancient icons such as the Colosseum, Roman Forum and Pantheon recalled Rome's time as the fearsome hub of the Roman Empire, while catacombs and clandestine churches harked back to the early days of Christianity.

Lording it over the Vatican was St Peter's Basilica, the greatest of the city's monumental basilicas, a towering masterpiece of Renaissance architecture and clearly visible from where they sat.

Paddy had at first been a bit disappointed that there was no Guinness and the only beer available was bottled Peroni, but being able to look out at such a glorious view seemed worth it.

He sat with his wife making small talk with Ben's parents whom he wasn't all that keen on.

"So," he said, a bit awkwardly, "have you been to Italy before?"

"Oh," Patricia said, with something that sounded vaguely like a combination of a forced laugh and a throat-clearing, "*many* times. We used to take Ben and Mark to the Amalfi Coast on holidays when they were little. Stopped a few times here to see the sights and take in the art and culture. But if you're to do anything in Italy, you simply *must* visit Tuscany. The wines..." she nodded towards her half-full glass, "...are much better than *this* swill."

The awkward silence resumed until Ben's father spoke up. "So then, Paddy my good man, what is it that you do again? Forgive me - I've forgotten."

Paddy took a sip of his beer. "Well, I worked in courier delivery for a number of years, mostly delivering packages locally. DHL bought the company a few years back but I still run the delivery service - I just don't have to actually *go* on the deliveries anymore."

James sat upright. "So," he said interestedly, "you used to pull out packages from a van or something like that?"

"Well," Paddy replied, his eyes narrowing somewhat, "it was something *like* that in that the job title was *literally* pulling packages out of a van so... yes."

"I think I need another glass of wine," Patricia interjected, swallowing a large gulp from her glass and hailing the waiter.

MOLLY WAS FEELING CONSIDERABLY HAPPIER after a bath and a few glasses of chianti with Caroline.

She now sat on the hotel's beautiful rooftop terrace curled up on a wicker sofa alongside Ben, munching absentmindedly on some Italian cheeses and grapes, while Caroline relaxed nearby.

"You know," she said, "Santa Maria church is very small. Mum and Dad won't know what hit them when they see how tiny it is."

Ben snickered. "You think *your* parents will be surprised?" he asked. "Mine will simply be livid. I can hear it now: mother getting her nose in a snit, saying things like, 'Huh! It's so dusty in here,' and father with his upright disapproval, wondering where the 'right honourable gentlemen' of Italy are supposed to get married." He exhaled through his nose dramatically. "It's going to be *classic*."

Caroline, seated across from them, giggled. "You two," she smiled. "You're so... so *perfect* together. I'm just... I'm just..."

"Drunk?" Molly suggested, laughing. "We did go through that wine Fabrizio sent to the room awfully quickly."

"Speaking of which," Ben noted, looking at his watch, "where *is* Fabrizio? He's over an hour late."

"Dunno," Caroline said. "Want me to go look for him?"

"Would you mind?" Molly asked gratefully.

She patted her friend on the knee. "I'll be right back," she promised. She got up and made her way towards the lift, heading down to the lobby.

At the desk, she asked the clerk if she'd seen Fabrizio, but he apparently hadn't been around since earlier.

Annoyed, she returned to the lift but as she exited the lobby, she noticed a man sitting by the downstairs bar, flashing a big smile and flirting with the pretty young bartender.

Caroline marched over to him with a full head of steam and tapped him on the shoulder.

"Excuse me," she said, "exactly what do you think you're doing?"

Fabrizio turned to look at her and smiled. "Ah, *Bella*" he greeted energetically, "so wonderful to see you again."

"Don't give me that crap," she said sternly. "We've been waiting upstairs on you for an hour. And I find you sitting down here, drinking and – and – *flirting*?"

Fabrizio took her by the hand. "Signorina," he said, dramatically, "I did not mean to offend. But life is too short to worry about being a little late. Sometimes, we must go where the moment takes us."

Caroline pulled her hand back brusquely. "Well, buddy" she replied her voice terse, "the 'moment' had better take you up there to talk to Molly and Ben about their wedding in short order, or we're going to be finding another planner *and* another hotel."

The Italian put his hands up defensively. "Okay, okay," he said, "but tell me, Signorina... are you more upset that I am late, or more upset that I was speaking with a woman whose beauty is so inferior to yours?"

Caroline blushed slightly but didn't break her icy stare. "Don't think for a second that nonsense is going to work on *me*," she said fiercely. "I've heard all about you swarthy, Italian charmers."

Fabrizio raised an eyebrow. "Swarthy?" he repeated bemusedly.

Caroline continued without breaking stride. "You're all 'passion' and 'fire' and 'embrace your inner blah-blah-blah' for foreign women – and then when you get what you want you never speak to us again. So don't try your tricks on me, mister."

Fabrizio nodded curtly. "Yes, Signorina," he said, his face a picture. "I will no longer comment on the radiance of your beauty, which puts a sunset to shame…"

Caroline rolled her eyes. "If you're done doing… whatever it was you were doing here, I'd appreciate it if you'd come now and talk to my friend about her wedding. She could really use your help."

Fabrizio downed the last of his drink and pushed out his stool from the bar. "After you," he offered.

"Oh, no," she said sarcastically, "I insist – after *you*."

Caroline was pleased with her performance; she'd successfully done exactly what she set out to do, performing her bridesmaid duties well.

But despite herself - and feeling like a bit of an idiot for feeling that way - she couldn't help but admit that there was something about Fabrizio's smile that made her insides tingle.

CHAPTER 7

"*I* don't think you understand …" Molly said tersely.

They'd been discussing her plans and expectations leading up to the wedding on Christmas Eve, but Fabrizio's nonchalant attitude was now seriously rubbing her up the wrong way.

No matter what she suggested they do, the Italian gave off an air of frustrating carelessness, and resisted giving their days any structure whatsoever.

"We really want to see the sights of Rome - show the wedding guests some of this wonderful city."

"Of course, *Signorina*, of course," he responded gently, again flashing his debonair smile. "But *Roma* – she is not like other cities. She demands a certain… spontaneity. You must listen to her to see where she takes you."

Molly's father had had just about enough. He threw his napkin onto the plate in front of him – still full of small, white *calamari*, which Paddy couldn't bring himself to eat, considering the look of the tentacles – and jabbed a finger at the man sitting across from him.

"Now, listen here lad," he scolded, "I think we have been very patient so far with you. There's a lot we want to see and do while we're here, and I think we have the right to have some sort of plan. For God's sake man, this is our daughter's wedding!"

Helen put a hand on his arm, and he calmed down a bit. "What my husband is trying to say," Molly's mum began, "is that we want to make sure everything about the trip is being taken care of, and right now you aren't reassuring us that it is."

"*Signores*," Fabrizio responded apologetically, "Please, listen. All will be fine. We have the church, we have a priest – Padre Beppe, he is the best – and afterwards, we will have a wonderful dinner here on the terrazza. It is also Christmas, yes? We will drink some wine, eat some delicious Italian food, and have some fun."

Patricia cleared her throat. "I certainly hope so. In the meantime, if you would be so kind as to bring us a bottle of the '67 Conterno Monfortino, we'd like to buy a bottle for the table."

"And perhaps a few packets of crisps as well?" Molly's father added hopefully, as Patricia glared at Paddy as if he was something she'd scraped off the bottom of her shoe.

Fabrizio stood back and bowed his head. "But of course, *signores*. Would anyone like anything else? Caffe? Limoncello?"

"Could we get a pot of tea as well?" Helen inquired. "I could really go for a good strong cup right now."

"Ah," Fabrizio frowned, "I am afraid the hotel will likely not have any tea to speak of. Perhaps a caffe – erm, espresso?"

"Coffee?" Paddy gaped incredulously. "At this hour? Are you mad? We'd be up all night."

Fabrizio eyed Molly's mother. "Perhaps that is a good thing, yes?" he joked.

Caroline snorted and Molly blushed, but Paddy was not amused. "Now, see here lad …" he insisted, evidently offended.

Fabrizio looked abashed. "I am sorry, signore," he said with a feint towards apologising, "it is only that I am, how you say, hot-blooded and your wife, she is so beautiful. I joke."

"Well, it's not amusing, nor is it appreciated," Paddy replied curtly.

Fabrizio again flashed an apologetic look towards Helen, then he turned to Caroline and winked before walking off to get the drinks.

"Well ..." said Caroline after Fabrizio was out of earshot, "He's a saucy one, isn't he?"

"Very much so," Helen agreed, sipping from a glass of still water on the table. "He just seems so… forward." She sighed and blushed a little. "Though I have to say, it's been a while since a strange man looked at me like that."

"Mum!" Molly was aghast. "Anyway," she said wickedly, "I think he's much more interested in Caroline."

Caught off-guard, Caroline began stammering. "Wha – I – I wasn't – I – that is—" She was completely flustered, and she fought down a fierce burning in her cheeks. "I don't think so," she said finally, attempting to salvage what was left of her pride.

"Methinks the lady doth protest too much," Ben teased.

"Oh come *on*," Caroline protested. "Sure, he's … erm, good-looking… but you know how these Mediterranean men are…"

"*I* don't," Molly said with a grin. "Enlighten us, Caroline since you seem to know it all."

"I've heard the same stories you have," she sighed, looking around the table for support but not getting any. "Oh stop it, you know exactly what I'm talking about. There are stories – legends, really – about Italian men and their dashing good looks and well-cut jaw lines and *gorgeous* accents and – *ahem*—" She noticed she was getting a bit carried away and cleared her throat. "*Anyway*, they're always on the prowl, looking for a foreign girl to make their… conquest."

"Because they're Romans, and they conquer things?" Helen volunteered, with a glint in her eye. "Much like your dad over here."

"Mum!" Molly blurted, horrified afresh at her mother's brazenness, while Caroline and Ben laughed uncontrollably.

Patricia scowled. "My word," she said, disapproval dripping from her voice. "Is this *really* conversation for polite company?"

"Quite so," James agreed as Fabrizio returned with the bottle of wine. He stood up. "I think it's time we turned in for the evening, Patricia," he continued. "We've had… a very long day."

"Oh, come on, Father," Ben pleaded, "don't be that way."

"Was it something I said?" Fabrizio asked, coming back with the wine. When no one responded, or even met his eyes, he understood the implication. "Well, I will not keep bothering you. I shall see you all tomorrow then. *Buona notte.*"

He left again, leaving an air of despondent silence to settle on the rest of the group.

"You know something?" Caroline said, cutting through the rampant awkwardness. "I think I should turn in, too. We have a long day ahead of us tomorrow, and I think I've had enough wine for one night. Would you mind, Mol?"

Molly shrugged. "You're right," she said. She yawned as she got up, only now realising that, despite the abrupt way the Pembreys had exited, there might have been some truth to what they'd said, too.

And she was exhausted, and so disappointed that their Italian trip had started so badly.

Ben's parents were annoyed, her own parents out of their comfort zone, and what with the disinterested wedding planner, missing dress and best man still absent, it seemed nothing had gone right for them so far.

"Night all," she sighed, giving her parents a kiss on the cheek. "Hopefully tomorrow will be a better day."

CHAPTER 8

*B*en sat back in his chair, equally deflated.

Here they were, in Molly's favourite city in the world, during her favourite time of the year to get married– and she seemed miserable.

Helen put a hand on his knee, breaking his reverie. "Don't worry about her, love," she said warmly. "She's just nervous about … well, all of it I suppose."

Ben nodded. "Yeah, I know." He smiled at his future mother-in-law and stood to leave. "I'd better turn in, too. I've got a few things I need to take care of before bedtime. Hope you understand." He shook hands with Paddy and kissed Helen on the cheek. "You two have a good night."

Once Ben was gone, Paddy turned to his wife. "So… what do you make of the Pembreys?"

Helen rolled her eyes. "*He* doesn't say much," she began, "which I suppose is a good thing. Whereas *her* …"

Paddy nodded. "I know what you mean," he agreed. "She comes off as a bit … stuck-up, doesn't she?"

"Stuck-up, pretentious, condescending… So unlike Molly. Or

Ben, for that matter." She sipped her wine and sat back, gazing out at the glorious Roman skyline. "Paddy, honestly," she said sadly, "what on God's green earth are we doing here?"

"Supporting Molly," he answered. "She is young, and she's stupid, but she is wholly in love with that boy. And this city for whatever reason." He looked at the plate of *calamari* again, eyeing the tentacles suspiciously, as if they might begin to twitch and move at any second, "Despite that, we owe it to our daughter to give our love and support."

Just then, his phone buzzed, and he pulled it out to take a look.

"Well yes, of course," Helen pressed on, "but a Christmas wedding in Rome? A tiny church? These little—" she picked up a piece of *calamari*, "—*things*, with their tentacles and round heads? Bit of a disaster really …"

"What's that?" Paddy hadn't heard a thing his wife had just said. An email he had just received said that something had gone wrong with a delivery back home. His eyes narrowed towards the phone again as he began typing furiously. "Sorry love, I really have to check in with the office."

"Paddy," Helen chided, "you're in Rome. For your daughter's wedding. For God's sake, ditch the phone for the next forty eight hours at least."

"It'll just be a minute," he insisted. "I promise. I'll be right back." He stood and walked off to talk on the phone.

Helen sat in silence, gazing out over the city skyline.

She sipped her wine quietly for a few minutes, thinking. Paddy had always worked hard, but lately he'd become obsessive. Her husband simply was a workaholic. She'd held out hopes that he could put the phone away while they were here, but the indication already was that he wouldn't.

She waited nearly half an hour like that, watching the city lights from her perch on the terrazza.

When Paddy didn't return, she finished the rest of her glass and gave up, sighing deeply.

Once again, the work that was supposed to be easier now that he wasn't making the deliveries ended up being more difficult.

Helen called the lift and returned to her Roman hotel room alone.

The following morning, the sun shone brightly from the small hotel window, waking Helen from her sleep.

Paddy was already downstairs in the lobby sipping the one kind of tea he had managed to get from the kitchen.

She stretched her neck, trying to get the crook out of her neck from the lumpy mattress and quickly got dressed. She could only hope today's adventures in Rome would be nothing like the day before

The rest of the group drank their *caffè e latte* with bread and jam. Paddy could not believe that there was no eggs, rashers or sausages – bacon didn't seem to be in the Italian diet at all.

"What I wouldn't give for some black pudding," he whispered regretfully to his wife as she signed for the bill.

"I'll be hungry in an hour," Helen agreed. "Though I suppose it explains how all these Italians are so slim…"

IN THE LOBBY, the wedding party once again waited for Fabrizio to meet them.

Somewhat unsurprisingly (at least to Caroline), he was nowhere to be seen. She went up to the desk to inquire about their coordinator, but Fabrizio was absent.

Though she wasn't certain the desk clerk had fully understood her, routinely referring to their coordinator as *il capo*, which according to Caroline's iPhone translator app, meant *the boss*.

She chose to keep this from Molly and the others to avoid their stress. Instead, she asked the receptionist for some tour brochures, and arranged for a taxi to be called.

When she finally rejoined the others, she was completely armed with maps and tickets still warm from the hotel's printer.

"Okay," she said as she returned. "Turns out, Fabrizio isn't able to make it this morning, but we've got a whole itinerary here, so don't worry."

Molly opened her mouth to protest, but Caroline kept talking. "So first up, we're going to go check out the Forum of Augustus, followed by the Colosseum. After that, I suggest we get ourselves some lunch near the Piazza di Spagna, and maybe do some shopping, because why not? We're in Rome, so let's do this right. And if we're finished in time, we can go and see Santa Maria, where you two lovebirds—" she motioned towards Ben and Molly with a wide, gaping smile, "—are getting married."

The cars pulled up moments later, not giving anyone a chance to disagree with her last minute plans.

However, Ben held back a little and when they were alone, he asked Caroline intensely, "Where exactly is Fabrizio? I thought he was supposed to meet us here."

She shrugged. "Apparently, the guy is about as reliable as our reservations were," she said. "So I improvised."

"You did all this on the fly this morning?" Ben looked impressed. "That's … incredible. Thank you."

Caroline nodded. "That's what bridesmaids are for. But listen: don't tell Molly about this, okay? She's stressed enough as it is. And with your parents and hers… well, I think you can agree that we have to make this as easy on her as possible."

CHAPTER 10

*I*ncredibly, the weather was sweltering, and not at all the festive picture postcard Molly had been hoping for.

The unseasonable December warmth meant that just in walking around the Forum of Augustus, she found herself sweating profusely, even though all she was wearing were jeans and a t-shirt.

She took a look around, perched on the steps just outside the Temple of Mars Ultor, trying to see it for the first time through her parents' eyes.

She should have felt exhilarated – but instead, she seemed oddly let down. All around were tacky shops selling postcards, shot glasses, t-shirts, official Forum of Augustus chocolates – everyone looking to make a few euros off the tourists who passed through the gates each and every day.

Whatever the Forum might once have been, whatever its relationship to what Rome once was in the days of Caesar Augustus, it just wasn't authentic anymore.

An hour and a half later, as they walked around the Colosseum, she felt little better. Here was *the* place from her posters and textbooks and Roman histories, a building of Italian antiquity that had haunted her dreams since she was a child…

"What do you think Dad?" she asked Paddy who was shuffling along behind her, looking hot and bothered in his red woollen jumper and heavy jeans.

"It's nice, but I thought it would be bigger. I suppose it's kind of a skeleton of the football stadiums back home?'" he said, decidedly unimpressed.

Ben noticed her dejected demeanour and came up behind her, wrapping his arms around her waist.

"Hey," he said, kissing her on the cheek. "Having fun?"

"Actually, no," she replied sullenly. "You know, I've adored this city since I was a little girl, and I loved it when I first came here back in college too, but whatever I'm seeing doesn't seem to at all translate to my parents. I so want them to understand why we chose this wonderful city for our wedding. "

"Yes, but what can you do only show them around?" he asked. "Maybe organise some gladiator battles? A few lions?" His eyes twinkled.

"I don't know," she replied glumly. "Maybe they have a point too. To a lot of people, this seems like just another Italian tourist site, something to be catalogued on Instagram photos and Facebook check-ins." She sighed. "Or maybe I'm just stressed or overtired or something."

Ben released his arms and took her hand in his. "Listen, Mol," he said in a low, voice. "It's not about where we are but where we're going. You and me, we're getting married in a couple of days. And I don't care if we're in Dublin or Rome, New York or New Delhi – all I want is you as my wife. This will be great because of you. And because of us. What matters isn't this," he explained, pointing to the ancient ruins surrounding them. "What matters is how we feel about each other now, and when you walk down that aisle on Christmas Eve."

Molly stood on her tiptoes and kissed Ben on the lips. "You know," she said, smiling, "you're very sweet sometimes."

"I do what I can, Mrs. Pembrey," he replied, kissing her again.

She laughed. "I'm not Mrs yet, *Lord* Pembrey."

"Ugh, don't remind me of the title. My mother does enough of that for both of us."

CHAPTER 11

After leaving the Colosseum, the wedding party headed towards Piazza di Spagna.

Molly took their driver's suggestion for a classy, tasteful *ristorante* for lunch, after which they planned to break off and walk around the stores in the area – Gucci, Armani, Prada, and all the other high-end Italian designers with storefronts nearby.

Sitting next to Paddy on the way was a chore for Helen. Once again, her husband spent the whole time on his phone, spitting directions at his assistant, tapping out emails and seeming extremely stressed over what sounded like minor issues.

Bad weather in Dublin had caused a delay on a major shipment, and never once did Paddy look up from the screen, so engrossed was he in trying to fix the unfixable from afar.

A few times, Helen tried to point out some of the sights ("Look, the Opera House. "We *must* remember to come back and walk through this park while we're here"), but to no avail; Paddy was in his own little world, consumed by work as usual.

At the restaurant, Patricia and James insisted on paying, and proceeded to order the most extravagant things on the menu in highly affected (and to Molly's ear - poorly worded) Italian.

Soon, buttered quail arrived on their table, followed by spaghetti with anchovies and squid as their *primi*. The younger ones gamely kept up with the Pembreys, but Paddy and Helen found themselves once again at a loss.

"How are we supposed to eat this stuff?" Paddy whispered.

They tried to munch on what they could, but he felt a cold shudder go down his spine each time his nose even caught wind of an anchovy.

As if that weren't enough, the *secondi* course came out blazing and steaming with a smell that Helen found stomach-churning. "What on earth is that?" she asked Patricia.

"Beef cheeks," Ben's mother said reverently. "They're quite the delicacy - you'll love them."

"Actually," Helen said, "I'm not feeling very well just now…"

"Oh Mum," Molly said, "do you want us to call you a taxi or—"

"No, no," she said, "I think a bit of fresh air might do me good. Paddy, can you…?"

"Of course love," he said. They exited together, a look of disapproved consternation overtaking Patricia's face.

CHAPTER 12

Outside the restaurant, Paddy was famished. "This is all mad stuff, isn't it?" he said glumly as they walked down the cobblestone street. "I'm starving."

"I don't understand why Ben's parents can't just eat normal things," Helen added. "Who in their right mind would eat a cow's cheek when you could have steak or roast?"

"The same people who order for the whole table without asking, I'd say," Paddy joked and the two of them laughed together.

They stopped at a nearby cafe and picked up a couple of cold-cut sandwiches. Without even a passing familiarity with Italian, ordering was difficult, but they were able to point at the meats that they wanted, and it did the trick.

Helen guided Paddy back towards the park she had seen on their way over in the taxi, and Paddy picked up two chocolate gelatos from a shop just outside the entrance.

She felt her heart melt along with the gelato as she walked along on Paddy's arm. It was almost like she was a teenager again, meeting him on a first date.

The park – which turned out to be the famed Pincian Hill, or *Pincio* – could not have been better for a romantic stroll. A beautiful lake surrounded by trees strung with fairy lights, sparkled in the late afternoon sunlight.

Latin columns, street lamps and statues lined the winding paths, where children giggled and played while their doting parents dashed off after them, ensuring they were never completely out of sight.

Helen sighed, taking it all in. It was perfect – exactly the kind of authentic Italian experience Molly was always taking about.

But it didn't last.

Shortly before they were supposed to rejoin the rest of the wedding party, Paddy got yet another phone call from Dublin.

"Paddy," she pleaded, "can't you just ignore it? Felicity and the others can handle it. Isn't that why you employ them in the first place?"

"I'm not just a worker anymore, love," he replied. "I'm the *manager*. If something fails, it's not just a problem for me – every one of our employees could be at risk. This is our busiest time of the year too. I have to take this. Sorry." He walked off a few paces ahead of her.

Helen sighed sadly and continued walking, watching the late winter sun cast magnificent light over the Eternal City in these glorious surrounds, all by herself.

When that evening, the group returned to the Hotel Marliconi, they were greeted by a familiar form with ruffled hair and a winning smile.

Fabrizio was standing by reception and grinning at them.

Caroline was not amused. "Stay here," she told the rest of them. She marched over to the Italian, her jaw set and determined. "Where in God's name have *you* been all day?" she demanded.

"Ah, Signorina Caroline," he said, letting the word roll round on his tongue, "how has your day been so far?"

"How – has – our – day – been?"

"Yes, that is what I asked," he replied pleasantly.

"*I* planned the whole day, Fabrizio," she exploded, jabbing a finger towards his chest. "I did it to keep the bride that *you're* supposed to be working for, sane. I arranged *every*thing. And you helped with *nothing*. I have been improvising all day, because *you* - Mr Wedding Planner can't do your job."

"Ah, signorina," he soothed laconically, "you really must relax. I am sorry you thought I would be here today. I did not mean for you to have such difficulty."

"That's the point, you absolute *arse*," she continued yelling. "Molly and Ben are *paying* for a service, and you're not providing it. I'd fire you right here and now if it was up to me, but I don't have any say in the matter."

"Signorina – Caroline – please, allow me to make it up to you." Fabrizio put his hand around her shoulder. "If you'll go up to the terraza…"

"We've already *done* that. I'm not waiting up there again all night expecting to hear plans, only for you to sit at the bar flirting."

"Please. Come with me. And bring the others, too. I will go now – meet me up there as soon as you can, yes?"

Caroline sighed angrily. "I swear to God, Fabrizio, if this turns into another one of your 'let's-meet-ups' where we wait for an hour for you to show your face…"

"I promise you, it will not," he said solemnly. Then he bowed and headed upstairs without another word.

Caroline gathered the others and headed to the lift.

On the way up, she was stuck with the endless prattle of Patricia Pembrey, who was having a very one-sided conversation with Helen O'Brien.

"Yes, the Dolce & Gabbana store was fine, but Prada was incredibly disappointing. 'So many shoes, so little time,' I thought, but really, it was about fifty variations on the same shoe. And the handbags? Pssh. Nothing worth mentioning. Now, of *course* I walked out with a new pair," she slapped a shopping bag, "but I wasn't particularly impressed, at any rate. Now Gucci, on the other hand, was something special. I simply *had* to pick up a few scarfs, and then a shirt to go with them and before I knew it, I was so weighed down with clothes that I could hardly move! It was—"

The ding of the lift cut Patricia off, much to the others' relief.

They exited and were immediately shocked: there, in front of them was a table set up with seven places, along with twinkling wine glasses, and that perfect late evening view of St. Peter's Basilica below.

Candles on the table and fairy lights strung overhead completed the scene of romantic Italian serenity.

"Did you…?" Ben asked Caroline, pointing at the table.

She shook her head. "No, I – I had no idea," she said in wonder, glancing over at a beaming Fabrizio, who held out a chair for Molly.

"Come, come," he said. "Pembreys, O'Briens, and the beautiful Signorina Caroline, come! Sit! Eat!"

He pointed at the salad set out in little bowls on the table. "Here we have salad with lettuce, onion, green pepper, tomatoes, and crumbled gorgonzola cheese. We will pair this with a sweet vermouth *aperitivo*. Please, enjoy."

Caroline couldn't believe it. She had been raging at Fabrizio all day long, but here, he had outdone himself. This was beautiful, and she could tell by Molly's face that it was a lot more like her Italian dream.

When she saw him head back to the kitchen, she excused herself and followed him. "Fabrizio," she called when she was far enough away that the others couldn't hear her.

He turned and smiled. "Ah, Signorina Caroline. Is there something not to your liking?"

She shook her head. "No, I have to say… I did not expect this at all. The lights, the food, the wine, the view… It's fantastic. Molly and Ben are thrilled. But I have to know… when I was yelling at you before, downstairs, why didn't you tell me you had this planned?"

His smile grew wider. "Because then, I wouldn't have the opportunity to speak with you now," he said, laying the charm on even more thickly.

Caroline blushed slightly. "Well, I think I owe you an apology. This is truly wonderful. You've done a very good job."

He nodded. "Now, if you will excuse me, signorina, I must get back to the kitchen to bring out the *primera*."

"Can I ask what we're having?" she asked.

"And what kind of surprise would that be?" he winked.

She watched him walk away, thinking to herself, *Okay, so maybe he's not completely cheesy.*

And even if he is, maybe that's not so bad...

CHAPTER 14

*T*rue to his word, Fabrizio's presentation was superb.

The *primera* of pasticcio al forno, "a traditional Christmas pasta bake," according to their host, delighted the guests. Layers of rigatoni, ground lamb, tomato sauce, and generous helpings of cheese were a welcome way to replenish after a day of sightseeing.

The tender slices of veal and delicious roasted potatoes that comprised the *secondi* were an absolute delight, too. When Helen O'Brien raised a faint objection to eating veal, Fabrizio noted that, "little animals are the sacrificial victims of the Italian lust for meat at Christmas. It is… tradition."

One bite later, Helen's moral qualms melted away like the meat in her mouth.

So delicious was everything that no one seemed to notice just how much wine was being consumed.

This was partly Fabrizio's doing: rather than leaving a bottle of wine for the table, he insisted on pairing different wines with each course.

By the time dessert rolled around, everyone had had more than their share of delicious Barberas, Sangioveses and Vermentinos.

It was after Fabrizio brought out a delightful-looking *zuppa inglese* that things started going downhill.

The festive dessert, made of rum, jam, pastry cream, whipped cream and fruit, reminded Paddy of sherry trifle, easily his favourite dessert.

He hadn't been particularly impressed by the wines nor the *limoncello* Fabrizio had foisted upon the table, but this – this was a rare slice of home, and Paddy was simply delighted.

"Nothing beats a good trifle," he said, his mouth watering.

Patricia shot him a look. "Trifle?" she repeated, amusedly. "How... *quaint.*"

"Now, don't get me wrong," Paddy continued between mouthfuls of *zuppe*, "it's nothing compared to my Helen's here. No one does it better. But this isn't half bad at all."

"I can't say I've ever had trifle before," James mused.

Patricia nodded. "Of course you haven't, dear," she said haughtily. "It's a rather ... common dessert, no flair or artistry needed."

Helen's gaze shot up. "Really ..." she said decidedly unimpressed.

"Oh darling," Patricia insisted, "that wasn't meant to be insulting."

"Good," Helen replied flatly. "Because it certainly sounded like that."

Patricia wasn't finished. "I just think," she continued, "it speaks to a certain... *kind.*"

"Mother..." Ben interjected warily.

"No Ben," Patricia continued, holding up a hand to silence him, "I am tired of having to hold my tongue. You are asking me to be something that I simply am not. And I also resent being told that I have to pretend to think this....Italian charade... is all okay when it simply is *not.*"

Ben shook his head apologetically at Molly. "Father," he motioned towards Patricia, "couldn't you..."

James merely looked down as his wife continued on. "Ben," she said, softening as she gazed concernedly at her son, "this can't truly be what you want - a hush-hush ceremony in a tiny church in a foreign country? You are entitled to so much *more*. You are the son of a lord, and heir to an important title. One day, you will be the 16th Earl of Daventry. Our family has certain *standards* to uphold. And however pleasant this young lady," she motioned towards Molly, "might be, I simply do not believe she understands what inheriting such a title might mean. Of course, I cannot blame her for that. Manners are taught as much as they are learned."

"Now, you hold on!" Helen exploded, shocking everyone at the table as she stood angrily. "I don't know who you think you are to insult my daughter and my family the way you have, Patricia, but this is *truly* beyond the pale. Your so-called English *title* does not bring with it the opportunity to look down your nose at *any*one's manners, at least not with the way you yourself are acting."

Helen's breathing increased in rapidity, and she felt her heart race in her chest. She glanced at her daughter, who looked on the verge of tears, and took a deep breath before continuing in a more relaxed tone.

"For Molly's sake, I am going to assume that you simply have had too much wine tonight, and it has loosened your tongue. I can be far more forgiving of an obnoxious drunk than I can the nasty person you are showing yourself to be this evening. I think we should leave now, before I say something I myself might *truly* regret. Paddy?"

Paddy looked at Molly, then to Ben, and finally stood and joined his wife.

"I – good evening," he said simply as Helen stormed off.

Molly stared at Patricia, who seemed unconcerned by their exit.

"Molly, dear," she said with a put-on smile, "I hope you know this had nothing to do with you…"

The bride-to-be looked shocked. She looked at Patricia quizzically. "Nothing… to do… with me?" she repeated.

"Of course not," Patricia shook her head. "We simply want the best for our son that's all."

Molly's jaw hit the floor. "So... what you're saying is... I'm *not* the best for Ben." She looked at her fiance, who said nothing. "How... *dare* you...!"

"See. Like mother, like daughter," Patricia muttered under her breath.

"And *you*," she exploded, turning on Ben. "That you could just *sit* there while this... *woman* insults me, insults my mother and my father while all we're here in Rome - for our wedding?"

"I – I don't—"

Molly narrowed her eyes. "You know what, Ben?" she snapped. "You can keep your titles, and your Lordship and your stuck-up parents. I can't be with someone who cares so much about a title and so little for his wife-to-be."

With that, she spun on her heel and walked off.

Caroline jumped up to chase after her – but before doing so, she turned to the Pembreys. "You're just... I can't even ..." she muttered before going after her friend.

Ben sat at the table in stunned silence. His mother sipped on her limoncello, a satisfied look on her face, while his father continued to stare off into the distance. "See Ben, this isn't—"

"Mother," he said quietly, "can you *please* give it a rest for once?"

"I'm only saying..."

"Not. Now."

"All right, all right," Patricia responded. "But at some point, you're going to have to face facts, Ben: that girl is simply all wrong for us. And her family is —"

"*Mother,*" Ben interjected hotly. "That is *enough*. You have been rude, pretentious, and condescending, particularly towards the O'Briens. And now, you've ruined the one thing that has made me happier than anything ever has. I want to *marry* Molly. I'm *going* to marry Molly - here in Rome on Christmas Eve. And there is simply nothing you can say or do that's going to stop me." He stood up and angrily tossed his napkin on the table. "Molly however, might well be a different story. "

CHAPTER 15

*T*ears streamed down Molly's face as she wound her way through the cobblestone streets and back alleys of the beloved city of her dreams.

The sun had set on Rome, and everywhere she looked, shops were closing up, their darkened windows displaying clothes of red and green and large, intricately decorated signs proclaiming, BUON NATALE.

It was too much to take. What had she been thinking, bringing her and Ben's families here?

Since she was a little girl, all she'd ever dreamed about was a romantic Christmas wedding in Rome.

She knew the place so well she felt almost like an honorary Roman. She knew the sites by heart, knew the history of the city and the empire that bore its name, the names of the great men and women who had made this the single most legendary Italian city in the world.

And one of the most important things she'd planned for her wedding day was bringing the guests to the Trevi Fountain after the ceremony, to carry out the famed tradition of throwing coins in the fountain.

But would any of her guests truly want to return to Rome? And more to the point, after this trip, would Molly want to?

She passed by the Pantheon, its columns illuminated by a row of Christmas trees lit up along the piazza in front.

It was beautiful and looked so magically festive in such glorious surrounds, but for once, failed to lift her spirits.

She continued walking, eventually crossing the Tiber and coming up on Vatican City.

St. Peter's Basilica glowed in the sun's fading light.

I'm usually so entranced by this, she thought glumly. *What's wrong with me?*

But she knew exactly what was wrong: Ben. Why hadn't he stood up to his parents back there? How could he let his mother say such things about her family – and to her?

She could never have imagined sitting idly by while Paddy or Helen said similar things about Ben.

How can we recover from this? she wondered as she found herself walking past the Castel Sant'Angelo.

She knew the answer to this, too: maybe they couldn't. This was *it*.

She was in her city of her dreams, at her favourite time of the year…supposedly to marry the man of her dreams, and now everything was ruined.

All because of stuck-up Patricia Pembrey and her penchant for wine and haughtiness.

Molly saw a tram coming and decided to escape for a while.

She bought a ticket and jumped randomly on the departing #19 and took a seat in the back.

She gazed longingly out the window, watching her beloved Eternal City passing by, wishing for something – anything – to give her that familiar burst of inspiration.

It wasn't forthcoming. Everywhere she seemed to look now, she saw commercialism, tourist traps, and big-city trappings.

There was no magic here anymore, she decided sadly; it was like just any another city.

The accents might be different, the language more melodic-sounding, and the skin tones a bit darker, but a city was still a city. Her parents were right; she should have just got married back home.

Married. She cringed. Was she still getting married? She loved Ben, certainly – but she simply couldn't handle his mother being the way she was. And if he wouldn't stand up to Patricia, stand up *for* his new wife, his new family, this simply was not to be.

She shook her head, and got off the tram to unfamiliar surroundings. The sign designated this area Piazza Buenos Aires, but she was pretty sure she'd never been here before.

She wasn't sure how long she'd been travelling, nor exactly where she was either. She shrugged and trudged on dejectedly.

That was when she saw it.

It wasn't quite a clock tower – there was no clock on it – but it nonetheless rang out, a bell tower dressed up in its festive finest, beautiful brown Tuscan architecture housing tresses that seemed to stretch up into the sky.

Molly walked towards the structure, entranced.

Suddenly, as the tower rose in front of her, she came upon an archway, lit up with fairy lights, a face in the centre almost gazing down upon her, beckoning her to enter. Where was this?

Balconies like something out of *Romeo and Juliet* adorned buildings that almost looked like miniature castles. Cars, apartments, trees, and green grassy areas were all smashed up against each other in a thoroughly confusing fashion.

The entire area was decorated with white fairy lights, while multicoloured bulbs hung from the tent coverings of pop-up cafes along the street.

She heard a rhythmic beating from somewhere nearby: a drum circle, replete with locals dancing in time had apparently sprung up in a nearby park.

The winter wind blew chilly now, but no one seemed to care.

Molly turned around in full circle, in awe of what she had just stumbled upon. She closed her eyes and breathed in deeply, taking it all in. *This* was the magic of Rome she knew.

It wasn't in the historical sites or the typical trappings of the ancient city she'd shown her parents – it was *here*, in *this* place, wherever it was, with these people, obviously locals, dancing and singing and being festive. The lifeblood.

She grinned as she found herself swaying to the beat, smiles of joy now replacing tears of heartbreak and frustration.

This was *her* Rome.

"*W*ell, where *is* she?" Ben demanded, breathing heavily and sounding more than a little panicked, as he paced his hotel room.

"I've tried phoning her, asked around the hotel – I even asked that dopey desk clerk if she had seen her. Nothing. No one knows where Molly went."

Caroline poured a glass of water and handed it to him. "Calm down," she said soothingly. "I'm sure she'll turn up. She was really annoyed by your mum. She probably just needs to blow off some steam. This is the city of her dreams, isn't it?"

When he looked even glummer at this, Caroline put a hand on his shoulder.

"Ben," she continued, "Molly's a big girl. She can take care of herself. Look, maybe we should talk about something else, help get your mind off things."

"Like what?" he asked.

"Like, what in God's name is wrong with your parents?"

Ben shook his head disappointedly. "I don't even know where to begin. My mother can be—"

"A heinous she-witch?" Caroline offered.

"—difficult. Hell, she's difficult in the *best* of times, let alone when she's had a few…"

"But we're here for your *wedding*." Caroline pressed. "What does she have against Helen and Paddy? And what was all that rubbish about dessert - and that whole trifle thing? I love trifle myself."

Ben sighed. "It's just …" he ventured, "my mother has always had issues with 'new' money."

Caroline cocked her head. "What do you mean, 'new' money?"

"Like, money that hasn't been inherited. Self-made wealth."

"Well, Paddy's hardly *wealthy*. I mean, he and Helen are reasonably well-off, I suppose, but nothing like—"

"Me?" Ben offered.

"Well, I wasn't going to say it, but your father *is* a member of the House of Lords…"

"*He* may be, but *I* don't want to be."

Caroline threw up her arms, exasperated with Ben's naivety. "Oh come, *on*, Ben!" she exclaimed. "You of all people *know* that's not how this works. When your dad passes away, that's it: *you* become the Earl of Coventry—"

"Daventry."

"—whatever. The point is, that English nobility stuff means nothing to the likes of us. We don't do gentry in Ireland as you know. And then for your mum to go around pretending like she's… I don't know, the Queen of England or whatever, is a bit much."

"I get that," Ben nodded. "But what's that got to do with *me*? Why would Molly be mad at *me* for how my parents act? She knows I don't agree with their values *or* their attitudes."

"Because, Ben, you didn't stand up for Molly or her parents back there! You're like a turtle: when confronted, you went right back into your shell. And if I know Molly, all she wanted was to hear you put your parents in their place."

"But I did," Ben insisted. "After you all left, I lit into them. Told them they'd better get used to the idea of Molly being around, because I'm *going* to marry her."

"Great," Caroline told him, "but does *she* know that?"

"She knows me," he replied. "She should know that about me."

"Molly's not a psychic, Ben," Caroline told him. "All she saw was you kowtowing to your mother's nastiness - and with only a day to go till your wedding. I'd imagine *that*, more than anything, is what set her off."

Ben slumped down in a chair. "I just don't know what to do Caroline," he said sadly. "If the wedding is called off —"

"That," she insisted, "won't happen." She grabbed her coat and headed towards the door. "Look," she told him, "I'll head out and see if I can find her, talk her round. You just stay there, and keep in touch."

Ben nodded glumly, and Caroline went back out to the hallway ... where she collided straight with none other than Fabrizio.

"Signorina Caroline," he said happily, "I am so happy to find you. Everyone left so quickly…"

She stared at him impatiently, waiting for him to explain what he was doing outside her room.

It was then that she noticed the clothing bag hung over his arm. "I bring good news: your dress has arrived. The wedding is saved!"

Caroline chuckled ironically as Fabrizio handed the bag to her. "Well," she said, "thanks anyway, but we're no longer sure at this point if there's actually going to *be* a wedding."

"What do you mean?" he asked, looking shocked.

She sighed. "Well," she explained, "everybody left because there was a big row over dinner between Ben's parents and Molly's, and it ended with Molly walking out on Ben."

"Oh no," he replied concernedly. "So where is she now?"

"That's the thing," Caroline said. "I'm heading out now to try and find her. She took off, and no one seems to know where she is."

"And you are going to, what, walk around *Roma* after dark calling out her name until you find her?"

Caroline shrugged. "She can't have gone far," she replied.

Fabrizio shook his head. "Of course she can. There are trains, buses, trams, taxis – she could be halfway to *Napoli* by now."

Caroline's face fell. "Oh God, Fabrizio," she said, panic rising in her voice, "you don't think she would do that, do you?"

"I do not know," he answered. "She is your friend, after all. You know her best."

Caroline nodded. "Right, right," she said. "Okay, let's see… where would she go?"

"Perhaps something related to the wedding?" Fabrizio ventured. "Maybe the church or to the *Fontana di Trevi* to think."

"At this point, I think the wedding is the last thing she wants to think about. You didn't see her, Fabrizio. She was very upset. She ran off before I even had the chance to to talk her."

Fabrizio nodded. "Okay, I have an idea. Go, leave your dress in your room, and meet me downstairs in a few minutes. We will drive in my car to a few places I know. Perhaps we will be lucky."

Caroline stared at him again – only this time, it was in admiration. "Fabrizio, that's very kind of you… I'm…"

"I know," he said, flashing her his increasingly charming smile. "I will see you downstairs."

CHAPTER 18

 a few minutes later, she stood outside the hotel, craning her neck to see where Fabrizio might be. Several cars passed by, but there was no indication any of them was being driven by the handsome Italian.

Her attention was struck moments later by a gorgeous yellow Lamborghini, sleek and stylish and very cool.

Boy, she thought to herself, *nice to have the money to afford one of those babies.*

The Lamborghini turned into the hotel turnabout, and the horn honked towards her. She squinted to see the driver.

It was Fabrizio. "Of *course*," she murmured.

He opened the door for her – opening it not out but *up*, which made her stand back.

"Come," he motioned.

The interior of the car was even more luxurious than she'd imagined. Gorgeous cream and black leather seats, a smooth, crisp dash, top-of-the-line stereo system… it was almost too much, and she said so.

"What," she teased, "you couldn't do well enough with a *moder-*

ately expensive car? You have to go with the one that costs as much as a house?"

He smiled. "My job," he explained, "causes me to have to drive quite a bit. I like... style when I do so."

"And you can afford this?"

"I can afford many things."

"How is that possible?" She herself had worked at a hotel before. Even at a luxury one like the Hotel Marliconi.

"The hotel at which you are staying," he said matter-of-factly, "is my main source of income."

"There's no way you can afford a Lamborghini on an event specialist's salary."

He looked over at her quizzically. "*Signora*," he said, "I am many things, but I am no event specialist."

"What are you talking about?" she asked, frowning. "Molly has been working with you for months now."

Fabrizio shook his head. "No," he said, "Molly was working with our event specialist, yes, but he is no longer employed with us. I fired him last week."

"What do you mean, *you* fired him? Are you his manager or something?"

"You mean... the Pembreys did not tell you?"

"Ben's parents? What did they not tell me, exactly?"

"The Hotel Marliconi," he said. "It is my hotel."

Caroline felt a shock ripple through her entire body. "Wait – *your* hotel? So that would make you..."

He looked at her and once again flashed his smile. "Fabrizio Marliconi. At your service."

"Wait, wait, wait," Caroline stammered as the car sped off. "This doesn't make any sense. Why would the owner of a luxury hotel be helping out a tiny wedding party like ours?"

"Lady Pembrey," he responded, "is an old family friend. Her mother and mine went to the same university in England. Cambridge. She asked me to step in to help with the wedding."

Caroline sat there in stunned silence. There was no way – there was simply no *way* that that horrible, vile, bigoted woman had stepped in and saved the day.

After all the complaining, the negativity and those awful things she'd said to the O'Briens... could Patricia really not be as terrible as everyone had thought?

A little while later, her thoughts were interrupted by the car jerking to a sudden stop.

"There," Fabrizio called out, pointing to a girl dancing in the middle of a nearby side street.

It was Molly.

Caroline jumped out of the car and ran straight over to her best friend. "Molly Rose O'Brien," she called out. "What on earth do you think you're doing?"

Molly just smiled, looking almost giddy.

"Caroline!" she cooed. "Oh, I'm so glad you're here. How did you – " She stopped when she saw Fabrizio standing by his car.

"Long story," Caroline said curtly. "Where have you been? We had no idea where you'd gone. Ben's been worried sick about you – literally."

Molly squeezed Caroline's hand in hers as they walked back towards Fabrizio's car. "I went exploring," she explained. "I hopped on a tram, got off completely randomly, and I kind of just stumbled upon this place. I have no idea where we are, but – Caroline, isn't it wonderful? *This* is what Rome is all about - this was the city I wanted you to see."

Molly was beaming with an enthusiasm Caroline hadn't seen since their arrival.

She took a look around her for the first time. She had to admit, this area, wherever they were, had a certain authentic charm to it, possessing more of a true Italian feel to it than other more heavily commercialised areas of the city.

"Fabrizio," she asked when they returned to the car, "where exactly are we?"

"Il Quartiere Coppedè," he said. "The Coppedè district. It is well-known for being more... erm... I am not sure of the English word... *svariato*... than any other district in Roma."

"It's wonderful," Molly said dreamily. "But now I think maybe it's time for me to get back."

"To your groom I hope?" Fabrizio inquired.

Molly nodded. "Yes, I suppose so." She turned to Caroline. "Is there any way I can have Ben's parents banned from the ceremony?"

Caroline squeezed her friend's hand again. "I don't think so love," she smiled. "But, listen... just leave everything to me. They'll be on their best behaviour, I promise."

"Fabrizio held open the car door. "After you, ladies," he said.

When they reached the hotel, Molly gave Caroline another hug. "Listen," she said, "I'm going to talk to Ben. I think we have some things to work out."

"You've only got a few hours left 'til your wedding, remember?" Caroline said. "Do talk to him. Explain it all, but don't forget that you love him – and he loves you."

Molly waved to Fabrizio as she walked away.

"Thanks for the lift," she called.

"My pleasure," he smiled, waving back.

ONCE MOLLY WAS GONE, Caroline went over to the Italian and kissed him on the cheek.

"You might just have saved the day, Fabrizio," she whispered. "Thank you for your help."

She turned to walk away, but he grabbed her arm and pulled her back towards him.

"*Signorina*," he said, his dark eyes boring intensely into hers. "Caroline. I do these things for you because I find you fascinating. I do not normally meet women like you," he continued.

Caroline trembled slightly despite herself. "Women like me?" she scoffed shakily. "You hardly know me."

"Few women are willing to speak their minds the way you do," he told her. "You are fearless and brave. You will tell people what you think whether they want to hear it or not. I... admire that."

With that, he took her face in his large, olive-skinned hands, and brushed her hair off her face.

A moment passed between them that felt to Caroline like an eternity.

"I'm telling you, Fabrizio," she said quickly, "I'm not—"

She didn't get the opportunity to finish, because she suddenly found his face against hers, her lips locked with his.

It was the kind of kiss that made a person weak in the knees, long and serious, blissful and playful – and when it was over, left an impression.

One hell of an impression.

Caroline's eyes were still closed when he broke away. "Fabrizio —" she murmured, momentarily awestruck.

"You see, *signorina?*" he asked.

Caroline opened her eyes, realising what had just happened, and shook her head. "No," she insisted quietly.

"No?"

"No," she repeated. "No, no, *no*. I'm – I'm *so* not doing – this can't – " She began to back away from him.

"Caroline," he pleaded, more intently.

"No, Fabrizio, look, thank you for helping me find Molly, but I – I have to – to go." She walked backwards away from him unsteadily, almost in a daze. "I'm – I'm sorry. I— "

Caroline didn't say another word, but instead, turned her back on him and picked up speed until she was almost running to the lift, her mind racing.

Oh God, she thought, *What in the world have I just done?*

*B*en was watching *Sky News* – Italy's Finance Minister was caught up in some sort of scandalous affair – when a knock came at his door.

He jumped out of bed, knocking over a less-than-sturdy nightstand (and taking down a lamp with it) in the process.

He cursed mildly over his stubbed toe and hobbled over to the door to reveal an absolute shock.

"Mother …" he said, irritably.

Patricia held her expression neutral, but he noted a slight smudge in her usually impeccably applied mascara. She'd been crying.

"Ben darling," she greeted, her voice wavering ever-so-slightly, "may I come in?"

He didn't answer, but left the door open and headed back into the room. Patricia followed, swallowing hard.

"I'd offer you a drink," Ben said coldly, "but I'm pretty certain you've already had quite enough."

She chuckled a little. "I suppose I should've stopped after that first bottle of wine."

"Mother, I don't give a damn how much wine you drank," he scolded her. "What you did – the way you acted – it was—"

"—unforgivable," she finished for him, nodding. "I know, dear. I know. I was only…"

"You were *only* thinking about yourself," he snapped. Patricia stayed silent and looked to the ground. "Is there something you needed?" he asked.

She shook her head. "I just – I want you to under—" she stifled a small heave in her chest before continuing, "—to understand all that comes with being the Earl of Daventry. Because it won't be—"

"Oh for God's sake, mother!" Ben yelled. "I don't care about being the Earl of Daventry, or the rank, or the title, or any of that. I care about *Molly!*"

He ran his fingers through his hair and paced a bit around the room. "Do you know what Caroline is doing now?" he demanded. Patricia shook her head. "She's wandering around the streets of Rome, hoping that maybe, somehow, she'll run into Molly, or Molly will answer her phone. And the reason I'm not out there with her is I'm afraid that seeing *me* will only make things worse. And you know what I have to thank for that? The damned Lord and Lady Pembrey! You, and your stuck-up, closed-minded, pretentious nonsense that makes you think that because you married Father, you're somehow entitled to better treatment than your so-called social inferiors."

At this, Patricia broke. She knew her son was right; he had every right and every reason to be upset with her. But more than anything else, she also knew *she* was right.

"Ben," she said, choking back a sob, "I know the title means nothing to you. But it doesn't mean nothing to everyone. In fact, it means a great deal. It imparts status and power – not for me – I grew up without it, obviously – but for your children. The only time I've ever invoked the title has been to help *you*."

Ben looked her in the eye, his blazing fiercely. "I never *asked* for that, Mother," he said darkly.

"You never *had* to," she insisted. "You are my *son*. Perhaps... perhaps when you have children of your own, you'll understand."

"If I have children," he said, "it's going to be with Molly. I only hope she can forgive me for not standing up to you sooner."

"Oh Ben," Patricia remarked, "I'm not concerned with whether or not you have children with Molly or – or – bloody Princess Beatrice!"

Ben arched an eyebrow. "Wha— why would I ever have children with— what?"

Patricia shook her head. "Never mind. The *point*, my dear, is that you can marry whomever you want – but you must choose carefully, because what you stand to inherit affects not only you but your children and your children's children." She fumbled with her fingers a bit before continuing, obviously searching for the right words to convey her feelings. "Do you remember Digadoo?"

"Digadoo?" Ben chuckled. "Sounds like a really awful kids' TV show."

"Digadoo," Patricia explained, "was your imaginary pony. When you were about three, you were absolutely *obsessed* with ponies, and you said you wanted one. When your father and I told you you'd have to wait 'til you were older, you invented this pony of your own, Digadoo. He was your friend, your confidante – and apparently, he could fly, too."

"Right."

"You and Digadoo were the best of friends for about a year. You'd do *everything* together. You even had me set a place at the dinner table every night for him."

"So whatever happened to him?'" Ben asked.

"Well, after about a year or so, we realised that you were still serious about this pony, so we got you riding lessons at the club."

"I remember *that*," he said. "But I don't remember Digadoo."

"That's because you don't need to, darling," Patricia said. "Digadoo faded into your memory the way imaginary friends are supposed to, and got replaced by reality. And the reality we were able to provide you with was far better than any fantasy you might have had."

"I don't recall the horse being able to fly," Ben said softly.

"No, but do you recall the fun you had?"

He nodded. "But that's hardly the point, Mother," he elaborated. "Money, wealth, power – they're all fine and well, but you can't buy happiness. And I can't remember, but I presume I was very happy with Digadoo."

Patricia shrugged. "You may have been," she admitted, "but you were three. You would have been happy with a bowl of custard and a few ladyfingers. Children can't appreciate what their parents can offer them. It's for the parents to provide the opportunities. And the Earlship provides more opportunities, opens more doors, than you can possibly imagine."

"That may be, Mother," Ben agreed, "but that doesn't excuse how you spoke to the O'Briens. And it doesn't excuse how you treated Molly. She's a wonderful person, mother. If you'd only get past your own ludicrous biases, you'd see that."

"She might be," Patricia replied. "She could be the loveliest girl who's ever lived. But I just don't know that the… the societal *manners* she and her parents have shown is compatible with giving your children, my grandchildren, the very best of lives."

"God, Mother!" Ben complained. "This isn't a Jane Austen novel. Manners and discipline and polite society? It's all nonsense. To say nothing of the fact that none of that gentry stuff even exists in Ireland. The only thing that's important is how we treat each other. That's what all the sermons at all the masses we attended when I was a boy said. *Do unto others* and all that. It doesn't matter if Molly wanted to get married in a foreign city, or that her parents tell saucy in-jokes. They are good people. They are kind people. And they deserve far better than how you've treated them." Incensed afresh, Ben rose and opened the door. "I think it's best if you leave now."

"Ben," she pleaded, panic overtaking her face, "I wish you would only try to understand. I'm not against Molly or her parents. I simply want what's best for you."

"What's best for me, Mother," he responded flatly, "is to be happy. And the only way that's going to happen is if Molly comes back tonight, safe and sound, and we get married in this city tomorrow. You and Father can come or not come to the ceremony – that's entirely up to you – but if Molly will still have me, we're getting married tomorrow."

Patricia nodded curtly and left the room without saying another word.

BEN CLOSED the door behind her and collapsed against the door. He knew his mother cared – the fact that she'd remembered an imaginary friend he'd forgotten like Digadoo was proof of that – but her haughtiness and closed-mindedness were simply unforgivable.

He was startled to attention rather quickly by a brusque rapping on the door. He stood, straightened his shirt, and began opening the door. Patricia, it appeared, had more to say. "Okay, look," he began, "I need you to hear me loud and clear: what you think at this point is imma— *oh.*"

It wasn't his mother standing in the doorway. Instead, it was a vision from heaven itself, an angel sent to guide him home. It was Molly, and she was grinning lopsidedly at her fiancee.

"Hey there, handsome," she said in her best American drawl. "Wanna get hitched?"

CHAPTER 21

*B*en took Molly into his arms and kissed her. "Where on earth have you been?" he asked. "I'm so sorry."

Molly smiled. "I went looking for something," she said. "I needed – I don't know – I needed to remember that Rome was the same city I knew and loved, I needed it to calm and heal me in the way it always did. And I needed to think."

"About my mother?" Ben asked warily. "Look, I need you to know – whatever she thinks, you are the woman I—"

Molly was shaking her head rapidly. "No, no, no," she insisted. "Not about your mum. About *me*." She took a deep breath before continuing. "Ben, I've been unfair to you," she began.

"No, you—"

"Please," she insisted, "let me get this out." She straightened her dress in front of her and continued, her voice barely above a whisper. "I've been very unfair to you and everyone. I wanted this wedding in Italy at Christmas. I pushed ahead with it despite what our families - both our parents wanted. And I tried to force my dream, my perfect vision of Rome on everyone.

And before you say anything, I know we both agreed on this, and that at the time it suited *both* of us. But if I'm being honest, you've given me everything I've wanted, while I haven't really given much back."

"That's not true," Ben argued. "Molly, you've been more than fair. Putting up with Mother – and Father – isn't even the half of it. Everything's seems to have gone wrong since we got here, and—"

"It's all gone wrong *because* of me, trying to make everything perfect. And when I walked out on dinner—"

"—which you had every right to do…"

"Perhaps," Molly admitted. "But it was still poor form. And after all your parents have done …"

A confused look overtook Ben's face. "What are you talking about?" he asked.

"It's okay," she said patiently. "Caroline told me all about what your mum and dad did. About how the wedding planner I hired messed everything up, and how Fabrizio is the owner of the hotel…"

"He's *what?*" Ben gasped.

Molly titled her head curiously. "Wait…" she said, putting two and two together. "You didn't know?"

"Know what?"

"That your mum asked for Fabrizio's help because she's old friends with his mum."

Ben sat down, mystified. "I – I honestly had no idea," he murmured. He looked up at Molly. "Mother was just in here. I read her the riot act because of how she'd acted. I… I had no idea she'd done that." He shook his head, recalling the conversation. "But that still doesn't excuse what she said to you and your folks."

"No, it doesn't," Molly agreed. "But Ben, whatever your mum said while she was drinking, I don't know if that means she actually *believes* it. She just wants the best for you, I suppose."

"*You* are the best for me," he said, standing and taking her in his arms.

"So then, you do still want to marry me?" she asked.

"Only if you still want to marry me," he said, adding, "and marry *into* my family."

Molly half-smiled. "I think I can make do," she mused. "Besides, we'll only have to see them occasionally. Every other Christmas or so."

Ben nodded. "If that, even," he said. "We could always move somewhere they'd never come, like—"

"—Naples?" Molly joked.

Ben laughed and kissed her. "I love you, Signorina O'Brien," he said, his heart filling up.

"And I love you, Lord Pembrey," she teased.

"Don't call me that," he insisted.

"I think I will actually," she said, smiling and holding him close.

*H*elen stood in her room, staring out the window at the glorious Roman skyline lit up against the darkness.

Behind her, Paddy sat on a chair, his laptop open in front of him and his ear glued to his mobile phone.

It seemed yet another shipment was running late, and rather than trusting that everything would be taken care of, as the others had been, he seemed to think he could will the packages to their destinations in time for Christmas by sheer thought.

"No, Felicity," Paddy said, irritation rising in his voice. "N-no— no— look, just get it done, all right? Now, where are we with the Jefferson Electronics account?" He typed a few notes on his computer, continuing back-and-forth with his assistant over the other end of the phone.

Helen had heard enough. "Paddy," she called soothingly, turning back to him. "We have barely hours until our daughter's wedding. Don't you think you can give the phone a rest? Can't someone else handle it?"

Paddy covered the receiver with his hand. "What?" he asked her, squinting towards her form. "What did you say, love?"

"Nothing," Helen sighed. "Nothing at all." She resumed looking out the window. Why couldn't she get him to put down the phone for more than a few minutes at a time? He hadn't always been this way. Only when DHL had taken over the business did his penchant for working constantly become an issue.

Here they were in one of the most beautiful cities in the word two days before Christmas, their daughter's relationship was in crisis, and all he could think about was computer part deliveries.

Helen stared across at the Vatican and St Peter's Basilica, silently wishing for a miracle.

CHAPTER 23

*I*n the room next door, things were only slightly less frosty. "I simply don't know what more to say to him," Patricia told her husband.

"Perhaps you shouldn't say anything," he counselled her. "Ben's a grown man. He needs to make his own choices, questionable though we may think them."

"But James," she whined insistently, "the O'Briens are... so..."

"Oh, they're all right, Patricia," he scolded her. "Paddy is a decent sort, and Helen is quite charming."

"But they're so... so..."

"Ordinary?"

"Yes!" Patricia exclaimed. "How can Ben settle for that when he can do so much better?"

"Do you even know your son?" James asked her. "He's far more comfortable with them than he ever was with us. He skipped out on Cambridge for Dublin, for God's sake. Let's let him make his own decisions. And I won't have any more of these hostilities. You will go and apologise to Molly and her parents."

"You can't be serious."

"Of course I'm serious," he said sternly. "This wedding is going to happen whether we want it to or not, Patricia, and I would prefer that we make the best of it, wouldn't you?"

Patricia sighed. "You're right, of course," she said resignedly. "All right. Tomorrow, over breakfast... I will... apologise."

"You know why I adore you, my dear?"

"Why's that?"

"Because you have more sense than any woman I've ever known."

"Tell that to your son," Patricia muttered.

"I plan to," James said, grinning and taking her into his arms.

*C*aroline paced around her room. What had she just done? This was exactly what she'd wanted to avoid – what she'd *tried* to avoid. Now, not only was it obvious Fabrizio was interested, but it turned out he was handsome *and* wealthy.

Good God, she thought to herself, *could I possibly be any more of a cliche?*

She was still pacing when Molly walked in, a smile plastered to her face.

"Caroline," she cooed, "I have to thank you. You've really gone above and beyond. Again." She went over to her friend, oblivious to her distress, and hugged her. She broke the embrace, however, when she noticed her face. "What's wrong?" she asked.

Caroline shook her head. "I can't even begin..." she said exasperatedly. "I'm just... I'm an idiot, that's what."

"You're not," cried Molly. "What are you talking about?"

"Oh," Caroline said, a note of sarcasm in her voice, "you have *no* idea, Mol. I've just been making, you know, fantastic decisions since I got here. Flirt with the suave Italian host? Check. Have a combative but strangely endearing relationship with him? Check.

Find out he's loaded? Check. Snog him in the lobby of his hotel? Check. Make a total gobshite of myse—"

"Hang on," Molly cut in, putting her hands up in a *stop* motion. "What's all this about snogging? And are you talking about Fabrizio?"

"It's not like I even *wanted* to," Caroline said manically as if Molly hadn't interjected. "I mean, yeah, I'd thought about it a bit, but he was so – I mean, he was just *there*, but then he'd been so sweet as to help me find you, and that smile – oh, that smile – but *no.* I can't be the stupid tourist on holiday who falls for the first Italian who gives her the glad eye. I mean, he's Roman. He'll flirt with anything that moves, probably charm the pants off them, too…"

"Caroline," Molly said, putting her hands on her friend's shoulders, "Get a grip. Are you trying to tell me something happened between you and my wedding planner?"

Caroline finally snapped out of her fit and looked at her best friend. "Your wedding planner …oh my God, Molly," she said with a half-smile, "you're getting *married* tomorrow…you are still getting married tomorrow, aren't you?"

Molly nodded. "Ben and I had a chat," she said. "Though really, a lot has been my fault too. But now, back to this… what happened with Fabrizio?"

Caroline pursed her lips and let out a long puff of air.

"Well, when you left to talk to Ben," she explained, "I thanked him, and I might have kissed him on the cheek. But only friendly-like," she added quickly. "And then… he twirled me into his arms, ran his hands through my hair… and … kissed me."

Molly positively beamed. "Oh my *God*, Caroline," she cried. "That's *so* romantic."

"It's not!" Caroline retorted. "It's cheesy and obvious and – and – *stupid*! It's exactly the cliche I wanted to avoid coming here."

Molly shook her head. "Oh come *on*," she told her friend. "Don't be ridiculous. He's *very* good-looking. And for the love of God, he owns the hotel. At the very least, you'd be able to come back to Rome any time you wanted and stay for free…"

"You see?" Caroline said, a wry smile coming to her lips. "This is why I never tell you anything. You always have to go from a simple kiss to a lifelong romance."

"It worked for Ben and me."

"Did not."

"Fair point. But *seriously*, if you were ever going to take a chance on love, now's the time to do it. I mean really, what is the worst that could happen?"

That question made Caroline pause. What *was* the worst that could happen? Certainly, things could be much worse than a holiday romance with a handsome, rich Italian who owned a hotel and drove a fancy car, and at Christmastime no less.

Still …

"Honestly?" she finally replied. "I think I'd lose some respect for myself."

"Whatever for?" Molly asked, incredulous.

Caroline sighed deeply. "I'm… I'm not like you, Mol," she explained. "I don't go all passionate about things and fall head-over-heels. Not that there's anything wrong with that, but it's just not my style. And I never, ever wanted to be a cliche. I absolutely *hate* that holiday romance nonsense."

"Okay," Molly assented, "but I want you to think about this: why do you think they become cliches in the first place?"

"What?"

"All those films and books with broad-chested, impossibly handsome men on the covers… They might be sensationalised fantasy, but in the end, do you think those cliches just sort of happened, like they were just created out of thin air? No way. They were inspired by things that really happened, or that we always *wanted* to happen.

A woman gets swept off her feet by a gorgeous, rich suitor in a romantic Italian city… what in the world is wrong with you that you *wouldn't* just jump on that ride and see where it takes you?"

Caroline was dumbstruck. She hadn't really thought of it that way. It wasn't just a matter of not wanting to be a cliche, she realised – it was her own pride that she'd been riding for last few days.

Fabrizio was a fantasy of sorts: impossibly handsome, incredibly wealthy, and rather sweet. And yet, here she was, pushing him away, just so, what, she could prove a point to herself? She had to admit, that seemed really…

"Stupid," Caroline said finally.

"What's that?" Molly asked.

"*Me,*" she continued. "*I'm* stupid. Molly, I've been an absolute idiot. This lovely man has been throwing himself at me, and I've pushed him away. What is wrong with me?"

Molly laughed at that. "There's nothing wrong with you, honey," she reassured her. "You're just as human as the rest of us. And sometimes, that means we do stupid things. But it's nothing that can't be fixed. You just need the opportunity."

"What kind of opportunity?"

"Well," Molly said, beaming, "I hear there's this big celebration tomorrow…"

CHAPTER 25

"*P*addy?" Helen called from the bathroom the following morning. "Love, can you bring me another towel?" She waited a few moments before calling her husband again. "Paddy? Are you there?"

Helen stepped out of the bathroom wrapped in a towel, a plume of steam trailing her. She rounded the corner into the bedroom to see where her husband was – only to find him barking orders into the phone.

Again.

"Felicity," he said sternly, "we need to – well no, I – don't make – well just go over it again then."

"*Paddy O'Brien!*" Helen thundered.

"I'm going to have to call you back," he said sheepishly into the phone before hanging it up. "Something wrong, pet?" he asked, turning to his wife.

Helen's face was red with fury. "Paddy," she said, her voice so low he had to strain to hear her, "today is your daughter's wedding day. It is a day for celebrating. For God's sake, Paddy, it's Christmas Eve! No one should even be at the office today."

"I hate to break it to you, love," Paddy replied patiently, "but today is the busiest day of the year for us. I can't just abandon them."

"Oh, you can too," she snapped. "I swear, if I see you on that phone *once* between now and the end of today, I'll break the damned phone – or your neck – or both."

"Yes, mammy," he chortled. He fixed his eyes directly on his wife. "Helen," he said, rising from his seat and approaching her, "I've never left Felicity in charge before. She's nervous, and I'm nervous, and we both just need everything to go smoothly."

"I realise that," she responded, "but the least your family can expect today is your undivided attention. Besides," she continued with a wink, "I'm going to need all the support I can get if I'm to deal with that – that – *woman*."

Paddy embraced his wife, who attempted to pull away. "Paddy, don't," she chuckled, "I'm all wet."

"I don't care," he replied. "We'll just have to be wet together, then."

"That's not *all* we can be together…" Helen said suggestively. "But for now," she added, kissing him on the nose, "I have to do my hair." With that, she returned to the bathroom mirror and turned on the hair dryer.

She left it on as she returned to the room to grab her hairbrush – only to find Paddy back on the phone again, barking orders.

Helen sighed, rolled her eyes, and went back to fixing her hair.

CHAPTER 26

*D*own the hall, Ben was practically screaming into his own phone.

"What do you *mean*, 'I forgot my suit?' Why did you not just wear it on the plane? … No, Mark, I don't. Just… just stop off somewhere and buy one. It is Italy after all, home of well-cut suits. Yes. Okay. Half-eleven. I'll see you there."

He hung up the phone and ran his hands through his hair. Once again, his idiot brother was throwing a monkey wrench into the best-laid plans.

How could Mark *possibly* have forgotten his suit? He was the *best man*. It was the one thing he was asked to bring. He wasn't even responsible for the rings. He – that was –

A sudden panic came to Ben's mind. *Oh God*, he thought, *what did I do with the rings?*

He first checked the room safe, but he didn't even remember using it, and sure enough, they weren't there.

Neither were they in or under the bed, in the bathroom, or on the desk.

He eyed his suitcase and, in a moment of pure hysteria, grabbed the entire case and attempted to flip it upside-down over his head.

Unfortunately, being less than coordinated on even his best day, he tripped on the suitcase table and went tumbling forward, knocking the side of his head on the edge of the cabinet and sending clothes and toiletries flying every which way.

He cursed loudly and stood, noticing a sharp pain at his temple. He went to look in the mirror for what he already presumed was there – and sure enough, a long trail of cut skin and blood streaked down the side of his face.

What a start to your wedding day...

He had just begun to clean up the blood with a washcloth and some soap when a knock came at the door. He opened it to find, much to his surprise, his father standing outside. The chipper look on James' face turned to horror when he saw his son's face – and astonishment when he saw the state of the room.

"Good Lord, Ben," James said, shocked, "what in heaven's name happened in here?"

"I – er—" his son stammered, "I couldn't find the rings. And I kind of – you know – panicked."

To his utter surprise, James burst out laughing. "Ben, old boy," he said, the sounds of his laughter echoing off the tiles in the bathroom. He was laughing so hard, he couldn't even get the next sentence out, so instead, he reached into his pocket and pulled out a small, black velvet box and opened it. Inside were two gold bands.

Ben closed his eyes in exasperation with himself. "Oh," he said slowly, "I... am such... an *idiot*..."

James shook his head and handed the box to his son. "Nonsense, my boy," he said, "you're just nervous. As you should be. Today's a big day."

"One you don't approve of," Ben said glumly.

"Now, whatever gave you that idea?"

"Oh, I don't know," Ben replied sarcastically. "How about *everything* that happened yesterday?"

"You mean, that business with your mother? Ben, your mother is the love of my life, but she and I are by no means a single mind.

Believe it or not, she's really just trying to help. And she's scared. She's losing her baby boy after all."

"What? But you've still got Mark."

"Mark is… a sweet boy. But you know as well as I do, he's incomparably stupid."

Now it was Ben's turn to laugh. "He is, isn't he?"

"Absolutely," James responded. "But Ben: your mother may have her faults, but she is also immeasurably sensible. And her worry isn't so much that Molly won't be good for the title; it's that she won't be good for *you*. All we want is to see you happy."

"But don't you see? I *am* happy."

"I know, son. I know."

"So why these shenanigans then, Father?" Ben asked. "Why allow Mother to treat the O'Briens like her inferiors?"

"Your mother is going to apologise to them this morning. Most of what happened was because of the wine. Your mother's tongue was loosened, and she made some very poor choices with what was being said. I seem to remember something similar happening a few Christmases ago."

"That business with the McGanns?"

"Precisely right," James agreed. "What started it all was your mother making an ill-advised comment on Lady McGann's – erm – *ample* posterior."

"Oh God."

"You have no idea. It took six dinners between me and that insufferable Earl of Cheshunt to get things back on track. 'Your mother has a history of saying ill-timed, ill-advised things. But she isn't bad by any stretch. In fact, she quite often has a very lucid understanding of the situation. And her worry in this case is that through your association with Molly – and the O'Briens generally – you will forget about the title, and hurt your children's chances at the finest things you always had access to."

"I never *wanted* access, Father," Ben insisted.

"I know that, but that's hardly the point. Don't you want the best for your children, whenever you may have them?"

"Of course I do."

"Well, that's all we ever wanted for you, too."

Ben closed his eyes and exhaled deeply. "I know, Father. And I appreciate it – *all* of it."

"Right then," James said, ready to change the subject. "Let's get you cleaned up and ready. It's not every day a future Earl of Daventry gets married in Rome."

"What do you think?" Molly asked Caroline as she came out of the bathroom.

Caroline clasped her hands against her face. Her best friend looked stunning beyond belief.

The dress was perfectly form-fitting, gleaming white like falling snow, with a stripe of red and green around it for a suitably festive feel.

Her silver high heeled shoes sparkled with tiny crystals, while red beads looked like holly berries expertly threaded throughout her elegant blonde chignon,.

"Molly," Caroline said, awestruck, "you look like a Christmas princess."

Behind her, a knock came at the door, which Caroline answered.

Helen walked in, grinning ear to ear. "Caroline, you look gorgeous this morning," she said – before she laid eyes on her only daughter. "Oh," she said, stopping dead in her tracks. "Oh – oh *my*... " Tears came to her eyes and she dabbed at them with a handkerchief and strode up to the younger woman. "Oh *Molly*," she said, now sobbing as she hugged her daughter. "Oh my little girl, my beautiful little girl…"

"Mum," Molly laughed through her own tears. "Stop, you're going to leave streaks on my dress."

Helen sniffled and pulled away. "Oh, I'm sorry," she said, laughing too. "I'm just… my goodness, Molly, you look so beautiful."

"I do, don't I?" Molly said immodestly and all three women laughed again.

Caroline went into the bathroom and came out with three glasses and a bottle. "Okay, girls," she giggled. "I got this downstairs earlier. It's grappa, not champagne, but same thing, I think."

Caroline poured three glasses and Helen raised a toast. "To my Molly," she said. "May your perfect winter wedding in Rome live up to all your dreams and be a delight …"

"…and may all your Christmases be white," Caroline rhymed wickedly.

The three women collapsed in a fit of laughter so cacophonous that they didn't hear the knock coming from the door, nor the creak as it opened.

Suddenly, Caroline straightened up, quickly followed by the others.

"I'm so sorry," Patricia said quietly, "the door was open a crack, and I didn't know if you could—" When her eyes caught sight of Molly, she smiled. "My word, dear," she said sincerely, "you look absolutely ravishing."

"Thanks," Molly said flatly.

"Caroline, I don't suppose…" Patricia said, motioning towards the door.

"Yeah… I'm – er – going to see if I can find some more – erm – ice," Caroline winced as she looked apologetically towards Molly and Helen. "I'll be back in a few."

Once the door was closed, Patricia inhaled deeply. "You're probably wondering why I'm here," she began.

"You could say that," said Helen coldly. "Though honestly, I'm wondering why I'd care, too."

"Right enough," Patricia conceded. "Molly, I should start with you. I was entirely out of line with what I said last night. I had far too much wine and far too loose a tongue, and I pushed my concern for Ben way, way too far. I apologise."

Molly nodded but said nothing.

"And Helen," Patricia continued, turning to the younger woman, "I—"

"Save it," she cut her off. "I don't want or need your apology."

"Mum," Molly said gently, "let her speak."

"No, love," Helen's iciness continued. "There is much I can abide, but Patricia, you aren't just a snob or a lush. You're mean-spirited. You think so much of yourself and your titles and your family, but you have no regard for those who don't share your obsession with nobility. You are conceited and self-interested, and I have no use for any of that. Particularly when it comes to the way you hurt my daughter."

Patricia swallowed her pride and pressed on. "Helen, I realise what I did. I know it's too late to take back, and I wish that I could, because it isn't something I actually believe."

"Oh it's not, is it?" Helen charged, her anger rising. "Come on, Patricia. Let's be honest here. Because of this English nobility business, you think yourself and James as being *better* than Paddy and me. You don't think Molly here is worthy of Ben. Isn't that right?"

"Do I think we're *better* than you?" Patricia repeated. "No, I don't think we're better than you, Helen. But do I think Molly is worthy of Ben? Of course not." Helen's eyes flashed, but Patricia continued, "We're being honest, here aren't we? So tell me – honestly – do you think Ben worthy of Molly?"

The words hit Helen like a stone into still water. She liked Ben; she thought him a nice boy and a fine catch, but was he *worthy* of marrying Helen's only daughter?

"No," she admitted quietly. "No, Patricia, you're right. I don't think he is, and I probably never could."

Patricia smiled warmly. "You see?" she asked, a kindred kindness in her voice neither Helen nor Molly had ever heard before. "We have at least that much in common." She eyed the bottle sitting on the table and poured three glasses quickly. "Whatever the case, dears, I would like to propose a toast: to new beginnings. May we all have the opportunity to wipe the slate clean and start today anew – as friends."

Slowly, Helen took up her glass, never taking her eyes off of Patricia. The two women clinked glasses and drank down the grappa, not noticing that Molly simply was watching them, not having her own.

"Oh *God*," Patricia winced. "That is simply *dreadful!*"

"Isn't it?" Helen laughed. "Disgusting. Ought to be outlawed."

"I need wine. Or champagne."

"Or both," Helen added.

Molly smiled. "Why don't you two go head out and find yourselves a drink then? And if you could, open the door carefully; I'm sure Caroline is right outside with her ear pressed against it."

With that, Helen and Patricia left, and to Molly's delight, they were talking.

Perhaps there was hope after all.

"*Y*ou can't be serious," Helen said to Fabrizio as he led her, Caroline, Patricia, and Molly to Santa Maria, a tiny church close to the Trevi fountain, "This is a *church?*"

From the outside, it wasn't much to look at; indeed, Helen would have walked right past it on any other day, thinking it an apartment or maybe a small hotel.

But a church?

"Wait till you see it, Mum," Molly responded cheerily. "It's absolutely *perfect.*"

Helen and Patricia exchanged skeptical glances – but those looks began to melt the second they stepped into the building.

The inside of Santa Maria was as far from its nondescript exterior as could possibly be.

It was certainly tiny – just a single row of wooden pews extended in front of the altar – but it was adorned in magnificent Italian opulence.

Paintings of the Virgin Mary and the crucifixion hung in ornately woven golden frames along the sides of the entrance. Renaissance-era archways held up walls reaching to the sky.

And most impressively, a large fresco, painted on the ceiling, showed the Assumption of Mary in vibrant colours that stood with even the great Sistine Chapel as a Renaissance masterpiece.

Molly had seen the church before, but to be getting married in it was beyond her wildest dreams.

"See, Mum?" she laughed at her mother's gaping mouth. "I told you this would be great."

"Well," Patricia told her, "I have to admit, Molly, that I was indeed a bit worried about this when Ben told me how tiny the church would be— oh my!"

Patricia was surprised by a man dressed all in black, standing quietly and solemnly in the back of the church next to the Advent wreath. It took her only a moment to realise he was the priest. "Beg your pardon, Father," she said apologetically.

The priest waved his hand as if to say, *don't worry about it*, and summoned the four women and their companion to him.

His face was serene, but it suddenly became quite expressive, a smile breaking out across his wide face. "*Buongiorno! Buongiorno!*" he said excitedly, "*e Buon Natale!*"

"*Buon Natale, Padre,*" Fabrizio replied. "*È tutto pronto per il matrimonio di oggi?*"

"Please, Fabrizio," the priest said happily, "For respect of our guests, let us speak in English." He went straight up to Molly. "And you, I imagine, must be our beautiful bride."

She smiled. "I am," she said happily.

"Wonderful. *Wonderful!* Well. I am Padre Giuseppe Mazzolo, but please, call me Padre Beppe."

"Padre Beppe," she cooed, "I'd like to introduce my mum Helen, my best friend Caroline, and my fiance's mother Patricia."

Padre Beppe seemed absolutely tickled. "It is so good to see you. We so rarely get to have non-local weddings here. This is very exciting for me."

"For us, too," Helen replied.

"I am certain," Padre Beppe said. "So," he continued, slapping his hands together, "We have a little sanctuary in the back where you can get prepared and so that your husband does not see you before we start. Since there is only a small congregation today, I have done away with much of the boring stuff. We will make this very *bam-bam-bam,* quick and painless, yes?"

The women laughed.

"That sounds … perfect, Padre," Molly said, gulping a little.

"Well," Fabrizio told the group, "it seems you have everything you need here. I must go and prepare something for the groom, and then bring the men over here. I will see you ladies shortly." He turned to walk out the front of the church.

Molly nodded in her bridesmaid's direction and then jerked her head towards Fabrizio.

Caroline took her meaning. "Excuse me just one moment," she said, "There's something I need to, just really fast…" With that, she hiked up the bottom of her dress and shuffled down the aisle quickly. "Fabrizio," she called. "Wait up a second, would you?"

Fabrizio paused and turned around on the steps outside the church. Caroline joined him outside and caught her breath. "Is everything okay, *signorina?*" he asked.

Caroline took a deep breath before starting. "Look," she said, "I wanted to explain myself. About last night…"

"Ah," he said, holding up a hand, "there is no need. I realise I overstepped."

"No, Fabrizio," she said, slightly abashed. "That's not what I meant at all. I was … I've never been very good at romance. I've always been… guarded. Especially when it comes to something spontaneous like this."

"But how could one live without spontaneity?" he asked sincerely.

Caroline shrugged. "I guess I just like to have a plan," she replied. "Or at least an exit strategy. I don't just go on flings. And I certainly don't just fall for random strange men."

"Fall for?" he repeated bemusedly.

"Yeah. That's not me. I'm not the kind to fall head-over-heels for a guy I've only just met. And yet…"

Fabrizio grinned. "And yet," he said quietly, "you find yourself… falling for me?"

Caroline looked down at her shoes, feeling stupid. "Yeah," she whispered, feeling her face go hot like she was a teenager.

Fabrizio placed his index finger under her chin and lifted her head up to face him. "Caroline," he said, "I do not know where this path will lead us. But I do know one thing: if I did not at least follow the path as far as I can, I would regret it the rest of my life. Is this what you feel?"

She nodded.

"Then perhaps we should take the journey together," Fabrizio said. And with that, he leaned in and kissed her.

After what seemed like an eternity (but more likely was only a few seconds), he broke away. "I am very sorry," he said, "but I really do have to go. But I will return soon. And afterwards we can spend a bit more time together, yes?"

"I'd like that," Caroline smiled. "But yeah, go. Go get the groom."

Fabrizio nodded and went off as Caroline returned to the church a huge smile on her face.

Inside the sanctuary, Molly cast her a furtive glance. "So…?" she inquired.

Caroline shrugged. "So… what, Mol?"

"Oh come *on!*" Molly nearly exploded. "What's the story with your Italian gigolo?"

Caroline only smiled in response.

𝒶n hour later, Ben stood outside the church with the other men – including, finally, his errant brother Mark.

"Ready to do this, big brother?" he asked, a glint in his eye.

Ben, visibly nervous, nodded tentatively and wiped the sweat from his palms onto his suit pants. "I could use a drink," he said.

James laughed. "So could I, son," his father said, "but there'll be plenty of time for that soon enough. Shall we head in? Paddy?" He turned to the bride's father.

"—and I don't care if they have to work 'til all hours of the morning, Felicity," Paddy spat into the phone, "I want that delivery there before their kids come down for Christmas morning." He held up a finger to ask the others to wait a moment. "No— No— Yes. Yes. All right, just heading off for Molly's wedding now, I'll call again later."

He hung up the phone to find all four of the other men with exasperated expressions. "Sorry, lads," he apologised, "couldn't be helped. Christmas and all."

"Okay then," Fabrizio said at last, "I think we are all ready then. Shall we?" He motioned towards the door, holding it open as the men went in.

Ben, Mark, and James took their places in front of the altar, while Paddy stayed back to await his daughter.

Molly surprised him by coming in behind him, unnoticed. His eyes fell to her dress first, then her face, and he found himself overcome with emotion.

"My God, Molly," he said, "You are a vision. I—" He wiped away a tear streaming down his cheek.

She collapsed in his arms. "Oh Daddy," she sniffed.

"I know, love," he said, patting her back. "I love you, Mol. More than anything in this world. And all this …" he gestured to the church and the beautiful Italian surroundings "you were right, this is perfect."

Molly wiped the tears from her eyes. "Okay," she said, straightening her dress. "Are you ready?"

"No," he replied honestly. "Are you?"

She nodded slowly. "Yeah," she said, sniffling away another sob. "Yeah, I am. Let's do this."

"Rightio," Paddy replied. He offered her his elbow, and, arm-in-arm, he and Molly began the procession up the aisle of Santa Maria.

CHAPTER 30

The priest called the service together and blessed them. "We are gathered here," he began, "on this nativity of the Lord's birth, to celebrate that special union between Ben and Molly. The readings today will focus on God's love, but we must not forget that love from on high is manifested so well in these two wonderful young people."

Molly and Ben smiled at each other as the priest continued the ceremony in Italian, as arranged.

They continued smiling through the readings, and even through the homily (though what the priest was saying barely registered for their guests).

Following the declaration of consent, Molly held her breath as they prepared their vows.

Ben went first, watching Molly intently, never breaking his gaze as he took her hand in his and spoke in perfect Italian: "I, Ben, take you Molly …"

Molly felt weak. Ben had been so good about all this, so determined to make this the perfect Italian Christmas wedding for her – and she felt she was going to break down at any moment.

She swallowed hard before beginning. "I take you, Ben, to be my husband .."

Ben smiled from ear to ear as the priest requested the rings, reassuring Molly that everything was going to be okay. She felt filled up, her heart rising as James handed Ben the rings.

Without warning, she heard a *clink! clink! clink!*, the sound of metal rolling down the steps of the altar and into the aisle. Ben groaned and Mark began to laugh.

He had dropped the rings.

He ran down the aisle after them, muttering to himself as he did. Molly couldn't help but laugh aloud. Whatever the case, whatever came next, *this* was her husband, the man she loved so dearly. He was strong, and he was brave – and sometimes, he was a complete klutz.

After finally catching the rings, Ben rushed back up to the altar. "Sorry," he lamented.

Padre Beppe laughed. "You would be amazed at how often that happens," he reassured.

"Really?" Ben asked, heartened.

"No," the priest quipped. "It has never happened before. Not once."

Ben groaned, but everyone else laughed.

"Okay, now, where were we?" Padre Beppe asked. "Ah yes… Ben, please place the ring on Molly's finger – carefully this time – and repeat after me …"

There were several more prayers in Italian, but Ben and Molly were in such a daze that they barely noticed anything until the priest announced, "Ben, you may now kiss the bride."

Ben took his new wife in his arms and gazed at her lovingly. He mouthed, *We did it*, and she nodded tearfully.

He then kissed her with a passion she'd never known before. She enveloped him, wrapping her arms around him. As they finally broke the kiss, he looked her in the eyes again.

"I love you, Molly," he said.

"I love you too," she replied before adding with a mischievous smile, "Lord Pembrey."

CHAPTER 31

little while later, the wedding party were out on the streets of Rome, everyone beaming at them.

"Okay," Molly called out to them, "time to make a wish."

Fabrizio nodded. "Does everyone have coins with them?" he asked the group. "I have some cents here if needed."

"Not sure Mark has any cents,'" Ben joked.

"That's a really awful joke," his brother mocked him.

"About as awful as your suit," Ben noted, appraising the royal blue and white pinstripes of Mark's jacket, which he clearly hadn't picked up in the Piazza de Spagna. "Did you think you were up for a role as a backup dancer for Lady Gaga or something?"

"That's funny," Mark jibed back, "as I assumed you were yourself going to be a guest star on *Boring Old Married Guys*."

As they rounded the corner, not far from the church to the beautiful baroque structure that was the Fontana di Trevi, they were surprised to find the area relatively quiet.

"It's because it is Christmas Eve," Fabrizio explained. "Not as many tourists now, and locals stay home. You have a perfect opportunity."

"Okay," Molly announced excitedly, "Now, according to legend, if you want to return to Rome, you have to throw a coin with your right hand over your left shoulder. Ready?"

The group turned their backs to the fountain, coins in hand. Just as they were getting ready to toss them in, however, Paddy's phone rang.

He reached into his pocket to answer it. "Hello?" he asked. "Oh, hiya, Felicity…"

Helen scowled and set her jaw. "That's it," she grunted. "I've had it." She grabbed the phone from him and said into the receiver, "Felicity, stop calling and go home. Happy Christmas."

She then took her husband's phone in her right hand and promptly tossed it over her left shoulder and into the fountain.

"Helen!" Paddy exploded. "That's my *phone*!"

"It *was* your phone, love," she said tenderly.

"But – but – I *needed* that!"

"And we need *you*, Paddy. It's time to give up the damned phone calls. It's Molly's wedding day. And it's Christmas!" Seeing the look of consternation on his face, she softened even more. "Tell you what, love: if we get back in a few days and the business is gone, I'll make you a trifle."

Paddy stared hard at her – and then a resigned smile spread across his face. "I'm sorry I've been ignoring you, love. I've been under an awful lot of stress lately…"

"I know pet," she replied. "But it's time to let it go. We're in this beautiful city on our daughter's wedding day - on Christmas Eve. And I don't know about you but I have every intention of coming back here. "

She reached for her husband and pulled his face in for a kiss.

"*AHEM!*" Molly cleared her throat loudly to catch her parent's attention. "Now, if you two lovebirds don't mind …?"

"Go ahead honey," her mother replied, smiling.

"Okay," Molly said again. "One – two – three!"

Eight pennies flew through the air in perfect unison, and clinked against the stone edifice before falling into the water.

Ben grabbed Molly by the hand and kissed her. Helen wrapped herself around Paddy, as Patricia and James grasped hands.

Fabrizio enveloped Caroline in a passionate embrace, while poor Mark just stood by, embarrassingly kicking at a stone on the ground.

Suddenly, as they all stood there, little white flakes began to appear – at first just a dusting falling softly, then more and more until they were pouring out of the sky.

"Snow in Rome?" Molly gasped delightedly. "But how...?"

Ben just smiled. "Merry Christmas, darling," he said to her. Seeing the confused look on her face, he continued, "I talked to Fabrizio, and he called in a favour from a friend who runs a ski resort up north. I wanted to make sure your dream Christmas wedding was perfect in every way."

Sure enough as Molly looked around, she spotted the snow machine a few yards away tucked behind a Fiat, shooting snow into the late evening sky.

"It's... it's perfect, Ben," she cried, hugging him close.

"All right, everybody," Fabrizio called out, "I think we are ready to head back to the hotel. In about ninety minutes, we'll begin dinner on the terrazza. I have reserved it specially just for you. I look forward to seeing you all there."

As the others made their way back to the hotel, Caroline hung back a minute. She nudged Fabrizio with her elbow. "You've really played a blinder on this, Fabrizio," she complimented. "I don't know how we could ever thank you."

He arched an eyebrow. "*I* know how you could," he said.

"How?"

"Come back to me, Caroline."

"What?"

He kissed her, a kiss full of meaning and promise. "I do not want this to be, as you said, just a 'fling,'" he explained. "I enjoy your company. I enjoy everything about you, Caroline. I want to enjoy you more. I want the legend of the Fontana di Trevi to work its magic and bring you back to me."

Her eyes widened. "I just... I don't know, Fabrizio. We've only just met—"

"—so let's continue meeting!" he said excitedly. "I do not make this offer lightly, Caroline. I make it only because I want to see more of you and..."

"...and see where this is going," she finished for him. "No, I get it. I do. And..." She watched her best friend and new husband walking away. Molly and Ben looked so happy, so contented, so perfect together. "Oh, what the hell," she said. "I don't know, maybe it's the romance of Italy, or the snow on Christmas Eve ..."

Caroline pulled her handsome Italian down by the collar and kissed him passionately.

Sometimes, being part of a cliche was a very good thing.

PORTOFINO SUNSET

CHAPTER 1

*A*nna Rhodes knew what she was doing; it was a pity her boyfriend didn't.

She had researched the best flights, the best hotels and the very best places to visit at their destination.

He, on the other hand…

"*Mark*," she called out yet again from the front door to their single-bedroom flat while looking at her watch, panicked. "We really need to go - *now*."

It wasn't that he was disorganised, per se. He could be sometimes. But he was brilliantly on the ball where it counted.

At only 31, Mark had quickly risen the ranks at one of London's largest banks, going from cashier to Director of Operations in the blink of an eye.

In the two years Anna had known him, she'd watched him work obscene hours with high levels of stress. But now, he'd finally settled into a role where he'd stick - for the time being at least.

She sometimes wondered what a rich, go getter like him could possibly see in someone who'd quit her beloved job as a bookstore assistant only a few months ago to get her first 'adult' job.

She puffed her hair up in the mirror, noting the black curls that hairdressers complimented all the time. She supposed she had looks, sure, and that had given her a fair amount of attention at university.

Her eyes, a deep chestnut brown, had always bewildered the men who approached her, though they were just as often put off by the slight gap in her teeth and her voracious laugh, as well as some of her other more annoying habits …

She sighed, checking her watch again.

Her phone buzzed in her pocket; she lifted it out to see her taxi app flashing. "Mark, seriously!" she called, this time much more forcefully. "The car is here. We need to go -- now!"

A second later, a shape emerged from the back room. Anna pulled her glasses down on her almond nose and squinted, forcing her eyes to adjust.

Mark stood there, in his usual three-piece grey suit, a perfectly starched white shirt set off with a jet-black tie. His blonde hair was nicely quaffed; his jaw was set in a goofy-looking grin, red-ruby lips set off against his golden locks and emerald-green eyes.

"Sorry," he said sheepishly. "I suppose you were right after all. I should have packed earlier."

She rolled her eyes good naturedly. "Well, there's no time for that now," she insisted, "the cab is here. I don't think they like waiting."

He strolled up and kissed her on the temple. "Darling," he said, "We've been waiting so long to take this trip, surely they'll wait five minutes at least? And it's not like Portofino is going anywhere."

"Hmm." She narrowed her eyes playfully. "If you've been waiting so long to take this trip, why'd I have to be the one to book it?"

"Well," he grinned back, "for one, you're a travel agent now, so it's kind of your job…"

"When I'm getting paid, it is. Were you going to pay me?"

At that, his face broke into a wide mischievous smile. "I'm sure I can find a way …"

CHAPTER 2

*A*nna curled up into Mark's arms as the taxi sped out and onto the road.

"What are you thinking about?" he asked.

She sighed contentedly. "The first time we met actually," she said. "I was an idiot."

"I think you made pretty clear that *I* was the idiot," he replied.

"You didn't fall off a stepladder though."

"No, but *you* didn't blurt out a date request."

"If you hadn't, we might not be on our way to Italy at the minute," Anna giggled. "I'm glad you did."

He kissed the top of her head. "Me too, darling," he responded. "Me too. I could do this forever with you."

"Could you though?" she asked, looking up at him. "You know how much I love to travel."

He gulped a little. "Let's just get through this flight first, though, shall we?" he said. "If we can make it through our first sunshine getaway, we can make it through *any*thing."

"Anything ..." Anna echoed satisfied.

That clinches it, she thought to herself, more certain than ever that Mark was the one for her.

. . .

THE CHECK-IN LINE at Heathrow was busy by the time they arrived, the line stretching halfway down the corridor, bending back in on itself, and looping around in a thoroughly confusing labyrinth.

The glare of industrial neon lights didn't help either of their moods, and by the time Anna and Mark finally got to the front of the queue some forty minutes later, neither was in much of a mood for what they heard next.

"I have to say," said the check-in attendant, "generally, we need you to check in your bags at least two hours prior to departure. You're just under that now."

"Well, we couldn't really help that, could we?" Mark snapped, his nostrils flaring. "We were here well before the two-hour mark, but we've been queuing for ages."

"If you'll just let me finish, sir ..." the woman responded patiently, "it seems you've hit a spot of luck, as it looks like your flight has been delayed about an hour and a half."

"You're joking ..." Anna said.

The woman shook her head. "It's actually quite good news," she explained pleasantly. "It means we'll be able to check your luggage on in time. The plane hasn't even arrived yet. It's still on its way in from Amsterdam."

"Well, that's just fantastic, isn't it?" Mark grunted.

The woman nodded. "Here are your boarding passes," she said, handing them to him, "just go through to the security check. Have a lovely flight!" she called out, with a burst of feigned enthusiasm neither she nor they could possibly have felt.

"Well ..." Anna said when they were out of earshot, "this is..."

"A disaster?" Mark quipped sullenly.

"I was going to say a stroke of luck actually."

Mark sniffed derisively. "I suppose, at least, we did make the flight in time," he said, attempting to look at the bright side.

"Exactly," Anna said, a bit more enthusiastically than she actually felt. "And soon we'll be on the Italian coast, sipping wine at a bar overlooking the Mediterranean…"

"Ligurian, actually" Mark corrected her absentmindedly. "And it won't be that soon. Portofino is about an hour's drive from the airport. We've a long way ahead of us yet."

"Mark," Anna said determined to stay optimistic, "OK, so this whole trip is off to an inauspicious start, I'll grant you that. But let's go get a cup of tea and some cake or something, and we'll relax for a couple of hours before we head off?"

He slowly nodded. "Yeah, that sounds good," he said finally. "You just know how I hate

"—travel?" she teased. "Yeah, I noticed. The minute we walked into the airport, you turned all ashen."

"Exactly," he said by way of agreement. "And crowds too. That's why we're doing Portofino instead of Rome or Barcelona or--"

"Mark," she said in a mock-serious tone, "you live in London. Lots of crowds."

He laughed genuinely at this. "If you can call Brodensbury Park 'London.'"

"It's still the city," she insisted indignantly.

Anna allowed a wave of relief to pass over her as Mark's spirits, so dour only moments before, seemed perked up by their light banter.

Given how long the queue to pass through security was, she knew she had to keep this up, if only until they got past the machines in order to keep his spirits buoyed.

That's why we're so well-suited, she thought to herself, smiling.

I can keep him grounded like no one else.

CHAPTER 3

The queue for the security machines took nearly as long as the one for check in.

By the end of it, Mark had moved on from wanting tea to something quite a bit stronger.

He and Anna quickly found their gate and, since their plane was still nowhere in sight, they went back to find somewhere they could get something to eat and a drink or two.

Anna felt a bit woozy after her second glass of wine, while Mark simply nursed an ale. He shook his head in annoyance and when she asked what was on his mind, he sighed. "I don't believe it." He pointed a short distance away at the departure screens. "It looks like we just got delayed again."

"Well," Anna replied, still trying to keep their spirits up, "I guess that means we should be ordering another round -- but I'm going to switch to coffee I think."

"Sounds like a good idea for you," Mark agreed "Save your stamina for all that lovely Italian wine later…"

She was glad to finally see him relaxing a bit. He'd been such a tense tangle of nerves all the way through the checkpoint queue.

When he'd finally come out the other side of the metal detector, he seemed as though a huge weight had been lifted from him, though he was still more pensive than usual.

They sat and drank some more, watching the screen and occasionally talking. But as the minutes passed, the flight departure time began to get later. It was nearing dinnertime when the screen finally flashed "Boarding."

By this point, Mark had gone from tense to downright anxious. Anna tried to soothe him to little avail, so she ordered a quick brandy for him before they boarded. He slurped the whole thing down in one gulp, and then rose, looking rather surly, as they both joined the queue for the plane.

It was another nearly half-hour before they finally made it to top of the line and then they were hit with the more irritating news.

"I'm so sorry," the male flight attendant said, sounding sincere, "I'm afraid we've double-booked a few seats."

"What does that mean?" Mark demanded.

"Well, we have two options," the man explained. "Either we can seat one of you in one of our remaining single seats -- there are two separate ones left, one in an exit row -- or we can rebook you onto the next flight."

"When is the next flight?" Anna asked, looking nervously at Mark.

"Currently scheduled for 10am tomorrow."

She shook her head vehemently. "No, no, we're getting on this one," she insisted. She heaved a great sigh and looked back up at Mark who grunted.

"Just put me in the exit row," she told the man, taking her boyfriend's grunt as assent.

He duly reprinted their boarding passes, and the couple entered the plane. Anna knew Mark was just about on the verge of exploding, so she stood on tiptoe and kissed his cheek. "Thank you," she said sweetly.

"For what?" he asked, startled.

"For not being a maniac to that poor man."

Mark nodded, but said nothing.

It was going to be a long flight.

"YOU HAVE GOT to be kidding me!" Mark considered himself a quiet, polite, mild-mannered man with an upbeat demeanour.

But something about this trip seemed to have broken him. The delays and seating situation on the flight had been bad enough, and the horrific turbulence over Switzerland certainly hadn't helped either.

But now, things had just gone from bad to worse: their luggage had been rerouted.

"How?" Mark demanded of the poor little Genoan man with a bald head and a wiry moustache, who clearly had only the most basic grasp of English. "How in God's name do suitcases bound for Genoa get rerouted to *Minsk?*"

"I very sorry," the man said painfully. "I do not know how it happen."

"So…" Anna chimed in, trying to sound reasonable. "When can we expect our luggage to reach us?"

"We fix this soon as possible," the Italian man replied.

"And you'll send it on to Portofino too, yes?" Mark said sourly.

The man nodded. "I drive myself if we need," he said, giving Anna a smile.

Sorry, she mouthed. She really felt bad for the poor man -- Mark was being quite unreasonable, though she entirely understood why.

"We'll have it by tomorrow, then?" Mark asked, still seething. "We're only here for four days."

"I cannot promise tomorrow," the man said sadly. "I very sorry. Can maybe promise two to three days."

Mark went from pink to purple at this. "Three *days?*" he practically exploded. "Our holiday is only four!"

"Maybe only two days?" the man backtracked nervously.

"Mark, come on," Anna said encouragingly, "let's go get the rental car." She turned to the man and said quickly, "Thank you." He smiled in response but said nothing, looking warily towards Mark.

Away from the luggage counter, Mark was absolutely seething. "I cannot *believe* this," he muttered. "This was supposed to be a relaxing, romantic weekend away, and…"

"And it still *can* be," Anna insisted. She grabbed him by the arm. "We can still have a lovely time here. Today's been awful, yes. But that doesn't mean our whole trip is ruined. Let's get the car, turn on some music, and watch the sunset as we drive. It'll be lovely."

"Honestly," Mark sighed, "I just kind of want to lie down."

"Do you want me to drive?" she asked.

"I can do it," he grumbled.

Anna shook her head. "No," she insisted, "we've both had a hard day, but you're clearly having a tougher time. It's okay. Everybody has these kinds of days. Let's get the car, and you can nap while I drive. It's only an hour or so, a straight run down the motorway yes? Shouldn't be a problem."

CHAPTER 4

*H*alf an hour later, Anna and Mark were finally on the road to Portofino.

She was immediately entranced by the vistas of Genoa, which, even from the motorway were stunning beyond belief.

There were mountains jutting up in the distance; steep, dramatic cliffs leading down to tiny towns where houses were smashed up against each other with little rhyme or reason; green, verdant trees; tunnels going not around or over the mountains but straight through them, the occasional gaps offering absolutely stunning views of a cerulean blue sea.

Anna desperately wanted to wake Mark up to see this, but almost from the moment he'd gotten into the passenger seat, he'd fallen dead asleep.

She pitied him, really -- he'd obviously had a horrible day -- but she was also rather disappointed. It was almost as if whatever spark he'd had before they'd left had disappeared immediately when they hit the airport, and try as she might, she hadn't yet been able to rekindle it.

On Anna drove, through small Italian villages with narrow,

cobbled streets. She gripped on the steering wheel tightly through these, nervous about hitting an oncoming car -- or a pedestrian.

Old women in two-storey buildings hung their clothes out to dry over balconies that looked like something out of *Romeo and Juliet*.

Vespas passed their car on either side, going faster than she thought possible on these narrow, winding roads.

The road -- if it could even be called that anymore -- turned and jutted and turned again, until she felt almost dizzy, as if she were scaling a mountain in the Alps.

And still Mark snored next to her, occasionally shifting in his seat for comfort.

Suddenly on Anna's left arose a beautiful body of water, the sun on the other side of the mountain making it sparkle an almost eerie bluish-grey.

Picturesque beaches stretched out before her, whetting her appetite even more to be finished with this journey and at a seafront bar sipping wine, her boyfriend relaxed and engaged.

It wasn't long before the trickle of water she'd seen became a sea, spread open wide and beautiful in the evening sun.

To Anna's right, rolling foothills dotted with green and brown stretched out as far as she could see, the crashing of the waves and the buzzing of motorcycles hitting her like a stereo cacophony that somehow turned these disparate noises into an orchestra.

The road began winding round again, and Anna became acutely aware of steep rocks to one side, sheltering the little bay-coves across the way.

They had to be nearing Portofino now. She checked the map on her phone. Sure enough, she had just a little way longer to drive -- this time up an even narrower road, uphill all the way in a little tiny car that didn't even appear to have four-wheel drive.

The car huffed and chugged its way up, up, up the mountain, until finally, at about the fourth plateau, she saw a perfect little chateaux, the insistent whiteness of its plaster walls standing out like a sore thumb against the greens of the surrounding trees and the reddish browns of the town below.

"Mark," she said softly when she'd pulled into a tiny parking space, "Mark, we're here…"

He awoke with a start. "Wh-- what? We're here? Already?" he asked, a confused look on his face.

"'Already?'" she parroted chuckling. "We've been driving for over an hour."

"Oh," he sighed. "I must've been really out of it."

"You were. Lots of snoring, but minimal drool."

Mark snorted. "C'mon," he said, "Let's go get checked in."

"Are you feeling better?" she asked as they exited the car.

He shrugged. "But I think I just want to chill out and relax in the room at this stage," he said.

Anna felt her jaw fall open. "What?" she asked, flabbergasted.

"We should check in, order a bottle of wine and maybe some food, and just chill in the room. By the time we get organised, it'll be nearly nine and the day's practically over now anyway."

Anna looked out towards the bay. "Mark," she implored him, "just *look* at this. I mean, the way the little ripples of sunlight are dancing on the sea… doesn't that thrill you?"

"You know what'll thrill me?" he said. "A nice, hot shower and a good night's sleep. We can regroup in the morning."

"But aren't you just aching to explore?"

"I *am* aching, Anna, from sitting in an airport for four hours, on a plane for three, and in a car for another. I feel like I should be halfway to Australia by now."

"But you *slept* the entire time!" she exclaimed. She couldn't believe him. She understood he was a little tired and possibly more than a little cranky, but the nap didn't seem to have done him any good.

Was the entire trip going to be like this?

Mark acquiesced a little "I did," he admitted. "And I'm sorry. But today has been a complete and utter disaster, wouldn't you say?"

"Surely not *everything* has been bad…"

"Maybe not, but *most* of it has been pretty terrible. I mean, from the moment we got to the airport, things… well… it just hasn't been our day, has it?"

"No," she replied, "no, I suppose it *hasn't* been the best."

Mark nodded. "So that's why I think now we should just relax, order some food, and get a bottle of unnecessarily expensive wine to share. We can have a shower and a sleep, and when we wake up, we can take in some of the -- er -- natural beauty of the place, or whatever. Sound good?"

"Yeah," Anna said, trying to sound more enthusiastic than she felt. "Yeah, that sounds like a plan."

"Right then," he responded, motioning towards the ornate doors leading into the hotel lobby. "Let's head inside."

CHAPTER 5

little later, with the moon hanging low over the cool black water, Anna sat out on the patio of their suite, a glass of red wine swirling in her left hand.

Her bikini, coverup, her sandals -- everything had been in her luggage. Instead, she basked in the moonlight in just her underwear, which she supposed from a distance would look just like a bikini anyway.

And besides, the only one around was Mark, who had downed two glasses of wine and passed out on the oversized king bed over an hour ago, the TV playing an Italian dub of *The Simpsons* softly in the background.

Anna knew she couldn't hide her disappointment forever. This wasn't what she had wanted for her first night of a romantic Italian trip with the man she was certain she was going to marry.

She knew he had some anxiety about being around large crowds, and she was well aware that travel in general was stressful for everyone. Hell, he might have just been thrown from not having had a proper meal all day.

The point was, there were all kinds of logical reasons for him to have been acting like a grumpy kill-joy.

Yet Anna couldn't shake this worry that perhaps he was revealing his true self to her now.

Maybe this was who Mark *really* was…

She took another slug of wine, then poured the remainder of the bottle into her glass. It was good wine, ruby red, tasting dry and sweet at the same time, almost like cranberries. And this was her third glass, making her feel warm in the mild chill of the evening air.

Maybe I'm just being silly, she thought as she sipped on her glass. It was *an awful day after all. And that flight was just a nightmare.*

She sighed, taking a long drink, and mused over their surroundings. *I do hope Mark can find something to like here, though. I mean, what's not to like? Portofino is amazing. The room is perfect, the view is impeccable, and so romantic.*

She finished off the wine and closed the doors to the patio, leaving the glass and the bottle outside. Then she shut off the remaining light and curled up in bed next to Mark.

Instinctively, she felt his arm wrap around her, and she smiled.

Tomorrow will be better, she assured herself.

I hope.

CHAPTER 6

*T*he sun was peeking just over the horizon as Anna stirred.

Beams of light broke through the shade on the glass doors leading out to the balcony, and she fluttered her eyes open, watching little balls of dust sit silently in a sun ray as she groggily dragged her head off of the pillow.

She rolled over next to Mark, turning her eyes to his large, muscular chest, which rose and fell slowly and softly. Suddenly, he turned onto his side, startling her and allowing a quick rush of adrenaline to flow through her veins, giving her a much-needed lift.

"Hey," she chided, hitting him gently with her hand, "I thought you were still asleep."

"Nope," he said. "Been awake a while. Did you sleep OK?"

"The bed's pretty comfy," she admitted. "And you certainly slept like a rock."

"I told you," he replied quietly, "I was shattered."

Anna snuggled up against him, content in the moment. "So how do you feel now?" she asked, an expectant tone in her voice. She kissed his neck and shoulder suggestively.

"Hungry," he answered honestly.

Anna stopped kissing him. "Are you kidding me?" she demanded, a note of frustration in her voice.

Mark grinned sheepishly. "I didn't mean I have to eat, you know, *now...*" he said. "I mean, we can..." He kissed her neck and moved up to her jawline, then to her cheek, and finally her mouth. "I'd be perfectly content to wait an hour for breakfast," he said, still smiling.

Anna giggled mischievously. "Ten minutes, tops."

CHAPTER 7

$\mathcal{H}$alf an hour later, Anna and Mark slinked out of bed, showered, and returned to the clothes they'd worn the day before.

Neither was particularly thrilled with the situation, but given that they didn't have any alternatives, Anna was convinced a vague smell had to be better than walking around Portofino naked.

She was astonished by the grandeur of the breakfast room, which they hadn't seen upon entering the hotel the night before.

But what was more surprising was that there didn't seem to be anyone dining there.

No -- scratch that -- one handsome Italian man, with perfectly coiffed hair and stunning olive skin, sat sipping an espresso and munching on what looked like a bread roll while reading a newspaper.

"Well," Mark shrugged, nodding towards the near-empty dining room, "it should be good service at least." He walked forward into the room and pulled out a seat for Anna. "What do you fancy, eggs? Bacon? Pancakes?"

A clicking sound came from behind them. Anna looked around,

and, seeing only the attractive Italian, shrugged. "I was thinking maybe sausages, and…"

The clicking sound came again and she turned towards the man, who continued to gaze intently at his paper. She turned back to Mark. "Is that guy tut-tutting at us?" she whispered.

Mark shrugged. "No idea. Tell you what, though," he said at a full volume, "I really could go for something decent. A full English would be--"

The sound came again and Anna whipped around, finally having had enough. "Is there something you wanted to say?" she demanded of the man.

The Italian folded his paper and took a sip of espresso. "You are British, yes?" he asked. His English was flawless, though heavily accented, which merely added to his allure.

"We are," she answered cautiously. "Is that a problem?"

"A problem?" the man beamed, looking directly at her. "Not at all! I *love* the British! So happy, Always wanting a drink. And tea. So much with the tea! I studied in Manchester for university. England is wonderful! Scotland is wonderful! Wales is -- well," he shrugged.

Then the man stood, and it turned out, he was tall and slim, but clearly built up, rock-hard abdominals visible just below his translucent white dress shirt. "My name is Ambrogino Basilio Bianchi. But you may call me 'Gino.'" He reached out towards Anna and took her hand, kissing the knuckles. "You," he added, speaking towards Mark without ever taking his eyes off Anna, "May also call me Gino, though we should not get too familiar, as I might end up stealing this lovely lady away from you."

Mark rolled his eyes, but Anna blushed. "Well," she said, "I'm Anna, and this is my f--" She suddenly caught herself, realising she'd almost referred to Mark as her *fiancé*. "--my boyfriend, Mark."

"The pleasure is all mine," Gino said suavely, winking at her.

She glanced at Mark, who was stifling a laugh. "So… " she ventured, "why were you tut-tutting us about breakfast?"

Gino shook his head. "I was -- er -- not, how did you say? 'Tut-tutting' you," he explained. "But since I studied there, I know that the English have rather unrealistic expectations of what *colazione* ought to be."

"Colazione?" Mark asked.

"How you say, 'breakfast,'" Gino answered.

"How *we* say?" he countered. "It's how *everyone* who speaks English say -- I mean, says."

Anna shot Mark an irritated look. "You'll have to forgive us, Gino," she said, turning to their companion, "we've never actually been to Italy before. What do you usually order for -- how'd you say it?"

"*Colazione*," Gino responded patiently. "We *italianos* prefer to eat light in the morning. Makes you stronger for *pranzo* and *cena* later in the day. *Colazione* is a simple meal. Bread and jam, biscotti, and coffee. Some of my friends drink *americano*, but I never go into Starbucks, and there's not even one close by that I know of. But *caffè latte* or just simply caffè will serve you quite well. Give you energy! Make you strong!"

"Er -- thanks, mate," Mark said, clearly trying to shoo Gino away. "I think we'll get just a bit of bread and a coffee and be on our way then. Can you --" Mark pulled out a five-euro note from the pocket of his trousers. "--can you get that for us then? Please?"

"Oh," Gino grinned, "I am not the staff, my friend. I am here as a guest, just like you."

Mark rolled his eyes. "Okay, fine then," he said in a hushed tone, "where'd you order your coffee?"

Gino's smile grew wider. "You don't need to order," he said in an identically hushed tone, as if the two of them were sharing some kind of secret, and he pointed to an automatic coffee machine and a basket of biscotti and rolls sitting a few yards away. "You help yourself."

Mark sighed, and it was Anna's turn to stifle a laugh. "Thank you, Gino," she said, grinning and shaking his hand. "Thank you very much for your -- er -- education."

Gino nodded. "I shall see you both again, yes?" he asked. "Perhaps tomorrow morning, we can share some *caffè?*"

"Sounds great," Mark said through gritted teeth. He shook Gino's hand lifelessly and went to get some coffee for himself and Anna.

"Ciao!" Gino said to them both, sounding delighted, and he walked out of the dining room.

CHAPTER 8

$\mathcal{M}$ ark returned with two small cups of espresso and
some bread and biscotti.

Clearly, he was not impressed.

"How can they live like this?" he said to Anna as he resumed his
seat. "I mean, seriously, haven't they ever heard that old saying:
breakfast is the most important meal of the day."

Anna shrugged him off. "It's a different culture, Mark," she said
soothingly. "We have to be open to new experiences. New ideas.
Meeting new people."

"What's that supposed to mean?"

She shook her head. "You could've been a little nicer to that
guy."

Mark took a bite out of his biscotti; then, realising how hard
and thick it was, quickly spat it out into a napkin. "Good God," he
complained, "how can they live like this?"

"For goodness sake, Mark," Anna reprimanded, "have you never
had biscotti before?" She dipped it into her cup, then ate the
crumbly remnants. "It's really not too difficult."

Mark mirrored her example, and was surprised to find he not
only liked it this time -- but loved it.

"Oh," he said, a hint of awe in his voice, "that's bloody delicious."

Anna grinned. "I knew you'd like it if you gave it a chance."

"Okay, okay," he said, putting his hands up defensively. "I admit it: you were right. Okay? You were right."

She leaned over and kissed him. "That sounds like something you should get used to saying," she replied chuckling.

They bantered back and forth for a while, and soon, they were making plans for the day: a quick call to the airline to inquire about their baggage; then, if it arrived in time, a late-morning dip in the salt pool they had seen out back, followed by a walk down the hill into the centre of Portofino to check out the pretty little shops and restaurants.

Lunch would be at a wine bar Anna's co-worker had told her about, a place that made their own wines and overlooked the sea.

Then they'd stroll along the beach for a bit, and perhaps visit one of the gorgeous, ancient churches before hitting a restaurant for an alfresco dinner.

It all sounded idyllic.

Too idyllic, it seemed.

CHAPTER 9

*A*nna was just about to suggest they head back upstairs and get ready for the day, when she heard about the last thing she had ever expected to hear on her romantic trip to Italy with the love of her life.

"Mark?" came a woman's voice from out of nowhere. "Mark Watt?" Then, more softly, "Mark? Is it really you?"

Her boyfriend stood, his mouth agape, stunned by something he was seeing while Anna looked at the woman attached to the voice.

She was … *stunning*.

The first thing Anna noticed were her luscious locks of blonde hair, mildly curled and hanging below a black Audrey Hepburn-style hat.

Her sunglasses had just fallen from her eyes, but her angular nose and rich, high cheekbones reminded her of some star of stage and screen.

She wore a snow-white single-piece dress, and she wore it *well* -- clearly, Anna realised, she came from money.

She held a black clutch bag in her hand, a gold watch offsetting the rest of the plain but stark colours she wore.

"No way …" she heard Mark whisper under his breath.

"Who's that, Mark?" Anna asked him, cautiously curious.

"I'm saying, it can't be. It's--"

"Mark!" the other woman cried, cutting him off. She ran to him and pulled him into a big hug. "I can't believe it! After all this time! My God, how are you, darling?"

Mark vaguely attempted to extricate himself from the situation. "I -- I can't believe you're here," he said quietly, gently pushing her back -- though, Anna noticed with some disdain, not with *too* much force.

"Hey, I need to introduce you," Mark said to the mystery woman. "This is Anna, my--" He trailed off, as if he were unable to remember the word.

"Girlfriend, Mark," she said reproachfully, "I'm your girlfriend?"

"Of course" Mark exclaimed a bit over-enthusiastically. "Yes. And this..." he continued, presenting the woman to Anna, "This... this is..."

She extended her hand towards Anna. "Pleasure to meet you," she said as Anna took her hand. "I'm Julia. Julia Chevreton."

"Julia?" Anna repeated, as if she had misunderstood. "You're... *you're* Julia?"

The other woman nodded.

Anna turned to Mark. "Your Julia?" she asked him pointedly.

He merely nodded in response, not breaking his gaze from the other woman. "What are you doing here, Jules?" he asked. "In Portofino."

"Well," she replied calmly, "same as you, I assume, darling. I'm on holiday." She looked back behind her, and from the corridor emerged a man -- but Julia's companion was nowhere near what either Mark or Anna were expecting.

The first thing they noticed was a tufting streak of whitish grey running through his hair. His face seemed kind, but older -- certainly a lot older than they. He wore a light blue dress shirt with the sleeves rolled up, revealing a single tattoo of a horse on his right bicep. His shirt lay untucked over khaki cargo shorts, giving him the appearance of an ageing Tommy Hilfiger model.

"There you are darling," Julia cooed, "Guys, I'd like to introduce *my* boyfriend. This is Stephen."

Stephen shook both their hands. "Chaam'd," came his voice, and

Anna couldn't place his accent immediately. "You're English too?" he asked.

She nodded slowly, only catching every other word. Mark picked up the slack though. "Where's that accent from then?"

"Dunedin," Stephen said, the first clear thing they'd understood; but he added, just for their benefit, "New Zealand."

"Well that's... that's great," Mark said, his eyes catching Julia's. "Won't -- erm -- won't you join us for breakfast?"

"Mark," Anna snapped, and realising she'd done so a bit too forcefully, composed herself before continuing, "I'm sure Julia and Stephen would like some privacy."

"Oh, nonsense!" Julia exclaimed. "So long as we're not intruding, that is..."

"No, no, not at all," insisted Mark. "Pull up a couple of chairs and sit with us, please. But you should know, there's not much in the way of breakfast."

"Oh, I'm used to it by now," Julia told him as she sat down at the table. "I've been living in Italy for the past two years."

"Is that right?" asked Mark, thoughtfully. "Whereabouts?"

"Milan, mostly," she answered, "Though I've had stints in Napoli and Torino as well. Torino is just *lovely*. If you're here for -- how long are you here for, anyway?"

"Just till Monday," Anna said, trying (and only somewhat succeeding) to keep her growing sense of annoyance from her voice.

"Oh," Julia gushed, "then I'm afraid you probably don't have much time to go to Torino, but next time you're back, you just absolutely *must*. It's incredible. The architecture is simply superb. So classic, lovely. And you can see the mountains all around you, the Alps, it's gorgeous, snow-capped, just absolutely delightful. You can go hiking -- do you hike?"

Simultaneously, Mark answered "Yes" while Anna replied "No."

They looked at each other, Mark in confusion, Anna with more animosity. "We're not really outdoorsy types, I'd say, Julia," she added quickly.

"Not that we're not fit or anything," Mark amended just as rapidly. "It looks like there are an awful lot of hiking paths around here."

"Oh, without a doubt, there are," Julia answered. "We've been in Portofino for, what, three days, Stephen?"

"Four," Stephen said.

"Four," Julia amended herself. "Sometimes we just utterly lose track of time. Don't you ever do that?"

"No," Anna said flatly.

"Oh," Julia said, but she continued undeterred, "Well, anyway, we've been here for a few days, so we've already seen quite a lot of the place. I simply *must* show you around, particularly with an old friend like you, Mark, and this *lovely* girl you've brought."

Anna saw where this was going, and she didn't like it. This was supposed to be her romantic weekend away with the man she had been certain up until twenty-four hours ago she wanted to be her husband.

Suddenly, it was being taken over by a blonde bombshell with delusions of being an extra in *Breakfast at Tiffany's*.

"Thank you, Julia," she answered gracefully after a moment, "that's a very generous offer but we--"

"--we'd love to find a good wine bar," Mark blurted out, cutting her off. "Do you know of any?"

"Do we..." Julia chuckled and looked at Stephen. "...do we know of any wine bars? Oh, dear Lord, Marcus, of *course* we know wine bars. As in, *all* of them!" She laughed with what to Anna's ears was mirthless and cold. "We would be happy to show you around, if you'd like a couple of experienced tour guides."

"That would be very helpful, yes, thank you," Mark responded like a little lost puppy dog.

Anna shot him an irritated look. "Mark," she said through gritted teeth, "as -- lovely -- as that offer sounds, I'd rather like to get my clothes back first before we go shuffling through town, wouldn't you?"

"Your clothes?' Julia asked, confused.

"Our bags apparently got sent to Minsk by mistake," Anna told her. "They'll hopefully be arriving today, but until they do, I--"

At this, the hotel concierge appeared in the dining room. "Is there a Anna Rhodes in the room?" he asked. Anna held up her hand shyly. "We have good news: your parcels are here."

"My parcels?" she asked, a wave of confusion spreading across her face; then, a dawning look of realisation as she translated: "Our luggage is here," she said to Mark, delighted.

"Well, that settles it then, doesn't it?" Julia said, looking satisfied. "We'll take you around Portofino on foot today. Shall we reconvene here in, say, an hour?"

"An hour it is," Mark said suavely.

Anna stared at him, then turned away.

Was he *serious*? They'd just randomly run into Mark's ex while on a romantic weekend away in Italy, and now they were making plans with her? What kind of sick, twisted joke was this?

And why was Mark so eager to go along with it?

As Anna trudged silently back upstairs to retrieve their luggage with Mark she realised that her greatest fear wasn't just the question -- it was that she was terrified she already knew what that answer would be.

"*Y*ou're being ridiculous," Mark said a few minutes later as he unpacked his suitcase. "This was all a huge coincidence."

Anna's nostrils flared. "You think I don't know this was a huge coincidence?" she asked, infuriated. "Of *course* I know this was a huge coincidence. What else could it possibly be but a huge coincidence?"

"Stop saying 'huge coincidence'. It's starting to sound weird."

"You *really* want to joke at this moment?" she snapped.

"Yes!" he laughed. "Yes, Anna, I *do* want to joke. Because this whole thing that's going through your head, this jealous streak or whatever it is--"

"Oh boy, was *that* ever the wrong thing to say …"

"Wait, wait," Mark offered softly, "hold on a second. Now, look, Yes, Julia and I used to go out. And--"

"No, *you* hold on," Anna replied harshly. "You didn't 'used to go out' with Julia. You wanted to marry her, isn't that what you told me?"

He shook his head. "I was young and stupid then," he said. "It was only--"

"It was only, what, three years ago?" After a moment, she composed herself enough to reply. "Mark," she implored, "all I want is quality time with you on this trip. But you seem more excited about spending time with your ex-girlfriend than your *current* one."

Mark, now clad in only a pair of boxer shorts, strode across the room and took Anna by the shoulders. "Nothing -- *nothing* -- could be further from the truth," he said sincerely. "Do you understand me? Whatever there was with Julia -- that's all in the past. Yeah I was a bit shocked to see her, because we were once very important in each other's lives. But that time is over now. We're just... going to catch up. OK?"

Anna looked down at the floor, but she nodded compliantly. "I guess I *am* being a little jealous," she said. "Julia -- she's known you longer, and been more intimate with you, and--"

"Known me longer, yes," Mark replied. "There's nothing we can do to change that. But been more intimate with me?" He gently tipped Anna's chin up with his index finger, and she looked up at him. "Never," he finished. "There has never been *any*one who knows me like you do."

She nodded again. "Well, I suppose I ought to get dressed then," she demurred. "For this expedition with another Brit and an Aussie."

"Kiwi," said Mark absentmindedly.

"What?"

"Kiwi. Aussies are from Australia. New Zealanders are Kiwis."

"Oh," she said. "I didn't know that. Why?"

"Why what?"

"Why are they called Kiwis?"

"Something to do with the birds, I think."

"Are they native to New Zealand or something?"

"Anna," Mark said, with an exasperated sigh, "why would I ever need to know anything about this, unless I was moving to New Zealand to study ornithology -- or sociology even?"

"That's a really weird sentence and a really stupid question, and I'm not going to respond to it."

"You're being deliberately difficult now."

"Yes, yes I am."

"Can we please get dressed and go?" Mark said, his lips breaking into a wide, toothed smile.

Anna nodded, but she didn't return her smile. Her thoughts kept going back to the blonde bombshell Julia. What was her game? And why was she here, really?

Anna didn't know, but as she slipped on her favourite polka dot shirt, she told herself that her first order of business was to find out.

CHAPTER 12

"As you can see," Julia told them, in a voice that was simultaneously haughty and instructive, almost like a mildly arrogant tour guide, "Portofino doesn't care much about things like paths or pedestrian safety."

She motioned for them to move single-file up against a stone wall lining the street as three Vespas, one right after the other, zoomed past.

"It's beautiful," she continued once the vehicles were out of range, "but you have to be alert, or it can be deadly. So no drunken stumbles back to the hotel, in other words."

Anna rolled her eyes and looked to Mark, expecting to see the same thing.

What she found instead was rapture. He seemed entirely enthralled by what Julia was telling him. Anna chalked it up to his finally being in the mood to explore, but the thought nagged her either way.

Julia led them down the street, past expensive-looking estates named in white-and-gold signs, down past boats anchored in harbour, reflecting brightly in the morning sun, which bounced off the water in a surreal haze of deep blue and golden orange.

They passed cars inching along, going achingly slow past each other on the impossibly narrow two-way street, themselves going slowly along an ancient stone wall to avoid a collision.

Smaller homes and apartments now opened up to them, the ancient sandstone showing carved patterns that looked like family crests. Balconies were the only thing separating one house from the next, as they smashed up against each other almost like town homes of antiquity.

Suddenly they came across a curious sight: an old-looking stone bell-tower attached to what looked like a newer-build church.

Anna was struck by the oddest feature -- the church was painted in stripes, alternating yellow and grey. Julia, who had been talking the whole time (though Anna hadn't paid attention to any of it), was prattling on about the local seafood when Anna interrupted her. "What *is* this?" she asked aloud.

The other three stopped and looked at her. "It's a church, Anna," Julia replied dully.

"Yes, yes," she answered, a hint of irritation seeping into her voice, "clearly it's a church -- thank you -- but I've never seen one painted like that, have you?"

"Yes," Mark said in slight defence of his girlfriend, "That *is* rather unique, isn't it? Julia, do you know anything about this church?"

"Hmm, let's see," she said briskly, "I know that... it's a church. You've seen one church, you've seen 'em all, am I right?"

Mark laughed, but Anna didn't. "Like I said," she continued, "I've never seen a church painted like this before. I wonder if it means something."

"I'm certain I don't know," Julia said, attempting to usher them away from the church and towards the road that lay before them. "Come now, it's getting close to lunchtime, and I'm famished, as I'm sure you are, too."

"You can say that again," Mark agreed. "What is with this Italian 'no breakfast' breakfast shenanigans?"

"It's Continental, darling," Julia noted absently. "Shall we...?" She turned, walking down the steps leading up to the church and towards a number of canopies that looked like pop-up shops.

Mark shrugged and continued walking, but Anna remained behind, gazing at the church. Something about it stirred something in her. She couldn't quite put her finger on *what*, but it was definitely something she wanted to pursue later.

"Anna," Mark called back to her, "are you coming, or are you going to stay for services?"

She forced a laugh and answered, "I'm coming. I just think this is really cool, is all."

DOWN AT THE HARBOUR, they made their way past shop after shop, little boutiques with well-dressed mannequins showcasing the latest in Italian fashion in the windows, until suddenly -- and quite without warning -- the road opened up to what could only be described as a cobblestone beach.

Small waves lapped up against the shore, with dinghies and sailboats bobbing gently just a few yards out. All around them were set up tents selling all kinds of touristy wares. In the centre of the beach area, two men stood doing combination juggling tricks, delighting a crowd of about fifty or so gathered in a circle around them.

Off to their left were set up rows of aluminium chairs and tables bedecked with white linen tablecloths. A few white-haired Italian men sat at one of these, smoking cigarettes and pouring each other glasses of a deep cherry-red wine.

Julia led the foursome over to this seating area, and Anna noticed a small yellow overhang advertising very easy-to-understand words in any language: WINE BAR.

"Anyone fancy a drink?" she asked.

"It's eleven in the morning," Anna said doubtfully.

"Then we've got a long way to catch up, don't we?" Julia joked.

Then, seeing the reaction on Anna's face, she added, "Come along now. You're on holiday. And a lot of these people woke up with a coffee and followed it up immediately with a grappa. When in Rome -- or Portofino."

CHAPTER 13

A young man of about twenty quickly came over to them.

He was clad in the strangest attire Anna had ever seen. His shirt, starched to the nines and ruffled, was buttoned with little black pips, all coming together at the neck in a black bow tie.

His vest was multicoloured, almost tie-dyed, making it look outrageous, particularly against his black pants. He had a little black pencil-thin moustache and greased-back black hair, giving him the look of a slightly psychedelic cartoon character.

Anna didn't have long to gaze, though.

Stephen, without looking up at the man, leaned back and said, "Due caraffe di vino della casa vostra, se possiamo."

The waiter bowed slightly. "Si signore," he said. "Grazie." Then he was off.

"Isn't it brilliant?" Julia said, beaming at Stephen. "He is absolutely fluent in Italian. Knows just what to order every time. It's amazing."

"What did you order?" Mark asked.

"Two carafes of wine," Stephen answered, staring out over the water.

"Seemed like there was more," Anna ventured.

"There wasn't." He still hadn't broken his gaze from the bay.

"Stephen is… a man of few words," Julia said gaily.

"So how long have you been together?" Anna asked, making small talk.

"Oh, it was just recent," Julia looked to Stephen, who was still watching the water, almost like he expected something to happen - - maybe he had been a lifeguard in a previous job, Anna wondered. "We met on the train coming down here from Torino. He said he had business in Portofino. And I just loved that accent. So adorable!" She pinched Stephen's cheek and he turned to her, giving her a smile.

"What kind of business are you in then, Stephen?" Mark asked.

"Stocks," he replied simply.

"Stocks?" Mark probed, hoping for more.

"Yes."

Anna cleared her throat and turned to Julia, hoping to alleviate the awkwardness of the conversation. "So how'd you end up living in Italy? Mark said you used to know each other at uni…"

Julia smiled. "Well, we did a bit more than just 'know' each other," she said slyly. "Marcus and I used to be… " She paused dramatically before continuing, making sure to make brief eye contact with both Anna and Stephen. "…lovers," she concluded with a peak of dramatic flair.

Anna nodded. "Yeah, I know all about that," she agreed, failing to repress her annoyance. "What I was asking was, what brought you to Italy?"

Julia laughed again, and Anna was even more irritated to notice that she'd resumed her haughty, cold, feigned laughter.

"Oh, I always told Marcus I wanted to travel the world," she said. "And I did. Went to Japan, and China, and Singapore, and even shacked up for a few weeks with a fellow who used to work in the Kremlin under Gorbachev while I was in Gdańsk."

"You seem to have a type…" Anna noted, glancing quickly towards Stephen.

"What can I say?" Julia shrugged. "I like my men... distinguished." Her eyes flitted to Mark. "Except Marcus here. He's always had such a sweet little baby face."

The waiter returned with two carafes of wine, and Anna immediately poured herself a glass and began sipping. "So, you were saying..." she urged Julia to continue.

"So I was in Gdańsk, with the Soviet, when I got this call from an old university friend. She had a job for me in Milan. It paid exceedingly well, and she even arranged for my flight from Poland. I couldn't say no."

"So what is it you do then?"

"I'm a travel writer," Julia replied.

"You're a writer?" Mark repeated his voice full of awe. "Wow, you did it Jules - you truly followed your dream."

Mark's behaviour worried Anna. In the last twenty minutes, he'd shown more passion for this woman than he'd shown towards her, his girlfriend, for their entire trip thus far.

Admittedly Julia was beautiful, glamorous and evidently successful, but what was going on? Was it possible that--

"So, how did the two of *you* meet?"

Anna smiled at this. "Well, actually," she began fondly, "you could say I fell head over heels for him."

"Oh really? Do tell."

Mark continued, smiling too. "I was looking for a book on finance, trying to understand my new job, and I ended up in this book shop where Anna was working..."

"Oh, so you're a--" Julia paused to take a disdainful sip of her wine. "--shop girl?" she asked after swallowing.

"Actually," Anna said, a defiant and defensive note sounding in her voice, "I'm working at a travel agency now. But yes, I worked at a bookshop for a while. What's wrong with that?"

"What? Nothing, no problem at all! I think it's *wonderful* that you were supporting yourself. Really."

"Anyway," said Mark, sensing danger in allowing this line of conversation to continue, "Anna was working in the shop, and she went to get a book from a high shelf, and she slipped and knocked herself out."

"Goodness!" Julia exclaimed.

Mark smiled, looking over at Anna. "When she woke up," he said, "she was in love with me."

"That is *so* not how it happened," Anna said, playfully slapping him on the shoulder.

"Well, that sounds perfectly lovely," Julia chimed in. "What a way to meet someone! And so cute together, you two are."

They continued talking as they slurped down their wine. The bells at the church rang out for noon, and then, after a lovely lunch, Anna was ready for some time with just herself and Mark. She attempted to excuse the two of them, but Julia didn't seem all that eager to let them go.

"Come now," she insisted, "we should go take a look at some of the shops. They're quite incredible. There's Louis Vuitton, Anna. Have you ever been in a proper Italian Louis Vuitton store before?"

"Never been high on my list," she answered honestly.

"Well, let's go check it out. Mark?"

He nodded. "Come on, Anna," he said cheerfully. "Let's look at some of the shops. Maybe you'll even see something in there you like."

Anna nodded, but inside she was torn. Why was Mark so eager to spend time with this annoying and clearly egotistical woman? What was Julia's magnetic power?

Was it possible her boyfriend was still in love with his ex?

CHAPTER 14

*L*ater that night, Mark and Anna returned to their hotel room absolutely exhausted.

"We must have walked about ten miles," he complained. "I did *not* wear the right shoes for this."

Anna slipped her own wedge sandals off and lay back on the bed, heaving a great sigh. She was tired physically, yes -- after a day of walking and wine drinking and shopping with the ever-manic Julia, who wouldn't be?

But also mentally depleted. The entire time shopping, she'd been forced to watch Mark try on clothes that Julia recommended, as if he were a dress-up doll there for her amusement.

And at dinner -- also with Julia and Stephen -- Julia and Mark had gone over every point in their relationship, while Stephen, ever stoic and silent, looked on, leaving Anna with nothing to do but push her ravioli around her plate.

The worst part was, Mark had barely even noticed. They had several more bottles of wine through dinner, and increasingly, it seemed Julia and Mark were the ones on a date, or even on a trip together. They seemed so natural, as if no time had passed since they were a couple.

Meanwhile, Anna was left effectively to drink wine on her own, which only added to her increasingly sour mood.

The worst part came right before what should have been a delicious, dessert of tiramisu and panna cotta.

Julia announced to the table that the following day she and Stephen were going to hike to the Abbazia di San Fruttuoso, a 10th century abbey that was supposed to be incredibly beautiful and was only accessible by hiking up a nature trail for about an hour and a half.

The hike sounded exactly like something Anna would love to do with Mark -- but not with Julia and Stephen.

Yet Mark had leaped at the opportunity to go along with them, not even pausing for a moment to consider how she might feel about it.

As she lay there on the bed, Anna wanted desperately to talk to Mark, to let him know why she felt even a bit betrayed and hurt.

But though the wine had made her a bit sloshy, she was still sober enough to know that everything would look different in the morning. At least, she hoped it would.

And perhaps she could make the best of it with Julia.

Barring that, she could always push her off a cliff.

CHAPTER 15

*M*ark and Anna were up bright and early, rising just ahead of the sun. This time, both wore far more comfortable trainers and jeans.

Julia and Stephen were already waiting in the foyer when they arrived down, and Anna was surprised to see them talking with another familiar face.

"Gino?" she said, as they approached.

"Ah!" he said, moving forward and kissing her on the cheek. "Miss Anna! Buongiorno, signorina, buongiorno!"

"Uh, I'm here, too," Mark said testily.

"Yes, yes I see that," Gino said grimly. "So!" he continued, clapping his hands together without greeting Mark at all, "I am to understand that you are going to see L'Abbazia di San Fruttuoso, sì? It is a great journey. I have done it several times myself. Difficult, but beautiful. I will show you the way, yes?"

"Oh, I think we can handle it," Mark retorted.

"Nonsense!" Gino insisted. "You English, sometimes, you don't know the way. Or you get lost. And I don't want you to go missing!"

Unless it's Julia, Anna thought ruefully.

"Really," Mark said, "I think we can--"

"Oh, come *on*, Mark," Julia interjected. "Gino is a wellspring of information. We're so lucky we ran into him. He's coming with us - - I insist."

MOMENTS LATER, they were off, Stephen leading the way, with Julia and Mark behind, followed by Anna and Gino.

Once they were far enough away from the hotel, the first thing Anna noticed was how green and verdant the hillside was. The dusty, muddy road took them past small houses and what looked like vineyards or farms of some sort, trees and ivy and moss lining the way.

Though she was certain it had been used plenty of times before, Anna felt as if she and her group were some of the first people ever to walk this precise path, like it had been untouched by the ravages of time.

She was in deep thought when she felt a piece of gravel give way underneath her.

"Careful, signorina," Gino cautioned, grabbing her arm and helping her back up. "Some of these roads, they are not particularly strong." Then, turning to the rest of the group, he called out, "We must all watch our steps, yes? There are many things that can go wrong, and this hike can be dangerous if you are not careful. Okay? Okay."

They continued walking, Anna a bit more gingerly. After a time, they came to what looked like a small, red house with two park benches sitting outside it. It was a few moments before Anna realised that they were looking at a church.

"Is this it?" she asked Gino. "The abbey?"

"We can't be there already," Julia said. "It's probably just another old church."

"Yes," said Gino excitedly. "Yes, it is a church -- cappella -- chapel -- actually. It is usually used for small services for people who can't make it into town or to one of the bigger places for mass."

"It's so quaint -- like some kind of country church," Anna noted.

"I have passed it many times," Gino explained, "and I have never seen anyone inside of it. I don't know how often it is used anymore. But centuries ago, it would have been a perfect spot for daily masses. It looks like it would have been more for peasants, though. Likely, the priest would have said mass first at the abbey or a larger church, then come here to give communion to the lower classes -- the farmers, you know."

"Yes, yes, all very interesting," Julia said, a hint of exasperation breaking through her normally taciturn exterior, "but we have a schedule to keep, don't we? Shall we keep going?"

"Of course, signorina," Gino agreed. "After you."

They continued along the path, which quickly went from gravel and stone to chunky, turf-like dirt. Then, suddenly, they came to a flight of stairs, apparently carved directly into the earth and buttressed with stones.

"This way," Gino instructed, motioning for them to climb the stairs.

By the time they reached the top of the stairway, the sun was high in the sky, and Anna felt tiny beads of sweat dripping from all corners of her hairline. She wiped her forehead with her hand and felt the moisture splash off of it. It was hotter than she'd expected.

A bit further along the road, they entered what was clearly forest land. The path, though overgrown, became a bit clearer, and a small wooden fence lined the way, pointing them in the right direction. Gulls called overhead, while brambles and branches crunched beneath their shoes.

"Bloody hell," Mark suddenly called out. "Do you see that?"

They all turned to see what Mark was clamouring about. Sure enough, he had found something interesting: a small, black, hairy animal, with pointy ears and a snout, bearing a passing resemblance to a pig.

"Ah, yes," Gino smiled, stroking his chin thoughtfully. "*Un cinghiale*. A boar. Sort of like a wild pig, if you will."

"Oh, it's just a baby," Julia cooed. "If it weren't so hideously ugly, it would actually be quite cute."

Mark made his way closer, while the boar stared at him, sizing him up. "I wonder if he'll let me pet him," he said.

"I wouldn't do that, Mark," Gino warned. "Boars of this age are usually not alo--"

Everything next happened so quickly, Anna wasn't even certain it *had* happened at first. Just as Gino called out his warning to Mark, a second, much larger, boar appeared.

Mark only had seconds before it charged at him. It was far more enormous than he could have anticipated, probably about a hundred pounds or so, and it didn't back off. Instead, it opened up its mouth in what sounded like a squealing war cry, and it headed at him with such force that he had to dive out of the way to miss it. The boar mother and piglet ran off into the wood, while Anna and Julia both yelped in surprise as they ran past.

Moments later, Mark stood, attempting to dust himself off -- and then peeled over, howling in pain.

"Mark," Anna called, running up to him. "Oh my goodness, what happened?"

"I'm fine," he said, "I'm fine. Just seem to have..." He winced, rubbing his leg. "twisted my ankle. Let's get going."

"Oh, no, no, no," Gino said emphatically. "You're not going anywhere except back to the hotel. You cannot hike like this."

"Well what would you suggest?" Mark asked testily. "I can't exactly walk my way *down* the mountainside, either, can I?"

"No," Gino agreed. "I believe I must carry you."

"What?" Mark exploded. "No. No, not a chance. I'm not an invalid, Gino."

"At this point, my friend, I am afraid that you sort of... are."

"Mark," Anna said gently, "listen to the man. He's right. We have to get you back to the hotel. Look: I'll come with you." She then turned to the other couple in their group. "Julia, Stephen, you lot go on ahead. No sense us ruining your day, too."

"Are you sure?" Julia asked, and Anna noted a hint of relief in her voice as she did so.

Anna nodded. "Yeah," she said, "we need to get Mark back to the hotel, and there's really nothing you can do anyway."

"Well," Julia nodded, "if you insist…"

"I do."

"Right, then," Julia said. "You be careful. And feel better, Mark. We'll check in on you when we get back."

Mark waved but said nothing as Julia and Stephen struck on down the path.

"All right, Mark," Gino said as Julia and Stephen faded into the distance, "I'm going to have to carry you on my back. Have you ever had a pony back ride?"

"I think we call it a piggy back ride, Gino," Mark said flatly.

"What?" Gino asked in confusion (though Anna suspected he was mocking Mark just a little bit). "Who would try to ride a pig? That sounds like a bad idea. Especially given what you've just gone through."

Anna chuckled as the trio headed back towards the hotel, Mark holding onto Gino's back for dear life. Despite his obvious pain, she felt a bit relieved.

If this was what it took to get some alone time with her boyfriend, so be it.

CHAPTER 17

*L*uckily for Mark, the hotel were able to locate a doctor that was able to speak fluent English.

A brief, cursory examination revealed exactly what they had expected: he had twisted his ankle, likely in the dive away from the attacking boar.

The medic advised him to rest and keep his foot elevated for at least a day, and also gave him a handful of pills for the pain.

Mark took two, and ten minutes later, he was out like a light, nearly falling asleep in the dining room, forcing Anna and Gino to walk him groggily back up to the bedroom and lie him on the bed.

Anna closed the bedroom door behind her and shook her head, a pained expression on her face.

"I'm so sorry, Gino," she said. "I'm certain this isn't how you expected to be spending your trip."

"Nonsense!" Gino replied exuberantly. "I mean, yes, truly I did not expect to carry a man down a mountain today when I awoke." Anna laughed at that - he really was quite charming. "But really, Anna, I do not mind. I come to Portofino twice, sometimes three times a year. It is, if you will, my second home. I have seen enough of it to not feel I have missed anything. Okay. Now--" The Italian man grabbed her hand unexpectedly and began leading her out of the room. "--we should have some dinner, yes? I know precisely the place to--"

"Gino," Anna said, moving away from him, "I can't do that. My boyfriend is hurt, and he's--"

"Sleeping, yes?" Gino interjected. "He won't be up for some time, and he needs to rest. Come to dinner with me. I will show parts of Portofino where tourists do not usually go. Then, if you want to come back and dote on your injured boyfriend, I will bring you back. Okay? Okay."

As if that settled matters, Gino moved towards the door.

Anna thought it over a moment. She *could* go, at least for the time being, and it wasn't like Mark was going anywhere. On the other hand, what if Mark work up and found she was gone? What would he do? What would he think?

Spying a pad of paper and pen sitting on the desk opposite her, she picked it up and began writing:

If you're reading this, I hope you are feeling a bit better. I've just gone for a quick bite to eat. I'll be back soon. If you're hungry, order some room service. Don't go trudging down the stairs in your state. I love you.

Her note complete, Anna headed to the door with Gino. "I'm glad you decided to come with me, Signorina," he told her. "Now, let me show you the Portofino *I* know."

She followed him outside to the street, wondering what he had in store for them.

They walked back down through the narrow two-lane streets to the marina and its extravagantly expensive stores and waterfront wineries and tourist traps, but Gino continued on, narrating as they went.

"The Marina is really only for tourists," he explained. "You get all kinds here -- English, Americans, Swedes, Russians, Germans, Greeks -- but no Italians except the ones working in the cafes.

There are gelaterias just up the road that are wonderful, but like I say, it is mostly tourists and no natives who really go there."

They passed the marina and were suddenly walking directly next to the water, past restaurants crowded with people. Indeed, it seemed what Gino was saying was quite true. She heard conversations in several familiar tongues -- English, Spanish, and French -- as well as some she didn't recognise. But no one, not one, seemed to be speaking Italian.

"So do Italians just not come to Portofino on holiday?" she asked Gino as they walked at a casual pace along the waterfront.

"Oh, no, they definitely do," he told her. "They just know to avoid -- I am not sure how to say this in the correct way -- pale people."

Anna laughed hysterically at this. "'Pale people?'" she teased him. "Gino, that's the funniest thing you've said yet."

He laughed as well. "I do not know how else I would say that these people have the whitest of skin," he said. "Italians, we do not have white skin. We are dark, like olives."

"Now you're just being artsy."

"I do not know this word. 'Artsy?' It means I am like art, yes?"

"Kind of..." Anna said uncertainly.

"Well then," he said, "Perhaps I am like a sculpture. Like a well-built god, right?"

Anna shook her head in wonder. "I wouldn't go that far," she said, giggling.

"Ah!" Gino said excitedly. "We have arrived..."

CHAPTER 18

*A*nna looked around. Indeed, without her noticing, the crowd had thinned, and the restaurants had become more sparse.

Instead, she could see in front of her the ruins of a castle, and beside her stood a single *ristorante*, filled now not with the typical Northern European tourists but the darker, more expressive natives she had hoped to find to begin with, all of whom were carrying on loud, emphatic conversations in Italian.

Gino pulled out a seat for Anna at one of the tables, and he sat across from her. A waiter suddenly appeared, seemingly out of thin air, bearing wine glasses as well as two small, thin glasses with a reddish liquid in them.

"Signor Bianchi!" the waiter said, clearly familiar with Gino. "Ben tornato. Noi non abbiamo visto in mesi. Si sta facendo bene, spero?"

"Grazie, grazie, sì, sto bene. Questo è il campari per il mio compagno e io, immagino? Lei è inglese, quindi cerchiamo di parlare nella sua lingua."

"Oh, but of course, Signor Bianchi," the man said, switching from Italian to English flawlessly. "Signorina, I bring campari for you, yes? It makes -- er -- the appetite better."

"Grazie," Anna answered, smiling.

"Ah! Your accent, it is perfect!" the waiter complimented her. "So, may I suggest tonight that you begin with the *pesce spada* -- I am sorry, I do not know how to say..."

"Swordfish," Gino completed the sentence for him.

"Ah, suwordfeesh, yes, thank you, Signor Bianchi. Yes, it is quite tasty, and goes well with the Campari."

"We will have two, and a bottle of the *vino della casa*, grazie."

"Excellente! We will bring out a tasting menu as well, yes?"

Gino nodded, and the waiter went off. Anna sipped her Campari as the heat of the day sizzled off into an evening breeze. The drink was surprisingly bitter, and it made her mouth curl a bit. She must have made a face, because Gino immediately laughed.

"You have never had Campari before?"

Anna shook her head. "Oh, it tastes like -- I don't even know what. Like an extremely bitter lemon crossed with an orange rind."

"It is... an acquired taste, I suppose. Much like English beer."

"Oh, a pint doesn't taste near this bad, though I don't much like beer either."

"You prefer wine?"

Anna nodded. "Or cider, sometimes," she added. "On warmer days."

Gino tut-tutted, the sound now rather familiar and endearing. "No, this is not what you should do," he explained. "When it is hot, do not go for something cold. It makes you cool temporarily, but then, it warms you up, and you feel ill. No, you must drink something warm, like red wine, to make your body feel as warm as the outside."

"And what does that do then?" Anna asked.

"Makes you drunk faster," he laughed.

Anna giggled as well. Gino really was very good company. "So what do you do, when you're not showing British tourists the best local haunts in Portofino?"

"Mmm," Gino said, finishing off his Campari just as the waiter brought their swordfish and a bottle of red wine, "I drink, I eat, occasionally I shower…"

Anna laughed again. "No, really, though," she said, "what do you do for work?"

"What I must," he said vaguely; then, after a quick sip of wine, he commenced eating his fish.

"Wait, wait, that's not an answer," she persisted. "Come on. What do you do that affords you time and money to come to Portofino three times a year?"

"Ah, you were listening to me before, yes?"

"Well, yeah, obviously. But you're not answering the question. Are you, like, a spy or something?"

"Or something," he answered evasively.

"Really?" Anna gasped, dropping her fork on her plate with a clang. "No *way*. That's *so cool*."

"Relax, Anna," he said serenely, "I am not a spy."

"So, then, come on, what is it that you do? You must do something."

"Yes, I do. Okay…" He padded his mouth following his last bite of fish, and he leaned in close to her. "I work for an international law firm."

"So you're a solicitor then?"

Gino shook his head. "No, not as such," he conceded. "No, the law firm pays me to check up on people, learn if their claims are true or not. In Italian, this is called *investigatore privato*. In English, I think, 'private detective.'"

"A private investigator? Really?" Anna raised an eyebrow.

He nodded. "My usual job is tracking men who are, how you say, unfaithful to their wives. As I'm sure you can imagine, many men -- rich, usually older men -- bring their *mantenuta* to Italy for romance and passion, which is why I travel so much. And when I'm finished, I come home, and occasionally I need a holiday, so I come here, because it is so beautiful."

"I wouldn't have thought being a private detective would afford you that much… flexibility. And money."

Gino shrugged. "Sometimes it does. When one lives alone, one can often find more money than with a partner." He sighed loudly. "Unfortunately, this time, I am not here on holiday. I am actually here on business."

"You're working?" she asked, astonished.

He shook his head. "Not right now, clearly," he smiled, nodding towards his wine glass. "But yes, I am tracking down a person. They say he was headed for Portofino. He is … not a nice man. Left his wife, claims she was unfaithful, which means she will get nothing thanks to their *accordo prematrimoniale* -- er, their prenuptial agreement. But she says the opposite is true - that he is the one is unfaithful. So, I search for him and hope to prove this."

"That's… that's fascinating, Gino," Anna said, a reverent awe coming to her voice.

They spoke at length about for another hour or so, devouring both pasta and steak and another bottle of wine in the process. Anna found the Italian detective to be quite charming, and as the tenor of their conversation increased, she found herself ever the more bold in her line of questioning. Gino was supremely intelligent, and he truly had been all over the world. After completing his licensure in Britain, he had been heavily recruited, and his travels had taken him to Asia, then through Russia and Poland, always getting the results his firm wanted, before finally returning home to Italy.

It was all dreadfully exciting to Anna, who only a few months before had been working in a shop. Gino, she thought, was everything Mark wasn't. Mark had a life somewhat worked out already, what with his finance career and his promotions and all. He wasn't *boring* by any means, but this -- what Gino did -- was so much more engaging. Gino had seen the world; Mark had seen the office.

She quickly shook the thought form her head. This was absurd, wasn't it? She loved Mark. She wanted to marry him. And yet here she was,having a lovely dinner with a gorgeous Italian man she'd only just met, laughing and joking and learning secrets about his work life. How did this translate into a healthy, long-term commitment to her boyfriend?

"I'm sorry," Anna said, standing suddenly and pushing out her chair, "it's just -- I've just realised how long we've been here, and I'm a bit concerned about Mark waking up and me not being there."

"Ah, but you wrote him that note, didn't you?"

She nodded, "I did. But I still think I ought to go back. It's getting late anyway."

"The night is still young, signorina!" Gino disagreed. "Come, let us go dancing."

Anna shook her head stubbornly. "No, I don't think so," she said. "I really ought to be getting back."

Gino nodded. "All right then, Anna," he said properly. "Let me walk you back at least, yes?"

She nodded, gratefully accepting his extended arm, which she used to steady herself as they walked back to the hotel.

"Oh, thank goodness," Mark said when Anna entered the room. "I was starting to worry."

"No reason to worry," she said, swatting him away. "I was just out with Gino."

"With … Gino?"

"Yeah," she said. "How are you feeling? How's the ankle?"

"Fine," he said, but quickly followed up, "What were you doing with Gino?"

"Why?' she asked, "Are you a bit jealous, Marcus?'"

"Don't call me that."

"Why, because *she* calls you that?"

Mark swallowed. "Yes, actually," he said. "I don't like that she does it, either."

"But you've never told *her* to stop, have you?"

"Are you drunk?" he asked, watching her stumble around the room trying to take off her shoes.

"A little bit, yeah," she said. "He took me to a lovely restaurant, and--"

"Jesus, Anna!" Mark exploded. "You went on a date with an Italian gigolo?"

"It was *not* a 'date,'" Anna insisted. "He was just being kind to me -- kinder than you've been this entire trip, that's for sure."

Mark paced around the room, covering his mouth, clearly deep in thought. "Anna," he said finally, after a few moments of silence, "I have no idea what's going on with you, but it seems like ever since we got here, you've been so distant towards me. Cold.Thoughtless even."

Anna stopped short and stared at him blankly. "What?" she cried. "You can't be serious. *Me*? I'm not the one who's been cold and thoughtless, Mark. That award goes to you."

"How so?" he asked angrily.

"Mark, the first night, you were cranky and unreasonable. And I rationalised that, thinking that you'd been anxious, and the flight *had* been rough, and the wait had been interminable. I understood. But then..." Anna sighed irritatedly, collecting her thoughts, and sat down on the bed next to him. "Mark, I don't know how it worked out that your ex is here, but she is, and ever since that happened, you've been acting like her lap dog."

"I have not," Mark protested.

"You have," she insisted. "You've done whatever she wanted to do. You've never asked my opinion -- or she Stephen's, for that matter -- and you haven't any time at all with me - just the two of us."

"What about yesterday?"

"An hour, Mark," she said sadly. "That's all you've given me. And you've given her so much *more*. Do I need to remind you about dinner last night?"

"That was fun!"

"Yeah, maybe for you but it certainly wasn't fun for me. And it didn't look like it was much fun for Stephen, either. But who really knows with that guy -- he's awfully stoic, isn't he?"

"I haven't been able to figure him out," Mark agreed.

"Regardless," Anna stressed, "I have felt completely abandoned by you these last few days. This hasn't been even close to the romantic trip I was hoping for. I wanted. I wanted--"

What? What had she wanted? She wasn't entirely certain. When they'd been planning this trip, she'd envisioned a nice, romantic getaway.

As the weeks went on leading up to their departure, she had grown more and more certain that she even hoped Mark would get down on one knee and propose.

But now?

After his petulant behaviour, his attention to Julia, and his inattentiveness towards her, Anna wasn't entirely sure what she really wanted anymore.

"You wanted it to be just the two of us," Mark finished for her. She nodded, and he continued. "I do understand that. I really do. But perhaps you haven't thought about *me* in all this. I went along with this trip *for you.* You know me; I don't like to go abroad. I'd hate travel and would prefer to just stay holed up at home for a few days, watching TV and ordering takeaways and stuff. Maybe watch a few films, just chilling out. But I was determined to come here. *For you.*"

He stood up, and Anna was pleased to see that his ankle seemed to be feeling a bit better.

Still, that didn't make his poor temper abate. "I have to say, Anna," he added, "that I'm a bit resentful of how this has happened. You've been thinking of nothing but yourself this entire time, what *you* want, what would be better for *you.* Do I not count? Am I not part of this relationship too? Or is it only what *you* want that matters? And what is that anyway - me or is it that Italian gigolo?"

"Mark," she gasped, tears coming to her eyes, "I -- I don't..."

He threw his hands up in the air. "I'm going for a walk."

"But you can't," she cautioned, "your ankle--"

"I'll be fine." He proceeded to march out the door, slamming it shut behind him.

Anna fell over onto the bed pillows, tearful.

Had she been selfish? She hadn't thought so. In fact, she'd thought Mark was the one being thoughtless. If she was honest with herself, she *still* thought he was in the wrong here.

But maybe he had a point, too. He *wasn't* the travelling type. He'd gone on the trip strictly to make *her* dream come true. And he'd been the one to get hurt on the hike, after all. Perhaps he was right to be upset that she'd gone out with Gino too, at least without telling him first.

Clearly, something between them was broken, and Anna wasn't sure how to fix it -- if even it *could* be fixed. Her chest constricted as she lay there a while, clutching in frustration, still not entirely certain where her boyfriend was, or when he would return.

Finally, she stood up and straightened her clothes.

I have to find him, she thought. She grabbed her key and went straight out the door, not even bothering to lock it behind her.

Mark sat in the hotel dining room sipping on a bottle of Italian beer. It was weak stuff compared to what he usually drank, but it was all they'd had that wasn't wine or Campari, and he certainly didn't feel like either of those.

He wanted a proper pint, but barring that, he'd settled for the bottle.

How had this happened? he thought angrily to himself. Anna -- a woman he was prepared to spend the rest of his life with -- had simultaneously accused him of cozying up to his ex-girlfriend, and *then*, irony of ironies, had basically gone off on a date with some swarthy Italian she'd just met.

How, he wondered, could she so blind as to not see why he'd be upset by that?

At the same time, Mark was well aware that he'd been grumpy the entire trip thus far. He felt he was justified at points, but he certainly hadn't been easy on Anna either.

He took another sip off his beer and thought of ways he might make it up to her. He had an idea, but it would have to wait, at least until his ankle was healed up enough.

Just then, he saw someone moving around in the foyer. It was Julia, swaying a bit.

"Jules?" he called out to her. "Are you all right?"

She moved towards him and slumped into a chair. She was clearly drunk, and she was without Stephen to boot. "What's up Marcus?" she asked, an intoxicated smile coming to her lips.

"Just... " He didn't want to tell her he'd just had a blow-up with Anna, so instead, he said, "I couldn't sleep, so I came down here. What are *you* doing?"

"Hmm," she giggled, throwing her hair back behind her. "Celebrating."

Mark smiled gamely. "And what are you celebrating?"

"I had a big day, Marcus," she said. "Huge." She leaned forward and scratched the back of his head affectionately.

"Oh my God ..."

They both looked up at the same time, and Mark's face fell. It was Anna.

"Anna," he said quickly. "This isn't even close to what you think it is."

"But it could be..." Julia said drunkenly, a goofy smile plastered on her face. She grabbed for Mark, missed, and collapsed back into her chair.

"You walk out on me and you--" Anna's eyes were full of a fury and intensity Mark hadn't known before. "--you go straight to this... this... *horrible* woman--"

"Hey!" Julia cackled.

"Anna, I swear, she just came in here, half-drunk--"

"More than half, it looks like."

"--and she just sat down and started caressing my head. I didn't ask for it, I swear..."

"Look, you two," Julia hissed, standing on her own two wobbly feet. "You obviously have a *lot* of things to work out here. I don't need to be a part of your petty domestic, so if it's all the same, I'm going to go to bed."

Suddenly, the scene was broken by an even bigger cry that made them all jump.

"Oy!" came a thin, accented voice from behind them. "What're you doin' with my fiancee?"

The three of them whipped around to see Stephen standing, also a little wobbly on his feet, just behind Anna.

"Your *fiancee?*" Mark asked, incredulously, looking from Stephen to Julia.

"Oh, yeah," Julia hiccuped. "That's what I'm celebrating."

"She's going to be my wife," Stephen exclaimed, pointing menacingly towards Mark; then, slightly unsure of himself, added, "Well, as soon as I'm rid of my other wife…"

"*Other* wife?" Anna mouthed to Mark, who shrugged.

"*Only* wife," came a thundering reply behind her. The voice was worryingly familiar, and Anna turned around to see the last person she'd expected amongst this scene.

"Gino," she said quietly, a patient begging in her voice, "can you please tell us what the hell is going on?"

"Excuse me Anna and Mark," Gino said calmly, stepping right up to Stephen. "Mr Bryant," he continued in a stern voice, his demeanour a million miles away from the pleasant one they'd experience up to then, "on behalf of your wife, Mrs. Adelle Bryant, I would like to warn you that you are in direct and evidential violation of your prenuptial agreement. You sir, as the saying goes, have been caught red-handed."

CHAPTER 21

"My wife?" Stephen repeated eyes wide. "The *bitch*."

"She really is," Julia muttered from behind him.

"Jules?" Mark looked at her. "He's married?"

But she just flashed the biggest, most inebriated smile as she followed a fuming Stephen out the door.

"I'm sorry," she mumbled.

"I have been tracking the two of them for months," Gino explained when the others two had left. "It seems to have started in Singapore, when she met him in a hotel. When he proposed to her here in Portofino, things got a little... complicated. Now, Mr Bryant will be destitute and his new fiancee will end up with nothing."

Anna was flabbergasted. "Why didn't you tell us, Gino?" she asked. "Why didn't you tell me that it was them you were investigating?"

"I really wasn't sure I could trust you -- I didn't know if you were more closely connected. I have to be very careful in my line of work." Gino shrugged. "However some things happen for a reason. I feel that I might not have been able to build the case as well as I did here in Portofino without your help. So I must thank you for that, at least."

"So what now?" Anna asked.

"What do you mean? Now you go back to your room, and you forget this all ever happened."

"That's not going to work," Mark said, evidently curious about what had just happened as well as Gino's part in it all.

The Italian man raised an eyebrow. "You two are a young couple in love, aren't you? I'm sure you can find something to pass the time ..."

Anna blushed and met Mark's eye and when she turned back to Gino, he was walking out the door.

"Come back to Portofino sometime, yes?" he called behind him. "I'll show you both what it's like when I'm *not* trying to catch out cheating spouses."

BACK IN THEIR room a little later, Anna lay on Mark's chest as moonlight swept in through the windows. Both were still too electrified to fall asleep, yet nothing they'd done so far had managed to tire them out.

"I still can't get over it," he said. "I mean, I didn't know Julia was capable of something like this."

"It sounds like they're both pretty awful people," Anna replied, then added, with more than a touch of irony, "Looks like you got away lightly in the end."

Mark moved onto his side to get a better view of her, and she followed suit, looking directly into his eyes. "Anna," he began, caressing her shoulder. "I want you to know, there was never anything with Julia like what I have with you. I loved Julia. I did. She was my first love, and yes, at the time I expected her to be the *only* woman for me. But -- and this is going to absolutely blow you away," he added with a twinkle in his eye, "I am not always right."

"Can I get that in writing?"

He smiled. "What I'm trying to say is that Julia was wrong for me. We didn't fit, and I couldn't see that then. But I do now. And I'm glad."

"Glad she muscled in on our trip?" Anna asked.

"No, glad I got to see her again," Mark answered. "I honestly never thought I would, never thought I'd get the kind of closure I think I needed. But, I don't know, there's something about seeing your ex-girlfriend's dramatic life implode that makes you more fully appreciate what you have."

Anna kissed him. "That's all I need to hear," she said as she snuggled into Mark's chest. They didn't speak any more as they both drifted off into a warm, cosy sleep.

CHAPTER 22

"*A*nna," Mark called down the mountain path to his girlfriend.

She appeared, rising up the side of the hill, and stood beside him, huffing and puffing, attempting to feel her way forward.

"My God," she complained, "I need to get fit. This is ridiculous."

"You're a city girl," he said. "You're not used to these hills. But -- look at that view…"

She paused and looked out over the magnificent vista before them. Below, deep blue sea lapped up against the rocky coastline, and she could clearly see the beautiful dome of the ancient Abbazia just beneath, while in the distance the sun began its descent. The sky was ablaze with red orange and pink for a truly incredible Portofino sunset.

She took a deep breath, enthralled by what she was witnessing, and allowed herself to take it all in, closing her eyes in an almost state of meditation.

"This has been one hell of a trip, hasn't it?" he asked her, putting his arms around her waist. "We've been pulled every which way. My ex girlfriend, your Italian gigolo --"

"He was *not* my gigolo," Anna grinned.

"Be that as it may, we've had hikes and food and wine, and a lot of drama."

She laughed. "It *has* been pretty eventful, hasn't it?"

Mark smiled too. "Close your eyes. Feel that salty sea air against your skin and the warmth of the sun at golden hour. We're here in Portofino now, just the two of us, watching the sun go down. Doesn't it feel good?"

She closed her eyes again and breathed deeply. Without a doubt, this weekend hadn't been what she had expected, in any sense of the word.

But now, reflecting back, she could never say it hadn't been interesting.

"Now," he said quietly, removing his arms, "I want you to keep your eyes closed, but slowly, very, very slowly, turn around."

"What - why?" she asked hesitantly. "I sincerely hope you're not going to push me off the cliff."

Gamely, she shuffled her feet, feeling her way around and hoping against hope that she wouldn't take a wrong turn and end up falling off the edge.

"I feel dizzy," she said, a hint of worry in her voice.

"Don't be concerned," Mark assured her. "Just follow my voice, and you'll be fine."

Anna finished turning, and, not knowing what to do next, she smiled. The sun's depleting rays now felt gentle on her skin.

She heard the rustle of Mark's keys in his pocket. Had he rented a Vespa or something? Or perhaps he was setting them up to go cliff diving. She wasn't entirely certain she was comfortable with that. Sunset cliff diving, hang gliding -- wait, what was she thinking? Mark would never do something like that.

But maybe he had a horse for a horseback ride -- but no, she would have smelled a horse, or heard the clip-clop of its hooves. No, it wasn't a sunset horseride.

Wait -- could it be--

"Now open your eyes," he instructed quietly.

Anna's eyes flitted open. It took a moment for her to adjust to the light, but when they did, she nearly fell backwards -- which would have been very dangerous, given their current position.

Mark was down on one knee, holding up an impressive looking diamond ring.

"Anna," he started, "I love you. I've loved you since the moment you literally fell head over heels for me in your bookshop. I have never, felt this way about anyone -- *ever*. I want to spend every moment I can with you, for the rest of my life, and for the rest of yours, and from there ever after. Will you do me the great honour of becoming my wife?"

Anna could have fainted -- she swooned, certainly feeling light-headed enough to fall over. But Mark, almost preternaturally understanding what was happening, stood and put his arm around her. He held her close, and felt her begin to cry as he slipped the ring on her finger.

"Anna?" he asked hesitantly. "Why are you crying?"

"You were right," she sniffled. "From the moment we got to the airport, this was a disastrous trip. And now, I'm afraid you're proposing to me because you feel like you need to, because we--"

Mark held a finger up to her lips. "I've been carrying this ring around with me for a month and a half," he said. "I kept looking for the right time to ask you. And then, when you arranged this trip, I was going to do it when we got here, but then one thing after another, everything was -- well, you know."

"So you've been planning this for a while?" she asked, her tears abating.

"Anna, I've known I wanted to marry you since the day I met you. *You* are the love of my life."

She felt her face get hot with tears again. But this time, she wasn't crying out of frustration or sadness.

This time, they were tears of pure, unadulterated joy.

"So will you?" Mark repeated, looking concerned.

"Yes," Anna replied delightedly, throwing her arms around him while in the distance - with almost perfect timing - the Italian sun disappeared beneath the water in a truly glorious blaze. "Absolutely yes…"

FROM THE AUTHOR:

Thanks so much for reading the Escape to Italy collection.

If you'd like to continue your sunshine adventures, you might also enjoy the Escape to the Islands series; also now available in paperback and ebook.

If you'd prefer something longer length, read on for an extract of my brand new novel, THE SUMMER VILLA, out now.

Thanks again!

NEW FROM MELISSA HILL

THE SUMMER VILLA

Read an extract of Melissa's brand new No.1 bestselling novel - out now!

Villa Dolce Vita, a rambling stone house on the Amalfi Coast, sits high above the Gulf of Naples amidst dappled lemon groves and fragrant, tumbling bougainvillea.

Kim, Colette and Annie all once came to the villa in need of escape and in the process forged an unlikely friendship.

Now years later, Kim has transformed the crumbling house into a luxury retreat and invited her friends back for the summer to celebrate.

But as friendships are rekindled under the Italian sun, secrets buried in the past will come to light. Each of these three women will have things to face up to if they are to find true happiness and fully embrace the sweet life.

1.

It was just a little white lie. A way to kickstart her freedom.

And Kim Weston was now officially a runaway.

She couldn't help but laugh at the idea as she stared out the window of the airplane into the abyss around her. Thirty years old - an adult - and here she was, running away from home.

She'd boarded a flight from JFK earlier and watched as the sky turned from pale blue to black. They were already six hours into a nine-hour journey and she was tired but couldn't sleep.

There wasn't a star to be seen, no way to discriminate the ocean below from the sky above. Nothing but emptiness.

Ironic because it was exactly how Kim felt inside.

She had no reason to, or so everyone told her. She had every-thing – the luxurious Manhattan apartment, a personal driver to take her wherever she wanted to go, generous expense accounts at all the best Fifth Avenue stores, and a black Amex to service every last one of her spending needs.

She and her friends were the crème de la crème of New York's Upper East Side society set and partied with celebrities and VIPs alike. By all accounts she had the quintessential dream life.

So why was she running away?

She could still hear her parents' voices in her head and her own guilt in her heart as she sat quietly nursing a vodka and orange juice.

Most of the cabin passengers were asleep, and the crew was moving around less frequently, but Kim's mind simply wouldn't quit.

For once, she wasn't playing the role she'd been allotted. If she was expected to assume her part in the Weston family script for the rest of her life, then she needed a chance to play the rebel, even if only briefly.

Everything was planned to ensure that her parents wouldn't find her - at least not for a little while.

Her destination, (and certainly choice of accommodation) wasn't somewhere Peter or Gloria would ever think to look for her, since it was so far removed from the kind of places the Westons usually frequented.

No five-star luxury hotel suite awaiting Kim when she arrived. Instead she was staying at a tumbledown villa she'd found on the internet, where she'd be sharing living space and possibly even a room with other guests.

She shuddered involuntarily.

Kim was roughing it, in as much as someone like her could. The house had no onsite staff, there was apparently someone who'd come by daily to tidy and meet and greet, but that was it.

No concierge, butler, in-house chef – nothing. For once, she was going to have to cater for herself - in more ways than one.

That gave her some sense of unease; she wasn't exactly Martha Stewart, which was why she also planned to maybe enlist herself in an Italian cookery class as suggested by the booking site she'd used. Failing that, she'd just survive on pizza and pasta. It was Italy after all.

And she could afford that much, for a little while at least.

It was early afternoon when the flight landed in Naples airport and the transfer service she'd arranged (her final luxury, she wasn't going to rough it entirely after a transatlantic economy flight) picked her up outside the terminal.

"Signorina Weston?" the driver holding the sign with her name on it queried as she approached.

"That's me."

"*Buongiorno*. Right this way," the young Italian man instructed as he directed Kim to a waiting black Mercedes.

She stepped outside of the terminal, her long slender legs clad in white jeans which complimented her hot pink poncho. Sunglasses protected her eyes from the bright sun but she still held a hand to her forehead to shield them as she stared up at an almost cloudless Italian blue sky.

"I am Alfeo," the driver introduced himself as they walked, taking her luggage along with him. "How was your flight?"

"Long," she answered. She was bone-tired, a little cranky and not particularly in the mood for small talk.

Alfeo nodded and opened the car door for her.

"The journey will take just over an hour and a half depending on traffic. But we can stop along the way if you need anything."

"That's fine," Kim replied as she slid into the backseat and laid her head against the leather headrest. She closed her eyes, suddenly spent and exhausted from worrying now that she was here.

She was really doing this ...

It seemed as if only a few minutes had passed when she was awakened by Alfeo's voice announcing arrival at their destination.

Kim blinked several times as she tried to gather her bearings, then lowered the car window to look out at her surroundings. They were parked down some kind of laneway, and up ahead she could make out a grubby wall of peach coloured plaster, and a rundown paint-chipped wooden door the only interruption on an otherwise blank facade.

Unimpressed, she regarded the weatherworn door and its tarnished brass ring, and hid a frown as she dragged manicured nails through her tousled blonde mane, pulling her hair partially over her shoulder.

Her heart fell. This place looked like a complete dump. She sincerely hoped the inside was a helluva lot better.

"This *is* Villa Dolce Vita, right?" she asked, casting a beleaguered gaze at Alfeo as she stepped out onto the dusty gravel pathway.

"Si. Villa Dolce Vita."

"I'll need your number," she stated as she walked towards him with her phone in hand. "Just in case."

Assuring her that he'd be available whenever she needed, Alfeo complied, the suggestive grin on his face indicating he meant for more than just transportation. Were Italian men really such unabashed flirts?

"Can you maybe just help get my cases inside before you go?"

"Of course." He duly took her suitcases out of the boot, while Kim wandered further along the perimeter wall to where a break in the trees gave way to a view of the sea.

Realising that they were on an elevated site, high above the water, she glanced to her left to see a group of impossibly beautiful pastel-coloured buildings and terracotta roofs that seemed to almost tumble from beneath the surrounding clifftops all the way down to the sea, clinging and huddled together above the glittering Gulf of Naples.

The set up immediately put her in mind of a huge Piñata cake; the centre of the green and grey coloured mountain cut open to release a tumbling selection of irresistible pastel-coloured candy.

Now this was more like it...

Further along down the coast, rock promontories jutted out above diverging bays, beaches and terraces, all presiding over cerulean waters. Hills dotted with lush vineyards, olive trees and citrus groves looked down over the colourful shops, cafes, hotels and historic buildings scattered below.

Sailboats dotted the clear blue waters beneath and looking

down from where she stood, Kim could see snaking wooden steps leading all the way down to the rocky shore below.

The whole thing was dizzying in more ways than one.

By the time she returned to the villa entrance, Alfeo was gone, but the old wooden door had been left ajar.

Kim slipped through into the courtyard area to discover a hidden garden of sorts.

The dark pea gravel of outside gave way to a lighter coloured more decorative kind, and she noticed heavy stone planters dotted throughout the small courtyard area, housing rows of mature lemon and olive trees.

Coupled with vibrant magenta bougainvillea tumbling down the edge of an old stone building - evidently the villa itself - the garden was a riot of colour, and against the cerulean sky and glittering water on the bay, made for a picture perfect entrance.

Citrus scent from the lemon trees followed as Kim walked to the front of the property, her senses now well and truly awakened.

The villa was of the same blotchy peach plaster as the outside wall, a pretty but long past its prime two storey house with a terracotta roof and rustic windows trimmed with dull cast iron railings that had long since seen better days.

Turning to check out the view from the front of the house, Kim then noticed a terraced area beneath the gardens, accessible by four or five stone steps leading down to small pool bordering the edge of the entire site overlooking the panoramic bay.

Without the ornate bougainvillea-laden perimeter railings holding everything together, it was as if the entire site could easily slip right off the edge and plummet down to the rocky shore below.

OK, so this place was old, but surprisingly charming and while Kim didn't have high hopes for the quality of accommodation given the crumbling exteriors, she already felt a weird sense of calm at just being here.

It was as if Villa Dolce Vita had already cast a spell on her.

A chipped wooden front door with a black painted ring knocker at its centre stood wide open, and Kim hesitated momentarily as she listened for noise from inside.

She wasn't sure if there were other guests staying there already or if anyone was even expecting her, but there was no going back now.

She took a deep breath. She was really here. Doing her own thing, finding her own path.

Time to take the plunge.

Here goes nothing...

THE SUMMER VILLA is out now in ebook and paperback.

ABOUT THE AUTHOR

USA Today & international #1 bestselling author Melissa Hill lives in Dublin, Ireland. Her page-turning contemporary stories are published worldwide and translated into 25 different languages.

Multiple adaptations of her books are currently in development for film and TV with Hallmark Channel & Netflix.

The adaptation of A GIFT TO REMEMBER is airing now on Hallmark Channel US and Sky Cinema in Ireland/UK (as A GIFT FOR CHRISTMAS) with another Christmas movie planned for 2020.

www.melissahill.ie